PRAISE FOR THE BOOKS OF
LANI DIANE RICH

THE COMEBACK KISS

"An evocative treasure of a story . . . rife with passion, blazing hearts, and an intriguing mystery that goes to the heart of what makes a small town so very small, but so familiar and warm."
—**FallenAngelReviews.com**

"Outstanding! This book has sharp and funny dialogue that will hook you from the first paragraph. Combine that with a well-plotted story and interesting characters and you have a winner."
—*Rendezvous*

"Absolutely wonderful . . . a sweet story about the importance of family, be it untraditional, and past love and new love . . . I loved this book and recommend it to anyone looking for a fun and thrilling read."
—**MyShelf.com**

"A must read . . . page-turning, fun romance with a touch of suspense."
—**FreshFiction.com**

"Fast paced . . . Readers will enjoy this solid, secondhand chance at love [and the] roman
—*Midwest Boo*

MAYBE BABY

"What raises this novel above many other chick-lit titles is its depth . . . You'll read it quickly for its sweet sass, but you'll reread it to savor its bittersweet truths."
—*Ventura County Star* (CA)

"Sweetly engaging. B+."
—*Entertainment Weekly*

"A fast, fun read, especially for those who enjoy the quirky characters of authors like Jennifer Crusie and Eileen Rendahl. Strongly recommended."
—*Library Journal*

TIME OFF FOR GOOD BEHAVIOR

"I love Lani Diane Rich's thirtysomething heroine, Wanda. The world hands her lemons, and she snarls and throws them back at the world. Fast, funny, and always true to herself, Wanda is one of those heroines you want to have lunch with."
—**JENNIFER CRUSIE**, bestselling author of *Bet Me* and *Faking It*

"A sparkling debut, full of punch, pace, and wonderfully tender moments. I devoured it in one sitting. Lani Diane Rich's gutsy, wisecracking heroine, Wanda Lane, speaks to any woman who has ever doubted her right to be loved."
—**SUE MARGOLIS**, author of *Apocalipstick*

"A warm and funny story. A perfect read for a rainy afternoon. Or *any* afternoon."
—KAREN BRICHOUX, author of
Coffee and Kung Fu

"This effervescent debut novel will strike a chord with every woman who has ever been tempted to give her life an extreme makeover."
—WENDY MARKHAM, author of
Bride Needs Groom

"Rich has managed to skillfully blend serious topics with humor, and readers will love her for it."
—*Booklist*

"I recommend *Time Off for Good Behavior* to anyone looking for a good, at times hilarious, and meaningful chick-lit read. Don't miss it!"
—ChicklitBooks.com

"Terrific and absolutely hilarious . . . with a thoroughly original and delightful heroine."
—MELISSA SENATE, author of
See Jane Date

"Lani Diane Rich's first book is a success . . . with characters who have warmth and heart . . . presented well with humor and wit."
—Bookloons.com

CRAZY IN LOVE

Lani Diane Rich

FOREVER

NEW YORK   BOSTON

Copyright © 2007 by Lani Diane Rich
All rights reserved. Except as permitted under the U.S. Copyright Act of 1976, no part of this publication may be reproduced, distributed, or transmitted in any form or by any means, or stored in a database or retrieval system, without the prior written permission of the publisher.

Cover design by Claire Brown
Cover illustration by Michelle Grant
Book design by Giorgetta Bell McRee

Forever
Hachette Book Group USA
237 Park Avenue
New York, NY 10017
Visit our Web site at www.HachetteBookGroupUSA.com

Forever is an imprint of Grand Central Publishing.

The Forever name and logo is a trademark of Hachette Book Group USA, Inc.

Printed in the United States of America

First Printing: October 2007

10 9 8 7 6 5 4 3 2 1

Acknowledgments

To Samantha Graves, Robin La Fevers, Jill Purinton, Christine Merrill, Cate Diede, Rebecca Rohan, and The Cherries: I can't thank you enough for all your help and support. You are all as beautiful as you are brilliant, and that's saying quite a lot.

To my agent, Stephanie Kip Rostan, and my editor, Melanie Murray: I'm astounded at my good fortune to have such talent and dedication in my corner. You are wonderful beyond the telling of it.

To my fellow Literary Chicks: Alesia Holliday, Michelle Cunnah, Beth Kendrick, Whitney Gaskell, and Eileen Rendahl: You make the world a better place. And a hell of a lot funnier.

To Fish, Sweetness, and Light: There aren't words. I love you. Okay, there are three words.

CRAZY IN
L♡VE

Chapter One

Her hip was buzzing.

That didn't seem right.

Flynn Daly's left eye fought her, but she got it open. The right was far more stubborn. Didn't matter, because all she could see through the caramel-colored haze created by her hair was her white bedroom wall, which wasn't much to look at anyway. She gave up, closed her eye, and cursed her hangover.

Her hip buzzed again. *Gah.* She tossed herself over onto her back and shoved one hand into the front pocket of her jeans while using the other to shield her eyes from the sun, which was slicing its way through her blinds like a freakin' Viking invader.

"Yeah?" she croaked, not bothering to check the caller ID. It was too early for that level of coordination.

"Good morning." Freya's voice, prematurely leathered from smoking, scratched its way through the line. Flynn waited for her sister to finish dragging on her cigarette and deliver the rest of the greeting. "Or, if you want to get technical about it, afternoon."

"Afternoon? What time is it?" Flynn squinted against the sunlight, trying to focus on her clock. If she had bothered to set it after the last power outage, this might have done her some good. As it was, the blinking twelve o'clock seemed to mock her.

"It's almost two o'clock," Freya said. "How are you feeling?"

Flynn slumped back into bed.

"I'm fine," she said, although, truth be told, she'd left "fine" at the second of the six martini bars she'd visited last night. "Hey, did you know about chocolate martinis? They sound all interesting and exotic, but really, they're just strange. And they don't get better after the fourth one. That's a myth."

"Hey, babe, if the phrase 'chocolate martini' wasn't enough to tip you off, you got what you deserve."

"Should my extremities be all . . . crackly?" Flynn lifted one arm; it felt like a big sack full of dry sand. "That can't be right."

"You're dehydrated." Drag. Exhale. "A long night of chocolate martinis will do that to you. Get some water and open the door. I have news."

"Open the door?" Flynn dreaded the answer she'd get to her next question. "What door?"

"Your door, you doof. I've been standing out here knocking for five minutes. I almost left, but there's a shoe on your welcome mat. I figured it was the kind of thing you would have noticed if you'd left your apartment today."

"A shoe? Just one?"

"Glittery silver sandal with a wedge heel?"

"Oh. Yeah. I was wearing those last night." Flynn lifted up on one elbow and scanned her bedroom floor. Well, shit. Where was the other one?

"Look, babe, I know you're getting over this breakup with what's-his-face by spending some time with your inner sorority girl, and it's cute, really. But pull it together. We've got business."

"Business? What business?" Flynn pinched the bridge of her nose, trying to relieve the throbbing. She'd gone all of her life without hangovers, and just as she's staring down the barrelhead of thirty, BOOM. They hit. It was like getting her own personal flip-off from God.

Freya's voice came through the line, camouflaged in a harsh whisper. "Your neighbor with the crazy eye is looking at me like he'd like to lower me lotion in a basket. Would you please let me in? *Now!*"

Flynn stared up at her ceiling, praying hard to the angels or the gods or whoever was in charge up there to make something happen. She didn't much care what. They could start a fire, strike her with lightning. Floods, locusts, toads, whatever. Something to keep her from having to deal with Freya now. She loved her sister and everything, but two in the afternoon was too early in the morning to deal with her.

This is it, Universe, she thought. *Now's your chance. Bring on the toads.*

But, of course, there were no toads. No reprieve. She knew there wouldn't be. In a world full of wars, famine, and Bratz dolls, the angels or the gods or whoever had bigger things than her to deal with. She forced her legs over the side of her bed, and swore she heard a creak coming from her left knee.

Oh. That can't be good.

"Flynn? Are you coming or what?"

Flynn flipped the phone shut and tossed it behind her toward the bed. Judging by the clang-skitter of it hitting hardwood and shooting into the wall, she guessed she missed. She shuffled down her hallway toward her front door, pulling her hair up into a knot and staking it with a pencil from the hall table before going to work on her dead bolt and chain.

First to enter the room was a light cloud of smoke; second, dangling from Freya's pinkie finger, the wayward sandal; finally, Freya herself, looking like a fairy godmother, all glimmering blond curls and slightly overdone makeup. Her silk pantsuit was even pale blue, the preferred color of fairy godmothers everywhere.

Flynn coughed pointedly.

"You're not allowed to smoke in the hallway," she said, leading the way to the kitchen.

"I'm not allowed to smoke anywhere. So I smoke everywhere. Fuck 'em." Freya put the cigarette out on the bottom of Flynn's shoe and set them both on the breakfast bar as she settled onto a stool. "Baby, you look like shit."

"Gosh, I'm so glad you came over, Fray." Flynn whipped open the filter basket on her coffeemaker. "So. What possible business could we have on a Sunday morning?"

Behind her, there was a protracted silence, which was never the case with Freya. Freya almost never shut up, even in her sleep. Flynn dumped four heaping tablespoons of grounds into the filter, then added one more for good measure, and turned around to find Freya dialing on her cell phone.

"Hey," Freya said into the phone. "I'm in."

Flynn rested her lower back against the counter. After almost thirty years of being sisters with Freya, she felt pretty confident she'd be needing the support.

"Okay," Freya said. "Call on her land line." She glanced up at the old cordless phone on the wall. "That thing work?"

Flynn glanced at it, then back at her sister. She nodded.

"Freya," she said, "what's—"

The phone rang, cutting her off. Flynn stared at Freya, who motioned for her to answer it. Warily, as if it were a snake that might bite her, she picked up the phone.

"Hello?"

"Flynn." Richard Daly's voice came loud and clear through the phone. "This is your father."

Flynn slowly raised her eyes to Freya, who smiled encouragement. Freya never smiled encouragement.

Wow. This must be bad.

"Dad?" she asked. "What's going on?"

"This is an intervention," he said. "Your sister and I are worried about the destructive direction your life is taking. We feel it would be in your best interests to make a few basic changes."

Flynn had to squelch a laugh as the absurdity washed over her. Except, knowing her father and her sister as she did, it was a sadly predictable absurdity.

"You're doing an intervention?" she asked. "By phone?"

"I'm a very busy man, Flynn," he said. "You know that. Freya's there to give you all the details, but I felt it was

important that I talk to you in person and let you know
that I'm in total support of what she's about to tell you."

Flynn tightened her grip on the phone in her hand,
having strange flashbacks to her sixteenth birthday when
her father rented a carnival for her and her friends, then
sent his assistant to oversee everything while he hopped
a flight to Dallas.

"Wow," Flynn said, not bothering to mask her chuckle.
She'd learned, at about the age of sixteen, that it was easier on everyone if she just found the funny in these things
and moved forward. "An intervention by phone. Don't
you think e-mail would have been more efficient? Or text
message. Then you could use all that funky spelling." She
shot a glance at her sister. "So, it's *you two* who are going
to tell *me* what's wrong with my life? Am I getting this
right?"

Her father answered with his usual humorless stoicism.
"Freya will explain. If you have any questions, feel free
to call me."

Click. Her father was out of the intervention. Flynn
stared down at the phone in her hand, her eyes focusing on the end call button, which she pressed so hard her
thumb went white. The giggle started deep within, rose
through her throat, and by the time she released it, there
were tears and shaking and pains in her side.

Intervention by phone. This is one for the books.

"Flynn," Freya said after indulging her for a moment.
"Okay. That's enough."

Flynn wiped her eyes and straightened up. She'd have
to put on a serious face or this could take hours. "I'm
okay. I'm fine. I'm totally serious. Completely into it."

She squelched the last of the giggles and took a deep breath. "Go ahead. Tell me what's wrong with me."

Freya held up her hand and began ticking off her fingers. "You're almost thirty. You've never held a job for more than a year. You've never maintained even a casual relationship for more than six months. You live paycheck to paycheck, barely scraping by, living in a hellhole—"

"Hey!" Flynn said, mocking indignation. "This hellhole has free utilities."

Freya sighed. "Some things have opened up at the office, and Dad wants you to come work with us. We have a great opportunity that starts tomorrow. Your starting salary is excellent, and Dad has a new apartment all ready for you at the building he just bought in Brookline. We'll move you in while you're gone."

Flynn's amusement sank like a stone. "Excuse me? What? Are you crazy?"

"Oh, come on. This is *Southie,* Flynn. It's a miracle you haven't been killed already. And you're too old to be living like this. You're going to be thirty in, what? Four months?" Freya leaned forward over the breakfast bar, her voice more plaintive than Flynn had ever heard it. "Do you really want to be hopping from job to job? Living in Southie? In your *thirties*?"

Behind her, the coffeemaker slowly gurgled its way through the pot. Damn, but that thing was taking forever. For ten dollars more, she could have gotten a model that allowed you to pour a cup of coffee before the pot was done brewing.

But of course, she hadn't been able to afford that model.

"Look, Freya, I appreciate this and everything, but I'm

not a drug addict and, last night aside, I don't drink any more than you or Dad on an average day. I pay my taxes. I recycle. I vote. And this morning, I'm going to run out and get a paper and find a new job."

"Wait. What?" Freya's eyes widened. "You quit your job?"

Flynn shrugged. "What's-his-face—his name was Bob, by the way—took it kind of hard."

Freya laughed. "Oh, right. *You* broke it off with *him*. Should have known. Why? He didn't 'knock you over'?" Freya put the words in air quotes, making Flynn regret for the thousandth time the margarita night that had prompted her to confide that little gem.

"So, yeah," Flynn went on, "I quit. Working together would be uncomfortable for everyone. Besides . . . I was just a secretary there. And I'm excited about trying something new." Flynn turned back to the coffeemaker as a diversionary tactic, but it wasn't done yet. *Good God. This is the new millennium. There's no reason to live like this.*

If I worked for Dad, a betraying thought countered in the back of her mind, *I could afford my own espresso machine.*

"I know you made that promise to Mom," Freya said in a softened tone. "But you have to know you can't keep it."

Flynn turned to look at Freya. "This isn't about the promise."

Freya raised her eyebrows. "Oh, really?"

"Yeah, really." Flynn scuffed the floor with her toe. "If everyone found passion in their work, who'd clean up the bathrooms, right? It's great that Mom had it, but she was just lucky." Flynn met Freya's eyes and shrugged. "You know. If you don't count the cancer."

"Dad had a heart attack last week," Freya said suddenly, like a Tourette's patient off of her medication. Flynn stood frozen, stunned for a moment, then realized she wasn't breathing and gulped in some air.

"What?"

Freya waved one hand in the air. "Okay, fine, it wasn't a heart attack, per se. It was a little angina and by the time I got to the hospital, they were already releasing him. You weren't there, and when I asked him why, do you know what he told me?"

"Wait a minute," Flynn said, "he never called me. No one called me. Why didn't anyone call me?"

"He didn't want you coming out from Southie at night," Freya said.

The coffeemaker gurgled its death gurgle. The coffee was finally ready, but now the idea of getting out mugs was too much for Flynn. She stayed frozen where she was, feeling as though she'd just been slapped.

"I don't know . . . how am I supposed to respond to that? I mean, this is where I live."

Freya reached into her bag and pulled out a carefully assembled report. Flynn walked over to her and took it, running her hand over the clear plastic cover that protected the title page, which had *The Goodhouse Arms: Scheintown, NY* printed on it in a fancy script font.

"Great-aunt Esther died."

Flynn blinked, still staring at the report in her hand. "We had a Great-aunt Esther?"

"Grandmother Daly's sister." Freya nodded toward the report. "She left us this inn."

Flynn flipped through the pages, her eyes catching on pictures of tree-lined streets and a gazebo in the middle of a rose garden, her mind able to digest only a couple of random phrases. *Picturesque Hudson Valley location . . . locals refer to the town as "Shiny" . . . one of the oldest inns in the country . . . rich historic national treasure . . .* She closed it and dumped it on the counter.

"What does this have to do with me?"

"I want you to go."

Flynn let the silence hang for a moment before asking for the clarification she was pretty sure she didn't want.

"Go where?"

"To the inn."

"Dead Aunt Esther's inn?"

"That's the one."

"In upstate New York? Where they have cows and nature and no T?" Flynn paused for a moment, her head swimming. "What would I do there?"

"Maintain a presence for a few weeks until we sell it."

"*Maintain a presence?* What does that even mean?"

"It's nothing really. Dad and I talked about it yesterday, and we decided that it would be the perfect way for you to get your feet wet in the company business. Besides, I leave for my spa week in Tucson tomorrow, and there's no way in hell I'm missing that."

"Ah," Flynn said, smiling sideways at her sister, "the true motivations come out."

"Look, you go there for two, three weeks max, and when you come back, you'll have a desk and a real salary waiting for you at the office. It's total win-win."

Flynn tapped her fingertips on the counter. "It was really just angina? What is that? I mean, should we be worried?"

"We should . . . not make him worry."

Flynn lowered her eyes and bit the inside of her cheek. Her whole life she'd sworn to herself she'd never live off her father. She'd find her own way. She'd find a man that knocked her over and a job that she was passionate about and little woodland creatures would creep into her bedroom while she was at work and sew gowns for her. She sighed and glanced around her little apartment. Up until now, her lifestyle had seemed adventurous and romantic. Now, it just seemed selfish. Immature. Pointless.

"So . . . Dad doesn't know that this intervention is really about him, does he?"

"Oh, it's not just about him," Freya said with a smile. "Your life *is* totally screwed up. I just figure, two birds, one stone." Freya sighed. "Look. You broke up with your boyfriend. You quit your job. This apartment sucks. Will it kill you to just . . . try?"

Flynn met her sister's eyes and decided that no, it wouldn't kill her. Maim, possibly, but not kill. "How much should I pack?"

Freya's smile widened. "Enough for two weeks. Three weeks, max. All you have to do is go and make nice. Be a presence. Tell the staff we're not selling so they don't all freak out and run off before Dad closes the deal. It's hell to sell an active business that doesn't have a functional staff in place."

"Oh, God." Flynn cringed. "You want me to *lie* to them?"

"This is business, honey. Everybody lies." Freya raised a defiant eyebrow. "Don't look at me like that."

Flynn cleaned up her expression. "Like what?"

"Like you just sold your soul to the devil." Freya waved a dismissive hand in the air. "*Fine.* If you have to, you can go ahead and tell them we haven't made any decisions yet, but make them feel secure that they'll keep their jobs no matter what or we'll have a riot on our hands. A riot with no staff."

Once again, Flynn found herself asking a question she was pretty sure she didn't want the answer to. "*Will* they keep their jobs?"

"We have no control over that. But even if the new owner brings in some of their own people, they'd be stupid not to keep most of the staff in place, so probably, yeah." Freya patted Flynn's hand. "It's a total cakewalk. Trust me."

Flynn smiled, hoping she looked confident. Or at least not scared to death. "Sure. Sounds like fun."

Freya slid off the bar stool. "When you come back, we'll ease you into things at the office. Who knows? You might even like it."

Flynn walked Freya to the door, imagining herself having martini lunches with investors, referring to hotels and apartment buildings as "properties," and going golfing at the country club to help Dad swing a deal.

She didn't think she'd like it. But she hadn't liked being a secretary, either. Or an actress. Or a yarn shop clerk. Or any of the other seemingly endless list of things she'd tried.

If this kept Dad from worrying, then at least she'd be accomplishing something that mattered, which was more than she could say about anything else she'd done in the past eight years.

Freya pulled her pack of cigarettes out of her purse. "I have a hair appointment, but I'll be back in an hour to get your measurements and order you some real clothes."

"What's wrong with the clothes I've got?" Flynn said,

then followed Freya's pointed gaze down to her sparkly pink top, and the chocolate martini stain on her left boob. Flynn raised her head. "So, I'll see you in an hour, then?"

Freya nodded and left. Flynn leaned against the door and took a deep breath. This would be good. This would be a fresh start. And if she didn't love it, if it wasn't her passion, well so what? There was something to be said for responsibility. And security. And . . .

Her mind went blank as she realized that something momentous had just happened; she had finally run out of energy to rationalize. She pushed herself away from the door and headed down the hallway and into the bathroom. She opened the hot water tap and plugged the tub, then turned to the shelf next to the vanity to pull out a towel. It was slightly heavier than expected, but by the time it registered that something was on top of it, that "something" had already bounced off the top of her head and landed on the floor. When she looked down, there it was: the second silver sandal, lying sideways next to the tub. Flynn sat down beside it, staring at it for a long while before saying, "Now, how the hell did you end up here?"

"And you see? Here? *I only have three radishes left!*"

For any other guy, sitting on an industrial kitchen counter at three in the morning while a crazy redhead waved a handful of radishes in his face might be unusual. For Jake Tucker, it was just another Sunday night.

"Don't get me wrong, Merce," he said, tucking the notepad and pen she'd stuffed into his hands onto a shelf behind the biggest bag of beans he'd ever seen in his life, "I find root vegetable crime as fascinating as the next guy, but it's officially an ungodly hour, and during those I have a strict policy that it's either sex or sleeping. No exceptions." He hopped off the industrial metal counter he'd been sitting on. "Night."

"Wait." Mercy dumped the radishes and shut the refrigerator door, her eyes flashing desperation before she motioned to the metal shelves next to the stove, where she kept the pots and pans. "What about the hardware that went missing last spring, Jake? What, like a saucier just gets up and walks out of the kitchen on its own?"

He chose not to ask what a saucier was; it was beside the point, anyway.

"Look. I appreciate what you're trying to do." *Not really.* "Really. It's only the tiniest bit emasculating, and considering who I'm dealing with, that's saying a lot." He gave her a small round of opera applause. "Yay you. Good night."

He tried to leave, but she maneuvered around him and blocked his exit. She was a full-figured gal, his sister, but she could move like a snake.

"But the saucier . . ." she started.

"Give it up," Jake said, trying to keep his voice low and serious. People didn't take him seriously sometimes, and by people, he meant his sisters. "I don't need it. Just because I'm not a cop anymore doesn't mean my life is over."

She gasped, her mouth forming a little round *O* of horror. "Of course it doesn't!"

"Good. So drop it. It's no big deal."

"Of course it isn't."

Mercy clasped her hands together, and her face reddened with the extreme effort of keeping her opinions to herself. Jake counted the beats internally.

One.

Two.

Three.

Mount Mercy burst. "Except it is a big deal. You loved being a cop. And you were good at it."

"If I was really good, I wouldn't have gotten fired." Jake moved toward the refrigerator. "You got anything to eat in here?"

"If you'd just look at it from a different angle, I think you'd see there are other opportunities. For example, private investigations—"

"Oh, yeah, that would work. Shiny has a population of 4,128. There's no way—"

Mercy held up one finger. "That's 4,130. Janice Feingold had her twins yesterday."

"Well, unless the twins need a background check done on Janice—which, actually, I would advise, she's got the shifty eye—it's not enough people to support a private detective operation. So just let it go, will you?" He plucked three grapes off of a bunch and shut the door. "By the way, if the mystery of the missing grapes should come up, I've already solved it."

Mercy gave him an attaboy punch on his shoulder. "See how good you are?"

Oh, holy mother of all that is holy, Tucker women are impossible to crack. Even at three in the morning.

"I like the Goodhouse Arms. I like bartending. I like my life. Everything's fine."

"Everything's great!" Mercy's head bobbed up and down in time with the rhythm of her fierce loyalty.

"I'm"—he searched for a word that might make her back off—"*fulfilled*. I'm in touch with my authentic self, and it hasn't even made me go blind yet. I'm actually the most self-actualized man in America." He popped a grape in his mouth. "Not that I know what self-actualized means, but I know you girls are all worked up about it, so that's what I am. I'm better than that, actually. I'm happy."

"*You*," she said, emphasizing each word with a gentle but still uncomfortable poke to his chest, "are *ecstatic*."

"Good. We agree. So knock it off, okay?"

She blinked, feigning innocence. The youngest of his four older sisters, Mercy could bat an eyelash like nobody's business. "I have no idea what you're talking about."

"I just finished seven hours behind the bar and you're dragging me in here to talk about, what? Radishes? And sauciers? I mean, it was bad enough when you asked me to trail Derek, who is—"

Mercy held up one hand. "He was acting strange."

Jake raised his voice and continued over her. "—possibly the most devoted husband in the history of the world."

Mercy kept her game face on. "He'd had some late nights."

"He's an obstetrician. They do that. Besides, the man has seen every vagina in Shiny. I think he's secure in his choice."

Mercy's face set into a decided pout, and Jake felt a familiar niggle of guilt working its way into his head. Which was stupid. Four sisters and a mother, the pout should not work on him.

But it always did.

"Okay," he said, softening his tone a little. "I know you mean well, and I know it's just because you love me, but I don't need you to create little mysteries for me to solve. Okay?"

She gasped like a matriarch in a Tennessee Williams play. "I can't believe you think I would make all this up!"

Jake leaned back against the counter. "I know all about you girls and your secret meetings."

"Secret meetings?"

"Yes. Where the whole bunch of you sit around and talk about my life and how I've screwed it up and then you devise little plans to fix me when I don't need fixing."

"Secret . . . ?" She blinked. "What, you mean Sunday dinners?"

"Exactly."

"They're not secret. Mom invites you every week."

"Semantics. The point is, I'm not depressed about the way my life is going. That's just the sort of thing you girls make up in your heads because you can only scrapbook for so many hours a day."

Typically, in his family, a good sexist comment would change the subject right quick. Unfortunately, Mercy wasn't taking the bait.

"So, are you taking my case or not?"

"No." Jake tossed the last grape up in the air and almost caught it in his mouth. It rolled under the refrigerator, and he flashed Mercy his most disarming smile before going to retrieve it. "If you really think there's something going on here, go to the police and file a report."

"I can't go to the police," Mercy said. "They'd laugh at me. This is why I need a private detective."

Jake tossed the grape in the garbage and wiped his hands on his jeans. "What you need is a prescription. Good night."

He pushed his way out of the swinging door that led to Mercy's kitchen, and down the back hallway toward the bar, where he'd left his jacket. He could hear Mercy's feet as they padded determinedly behind him.

"You know what I've realized about Tucker women, Merce?" he asked.

"Wait. We're not done talking." Mercy huffed behind him. "Would you slow down?"

"Tucker women are like little terriers. They seem harmless, even cute sometimes, but then they chomp down on your pants leg, and you can kick as much as you want, but you're just never getting that leg back." He pushed through the swinging door that led into the bar and grabbed his jacket off the hook on the wall. "Go home. Derek's gonna worry."

There was a long pause, and Jake had to turn around to make sure his sister was still with him. She was, just standing there watching him, her eyes steeped in loving concern.

"We're not worried that you're unhappy," she said. "We're worried that you're obsessed."

Well. At least that was a new argument.

"I'm not obsessed." He leaned against the bar, not near foolish enough to think that would end the conversation.

"I saw you poking around in Esther's office," Mercy said, settling on a bar stool next to him.

He shrugged. "I was helping pack up her stuff."

"Really? Well, FYI, when you pack, you usually put files into boxes, not pull them out." She paused for a long moment. "You were looking for something on Gordon Chase."

Jake kept silent. He hadn't found anything, so there was no point in confessing.

"Look," Mercy said, a sigh in her voice, "I hate him, too. What he did was horrible, but he didn't kill Dad."

"He talked him into selling that land for almost nothing when he knew that developer was coming in," Jake said. "Then he turns it around and makes a million while Dad works himself to death? How is that not killing him?"

"Dad didn't work himself to death."

"He was killed at work. Same difference."

"Gordon Chase is not—"

"Let's talk about something else," Jake said. "Pick a root vegetable. Any root vegetable. How do you feel about turnips?"

"—responsible for everything that goes wrong in this town, Jake. He's not responsible for what happened to Esther." She shrugged minor acquiescence. "I might give you points on the thing with Elaine Placie, but still. It doesn't make this obsession healthy."

Ah, Elaine Placie. Now there was a topic he *really* didn't want to revisit, so he kept quiet.

"I loved Esther as much as anyone," Mercy went on, "but the woman was eighty-seven years old with a heart condition. She died in her sleep. It doesn't get any less suspicious than that."

Jake angled his body toward Mercy. "She tells me Gordon Chase is bugging her to sell, and then two weeks later, she dies suddenly in her sleep? At the very least, it's a hell of a coincidence."

Mercy looked at him skeptically. "So, what? You

think he had an old woman killed for a real estate commission?"

"Maybe. Maybe he's getting a kickback from the family, who had a lot to gain from Esther's death. This niece that's coming tomorrow. Maybe she knows something."

Mercy sighed. "You'll get no argument from me that Gordon Chase is a total shit, but I don't care about him. I care about you, and this isn't good for you."

Jake shrugged. There was no point in telling Mercy that the convenient way in which things seemed to work out for Gordon Chase was no coincidence. Nor did he think it was a coincidence that a laptop taken from the office of an associate of Chase's—a laptop that might have had evidence implicating Chase in a real estate scheme— went missing from the evidence locker the very night that Elaine Placie distracted Jake at the station, a distraction that ended up costing him his job. Mercy'd heard it all before, and arguing now would just make her think she was right about him being obsessed.

Which she wasn't. He wasn't obsessed.

He just wanted to take the bastard down. Hard. With bruising, and possibly the occasional whimper.

"We love you, Jake. We just think it's time for you to grow up."

Jake tightened his right hand into a fist. He hated this part the most.

"Look, I'm only thirty. There's still plenty of time for me to get a real job and find a nice girl with good birthing hips."

"That's not what we're talking about," Mercy said. "We're talking about you taking something seriously. Something besides Gordon Chase."

"Okay," Jake said, stretching out his fingers and forcing a smile. "It's late. I'm tired. You're delusional. Let's just call it a day and we can start with fresh haranguing tomorrow, okay?"

"If you need a mystery to solve—"

"I'm not investigating your fucking radishes, okay?"

Mercy's eyes widened and Jake knew he was real close to getting his ass good and kicked.

"I'm sorry. I'm a jerk." He put one arm around her shoulder. "I'm the jerkiest jerk in Jerkville, okay? I just don't want to talk about it anymore."

She reached up and cupped her hand around his chin, squeezing his mouth into an involuntary "O." She knew he hated this, and was doing it deliberately, but he had to put up with it because he'd been an ass.

Those were the Tucker rules.

"Look, you were stupid. You let Gordon Chase get the best of you and get into that evidence room."

"This is you being supportive, right?" Jake said, his lips still puckered under the pressure of Mercy's fingers as she tightened her grip.

"Gordon Chase is a big stinky turd man, but that's his problem. Karma will take care of him." She released his face and gave it a loving, if not particularly light, slap. "You need to drop it and move on with your life. And if that means investigating my fucking radishes, then that's exactly what you'll do."

She smiled her bright, cheerful smile, and Jake smiled back.

"All right. Can I go home now?"

She got up off the bar stool. "You are dismissed."

He motioned for her to go first, flicking off the light as he followed her out of the bar.

She was right. He knew she was right. It was time to let the Gordon Chase thing go. He also knew he had no intention of doing that, but it had to be worth some points that he at least knew she was right.

He was sure of it.

Chapter Two

♡Flynn checked her watch. *Again.* It was past two, and her driver was supposed to be there to meet her at the gate at one-thirty. The rest of the people disembarking with her at Scheintown—all three of them—had already gone on their way. *Their* people had been there, on time, to pick them up. Now the only people in the train station, aside from the workers, were herself and The Guy.

She stole a glance at him; he was still sitting on the bench across from her, reading a newspaper. When she'd first gotten off the train, he had smiled and said, "Excuse me . . ." but she'd been looking for a chauffeur type holding a big white card with her name printed on it, and had ignored him. The Guy was hardly a chauffeur type; he was wearing a maroon flannel shirt over a black AC/DC T-shirt and jeans, for Christ's sake. Besides that, growing up in Boston had taught her that you never smile at strangers.

Ever.

However, after dragging her travel suitcase behind her around the entire perimeter of the train station and finding no evidence of any genuine driver types, Flynn began to suspect that maybe The Guy *was* her driver. So, she went back inside, but by then he was sitting down, reading a newspaper. Which made her think that maybe he *wasn't* her driver, so she sat down as well, figuring that if he *was* her driver, he would approach her.

But he didn't. He just sat there reading, a slightly amused expression on his face. So, she thought, maybe he *wasn't* her driver after all. Maybe he was just the particular brand of homeless train station bum that sprouted up from the sidewalk cracks in places like Scheintown.

He didn't look like a bum, though. He was unkempt, but in that deliberate way that some guys did, which in the end kinda looked . . . kempt. His hair was brown and scruffy, but clean. His face held a slight five-o'clock shadow, but nothing excessively ragged. His eyes, in the one brief moment they'd connected with hers when she'd first gotten off the train, seemed bright and sharp. And he wasn't hustling the way bums hustled, asking for money or glancing around to see if anyone had tossed out any recyclables.

To be honest, he looked like a regular guy.

Correction: He looked like a regular guy who was waiting her out.

She checked her watch again. She'd been sitting there not fifteen feet from him for over twenty minutes. Argh. She uncrossed her legs; it was warm for October, and the pant legs of the sage silk suit Freya had loaned her were getting sticky. She tapped the pointed toes of her stiletto boots—also Freya's—against the stone floor. The sound echoed sharply through the empty station.

The Guy flipped the page on his newspaper. Flynn could see his lips tightening against a smile.

Oh, screw it.

Flynn got up, clip-clopped over to where he was sitting, and stood before him, arms crossed over her stomach.

"All right," she said, not bothering to mask the irritation in her voice. "I'm sorry. I made a mistake. My sister set this whole thing up and she's the type to get a limo driven by a guy in a tux."

He raised his eyes to hers. They were brown with flecks of gold, and they looked overly amused for the circumstances, but still kind. Despite her annoyance with him, the initial impression was a good one.

"Excuse me?" he said, barely able to contain his smirk.

Flynn rolled her eyes, mostly at herself. How could this possibly be going so badly so soon? How was that fair?

"You're here to pick me up. I ignored you. I thought they'd send a real driver. I mean, not *real* . . . You're obviously real. I mean . . . *Gah!*" She flashed her fingers out in frustration. "I apologize if I offended you. Can we go now?"

He folded the newspaper and set it down on the bench. "What makes you think I'm here to pick you up?"

She narrowed her eyes at him. Was he *playing* with her?

"You're here. I'm here. No one else is here."

He quirked an eyebrow at her. "With a line like that, it sounds like *you're* trying to pick *me* up."

She threw her arms down at her sides. "I don't mean

that kind of pickup. Look, are you from the Goodhouse Arms or not?"

He chuckled, pushed himself up from the bench, and walked toward her luggage.

"In my defense, I tried to speak to you when you got off the train," he said. "You zoomed past me like I was holding a copy of *The Watchtower.*"

"I thought they would send a real driver guy. You know. With the hat and the suit and a little sign that had my name on it. How was I supposed to know they'd send the . . . ?"

She trailed off. She had no idea what purpose this guy would serve at an inn. Maintenance, maybe?

He saved her, though, because he didn't seem to be listening, just looking around, holding her one bag in his hand.

"Where's the rest of it?" he asked.

"The rest of what?"

"Your luggage."

"That's it."

He lifted her bag as though it were as light as a shoe box, which she knew it wasn't. She'd packed it within an inch of its life.

"This is it?" he asked suspiciously.

"Yes, that's it." Flynn smoothed her hands over her suit jacket. "Why?"

"I was raised in a family of women. It takes no less than four suitcases for any one of 'em to get the mail. No way this is all you have."

"You know, some women do know how to pack." Which she did. The two thousand dollars' worth of label-wear that was being shipped to her the next day was

Freya's doing; Flynn had everything she needed—which pretty much amounted to jeans, sweaters, flannel lounge pants, and her favorite shampoo—in that suitcase. Still, the condescending look coming from the man holding it set her off.

"Do I need to remind you that my family owns the Goodhouse Arms now? Which makes me your boss?"

Flynn tugged her blazer straight and tried to stand a little taller. How did Freya do this all the time? No wonder she was so cranky. Flynn was already tired of playing the big, bad businesswoman, and it had only been five minutes. Freya did it all year round.

To make matters worse, The Guy wasn't buying it. He stood there, a half smirk on his lips, his eyes running over her face and then briefly down her body in an attempt to size her up as an enemy, and when his gaze met hers again, exuding confidence, she knew he wasn't the least bit intimidated by her even if she was his boss.

"You're selling it, aren't you?" The Guy said finally, his voice quiet.

Flynn felt her throat close a bit and cleared it quickly. "What?"

"The Arms," he said. "You're selling."

"No." Her voice squeaked a little on the word, so she cleared her throat. "What makes you say that?"

"So, you're not selling it?"

She stared at him. Why was the maintenance guy grilling her? "I just got here."

"Well, it's been a day or two since you got the news, right? You've had time to think about it. People like you usually have a plan for these things."

"People like me? What is that supposed to mean?"

"Rich people. People with money. People who get their money by buying and selling other people."

She narrowed her eyes and let her voice dip into warning tones. "Excuse me?"

"Your father is in real estate development, isn't he? Isn't that what he does—sells properties to the highest bidder?"

She put her hand over her heart, which was picking up speed. "Have you been researching my family?"

He chuckled. "A small town with Internet access is a very dangerous thing. We know everything but your bra size and your zodiac sign, although I'm guessing Pisces. You carry a lot of tension in this area." He gestured his hand to indicate her shoulders, then leaned closer. "I'm not going to guess your bra size. I think that would be inappropriate."

"Do you have some kind of medication you're off schedule for?" she asked.

"I notice you still haven't answered the question. Are you selling or not?"

Holy crap, he was unsettling. "What makes you ask something like that?"

"Well, evasiveness in answering questions, for one." He motioned toward her suitcase. "Minimal luggage, so you're not expecting to spend a lot of time here. You're dressed like you're about to hit the runway, not the office." He glanced at Freya's hand-me-down Kate Spade bag dangling from her fingers. "No briefcase, no laptop, just a purse. You don't look like you're here to work."

Flynn felt her stomach tighten. "What exactly do I look like I'm here to do, then?"

He cocked his head to the side and studied her for a

moment. "You look like you're here to appease the natives until the sale goes through."

She felt her mouth drop open, and her brain froze. She was sure there were a million poised, reasonable responses to his taunting, but "You're fired" was the only thing that came directly to mind.

Unfortunately, Freya had absolutely forbade her from firing anyone during the first week.

Fire the wrong person, she'd said, *and you'll start a stampede. All they'll find is your beaten, battered body under a thousand resignation letters.*

"Look, Mr. . . ."

"Tucker. But you can call me Jake." He grinned. How was it possible for him to be so mean yet look so friendly? He was like a polar bear, one of those really cute ones at the zoo that would carve you up for dinner in a heartbeat if it weren't for the bars.

"Well, Mr. Tucker—"

"So it's a *no* on calling me Jake, then, huh?" He nodded. "Trying to keep that professional distance. I totally understand. I will warn you, though. Everyone else calls me Jake. That's a lot of peer pressure to resist." His eyes were so filled with amusement, they were actually twinkling at her. "I'm right, aren't I? You're going to sell."

He smiled, keeping his eyes on hers, and she could see that underneath all the wise-ass crap, there was something more going on inside. That's when it finally dawned on her where that twinkle was coming from.

He was deliberately baiting her.

And he was enjoying it.

Jerk.

"Mr. Tucker, I've just spent five hours on a train, and

I'm tired. I'd like to go back to the Goodhouse Arms, get settled, and start working. Now, you can take me there, or I can call a cab, but either way, this discussion is over."

He kept his gaze locked on hers, but Flynn had no idea what was going on behind those speckled eyes. Hell. She'd been there less than a half hour and already she'd made an enemy. Well, that was fine. She wasn't there to be liked. She was there to do a job. And, eventually, she was sure, she'd figure out exactly what that entailed. In the meantime, if she could just get the maintenance guy to stop looking at her like that . . .

She took an unconscious step backward to put more distance between them, and the stiletto heel of Freya's left boot betrayed her, turning under her and sending her skittering to one side. She flailed both arms, but she knew it was no use. She felt herself falling, and closed her eyes as she prepared for the inevitable harsh clash between her ass and the cold stone floor.

Then, suddenly, she felt herself being pulled upright. She opened her eyes to see Jake Tucker's face just inches from hers as he set her right, his hands warm and secure on her upper arms. She stared up at him, swallowing hard. She didn't want to say, "Thank you," because that would imply gratitude and debt and she was still kinda pissed off at him, but she didn't know what else to say. *Good job? Well done?*

You can let me go now?

He released her suddenly, as though realizing himself that he'd held on to her a moment too long. He laughed self-consciously and motioned toward her boots.

"I never understood how you girls balanced on those things," he said.

"Well," Flynn said, "apparently not all of us do."

Their eyes met and there was another strange moment of . . . something. Flynn didn't know what it was, but it made her dizzy and she didn't like it. Maybe it was allergies? Was it possible to be allergic to a person?

Well, if her presence here in Scheintown had taught her anything, it was that anything was possible.

"Ready?" she asked.

Jake Tucker nodded. "Never been readier."

He turned and headed out of the train station, carrying her suitcase, so she had no choice but to follow him. He was moving at an easy stride, but his long legs carried him much farther per step than hers would have even without the stilettos, and Flynn had to hustle to keep pace. She finally caught up to him as he was laying her suitcase in the back of a huge, weather-beaten red pickup truck, which a kinder person than she might refer to as "classic." He opened the door for her and held out his hand to help her climb up, but she ignored it, managing to maneuver herself fairly well on her own, although there was a moment there where it was touch and go. *Stupid boots.* Once she was securely inside, he shut the door and walked around to the driver's side.

They enjoyed a verbal cease-fire for a while. Flynn had nothing to say to him, and it was obvious he was only interested in badgering her, so she stared out the window as they drove in silence. The road from the train station into the village was windy and green, lined by farms and trees and low stone walls that wound lazily around the hilly terrain. She knew it was supposed to be charming, but it just creeped her out.

"Nature," she muttered, imagining all the bugs and

rodents and slithery little things lurking in all that ma-
nure-fertilized green. *Yugh.*

"Hmmm?" Jake Tucker asked.

"Nothing," she said.

They passed through the village, and Flynn began to
feel better. Scheintown wasn't exactly the hub of civilization, but there were sidewalks at least, and cute little
boutique shops and charming Colonial streetlamps and a
brick post office and an honest-to-goodness general store
on the corner. There were still a fair number of trees, but
they sprouted up from little stretches of ground between
the sidewalk and the road, the way God intended. Flynn
released a breath.

She could do this.

Maybe.

Then the truck pulled up in front of the biggest, whit-
est, most unabashedly imposing building Flynn had ever
seen, which she swore looked down on her with marked
distaste. The tremendous wooden swinging sign out front
had *The Goodhouse Arms* hand-painted in swirly black
letters—which also, somehow, seemed to judge her. Below the big letters, similar but smaller ones spelled out
Inn · Restaurant · Tavern. Just below that, in letters so
small only Flynn could see them, was the simple line, *You
are in way over your head. Go home.*

"Oh, God," Flynn groaned.

The walkway to the front door was paved with stones
that had probably been there since Colonial days, and brilliant green bushes popped with roses on either side. Flynn
white-knuckled the dashboard and stared. She couldn't do
this. There was no way she could do this. She didn't know
anything about history or hotels or management or any-

thing. She'd had at least fourteen jobs in the last eight years, and while she could flip pizza dough and announce the weather on the radio and hand out flyers in a chicken suit, none of those skills prepared her for this. Places like this were run by uptight people in expensive suits who could pull off being condescending to snooty travelers wanting to sleep in the same bed as George Washington, not unemployed dilettantes like her who couldn't hold down a job her daddy hadn't safety-pinned to her shirt.

Flynn was so immersed in her panic that she hadn't even noticed Jake Tucker hop out and grab her luggage from the bed of the truck until he was there before her, suitcase in hand, opening the passenger side door.

"Wow," she said, barely able to take her eyes off the grand, disapproving columns that banked either side of the dark French doors at the mouth of this great behemoth of an inn. A bead of sweat trickled down the small of her back.

"Welcome home." His voice was softer than it had been at the train station, and Flynn had to look to make sure it was still the same guy standing there. It was. His expression was less condescending now, though, almost . . . sympathetic, like he could tell how panicked she was, and was making an effort to be kind. Not that she was going to let her guard down with him just yet, but she allowed the possibility that he might not be a total asshole. Only time would tell.

"Oh, and . . ." He reached into his pocket, withdrawing a set of keys. "Here. These are yours."

She glanced down. They were the keys to the truck. She looked back up at him. "Why are you giving me these?"

"The truck's yours. A small gesture of independence, from the inn to you."

She laughed out loud. "You're kidding, right?"

"Not at the moment. Why?"

"You don't actually expect me to drive that thing, do you?"

His eyes darkened, and the condescension returned. "Sorry, Ms. Hilton. Limo's in the shop. You'll have to slum it for a while."

Flynn clutched the keys tightly in her hands and looked up at him, anger coursing through her. She was leaning back toward *total asshole*. "Excuse me?"

His eyes met hers, and they weren't apologetic in the least. "Esther didn't drive, and this is the extra truck from maintenance. You want a town car and a driver, you're gonna have to make your own arrangements."

"That's not it," she said tightly. "I just . . ." She held the keys out to him. "I don't drive."

He blinked, the shock clear on his face. "You're thirty years old and you don't know how to drive?"

"Twenty-nine." She hopped out of the truck. "And I grew up in Boston. Anywhere I needed to go, it was either cab, T, or walk."

A smidge of contrition crossed his face, and Flynn figured that was as close to an apology as she was likely to get from this guy.

"Well, that's not the way it is here," he said. "There are a few basic things within walking distance, but sooner or later, you're gonna want the truck."

She released a breath, and stuffed the keys in her purse. "Fine. Thank you."

He nodded, hitched up her suitcase, and started down the sidewalk, away from the inn.

"We're not going inside?" Flynn asked, shuffling to keep up with his pace.

"You'll be staying at the cottage," he said, leading her onto a cobblestone path that curled around to one side of the inn. "It's where Esther lived. It's just around past the east wing here—"

"The east *wing*?" Flynn said, realizing as they walked that the east wing stretched a good thirty yards back. Hadn't Freya said it was a *little* inn?

"There's an east wing and a west wing. Three floors, thirty rooms, and two suites each. They're connected by the lobby, bar, and restaurant. The courtyard stretches out between the wings, going back to the rose garden. And at the edge of the east corner of the courtyard is . . ."

He trailed off as they reached a small cottage, painted white with green shutters. The cobblestones curved toward it, leading right up to the tiny little front door, also painted green. The porch held a two-seater porch swing, and the trees that flanked the cottage on either side were turning shades of brilliant red and yellow, except for the tremendous evergreen that shaded the front porch. Some leaves had started to fall, softening the walk as they moved toward the cottage.

They reached the first porch step and Flynn put her hand to her chest over her erratically beating heart. The cottage itself looked like it had hopped off the cover of the *Saturday Evening Post,* and that was nice and everything, but all the trees and the mulchy smell of the fallen leaves made Flynn's skin itch. Would a little cement kill these people? Seriously.

Tucker motioned down at the leaf-covered path. "Herman doesn't usually rake out here. Esther liked the leaves. I can tell Annabelle to send him over in the morning if you don't like it."

"No," Flynn swallowed, not wanting to admit that it bothered her. She could live with a few leaves. "It's fine. It's nice. It's . . . um . . ."

Flynn looked up to find him watching her, a bemused smile on his face. He knew she was freaked out. How did he know? Was she that transparent? She turned away from him, cleared her throat, and hardened her voice a touch. "This was my aunt Esther's?"

He nodded. "It was the manager's quarters back in the day, but Esther's been here as long as anyone can remember. Mercy—she's the chef—has put some basics in the kitchen for you, but if you need anything else, just let her know and she'll get it for you."

Jake unlocked the front door as he talked, then handed the key to her and moved to the side to allow her through. She stepped inside and . . .

"Oh, my God," she said without thinking. "It kinda smells like old lady in here."

Her suitcase landed with a thunk by the front door and she could tell when she glanced behind her that Jake hadn't appreciated the comment.

"You know, that kind of . . . peppermint smell. It's not bad. I wasn't being . . ."

He just stared at her, all virtuous and offended, as if he hadn't said a million mean things to her since picking her up at the station. She inhaled again, and decided it wouldn't kill her to offer a tiny olive branch. After all, she couldn't fire him for another seven days.

"I mean, it's beautiful." She glanced around at the little living room. There was lace everywhere. *Everywhere.* But the space was nice, and she was sure that once she opened the windows and cleared some of the knickknacks away, it would be fine. She took a step closer to the wall and squinted in the dim light to see if she was really looking at what she thought she was looking at.

Yep. It was a shelf dedicated entirely to ceramic cow creamers.

She crossed the room and poked her head in the bathroom. It was laid out in peach tile, which would take some getting used to, but it had a gorgeous claw foot tub, a stylish pedestal sink, and a door leading directly to what she assumed was the bedroom. She glanced over her shoulder as she walked toward the bedroom door.

"So, they, uh . . . they haven't cleared out her stuff, then?"

He shrugged. "Her clothes and personal things are packed away, but we didn't really have time to redecorate, no."

Flynn nodded, poked her head into the bedroom. A big four-poster bed, large cherrywood armoire, two ornate nightstands, a lace bedspread, lace curtains. It was pretty much an even mix of nice and *yargh.* She stepped back into the living room and found Jake Tucker, still standing by the door, watching her. Why wouldn't he just leave?

"Oh, sorry! Of course!" She pulled a twenty out of her purse as she crossed the room to him, then stuffed it into his hand. "Thank you. Bye."

He leaned against the doorjamb, his arms crossed over his chest as he stared at her. What? Was he holding out for forty? Greedy bastard.

"You still haven't answered my question about whether you're selling or not," he said.

She put her hand to her temple, which was beginning to pound. "Is everyone in this town so direct? Because if that's the case, I'm going to need to find a pharmacy."

"You've never lived in a small town, have you?" he asked, but didn't wait for the answer. "They all know I came to get you. The second I leave this cottage they're going to descend on me like locusts and ask me if I think you're going to sell the place."

"You're kidding."

"Would that I were," he said. "And right now, based on the way you've dodged my questions, I'm thinking you're going to sell."

"No!" Flynn said. "God, no. Don't tell them that."

"Is it the truth?"

"Well." She tried to keep a straight face as she parroted the company line Freya had given her. "We haven't made any decisions just yet. That's why I'm here. To help make the decisions."

"Right." He kept looking at her, that sly little smirk on his face, and her stupid traitor heart got all fluttery under his gaze.

Knock it off, she told herself. *Charming and handsome do not trump jerk.*

"Mr. Tucker . . ."

He smiled. For the first time, she noticed that his front teeth were slightly crooked. "Jake."

"I can't call you Jake."

His eyebrows quirked toward each other. "Why not?"

Duh. "Because then you win."

The sheer ridiculousness of it all seemed to hit them

both at the same time. They shared a smile, and once again, Flynn went all fluttery inside. She took a deep breath and mentally envisioned herself hosing the butterflies down with insecticide.

"Okay," he said, breaking into her thoughts. "We'll compromise. You can call me Tucker."

"Fine, *Tucker.* Thank you for the ride, but if we're done here, I'd really like to unpack, pee, and take a nap."

He chuckled. She raised her eyebrows and looked meaningfully at the door.

"Okay," he said, nodding. "Fair enough."

He tossed the twenty down on the half-moon table by the door and left. Relief flooded her entire body. Her reprieve wouldn't last long, though, she knew. Soon she would have to call a staff meeting and look them all in the eye and lie like a bastard. But for the moment, she was safe.

The hair on the back of her neck rose suddenly, and she got the distinct feeling that she was being watched. She glanced around, her eyes finally landing on the cow creamers. She walked to the shelf and stared them down.

"You guys? Will be the first to go."

Feeling marginally better, she turned and headed toward the bathroom, working hard to shake the absurd feeling that behind her, the ceramic cows were laughing.

There were three messages waiting for Jake when he walked through his apartment door. The first was, predictably, from Mercy, lecturing him on being nice to the niece, lest she sell the place and fire them all, et cetera, et cetera . . .

. . . et cetera. His sister had definitely inherited the
Tucker gene for excessive chattiness.

Pfft, he thought as Mercy rattled on. *Nice to the niece.*
Like he needed to be told. He was always nice. And he'd
been on his best behavior with the niece, if you didn't
count the badgering, which he didn't. It was a necessary
evil to see what he was dealing with in this Flynn Daly
person. If the niece was in it with Chase, Jake had to know
that. If it meant pissing off the niece in the process, so
be it.

The thing was, even after the badgering, he wasn't at
all sure what he was dealing with. His gut said she was
okay, and his gut was usually pretty reliable, but there
was definitely something weird about her. His research
had painted a pretty clear picture of what to expect; your
basic spoiled rich girl who's never had to work a day in
her life. She'd gone to Boston University, gotten a degree
in Liberal Arts with a minor in Theater, and had gone on
to be an actress for a while, with mentions peppered in
some regional papers outside of Boston. In recent years,
she'd disappeared off the radar, with the exception of occasional mentions in the Boston society sections, usually
for attending an event for one of her father's pet charities.
Based on all that, Jake had been expecting a spoiled so-
cialite out here to charm the locals while Daddy skewered
a deal back at Rich Dude HQ.

Instead, what he'd gotten was a mass of contradictions
with a heartbeat. She was both confident and insecure.
She stood straight, but walked with a tentative gait, like
a little girl in her mother's heels. She was sharp, but still
easily taken off guard. She had this crazy hair that was
tame and wild at the same time, hazel eyes that seemed to

see more than she let on, and a smile that reminded him
of a Disney heroine—wide, toothy, and with an uncanny
ability to knock his train of thought right off the tracks
every time.

She was . . . weird.

And Jake was pretty sure she was just a spoke in
this wheel; he really didn't think she was involved with
Gordon Chase. Of course, Chase would still be on the
prowl—Jake gave it twenty-four hours max before he
showed up at the Arms, ready to use Flynn Daly to get his
grubby hands on the sale. And she'd fall for his act. Most
women were helpless in the face of men like Gordon
Chase. Which could actually work for Jake; if he stuck
close enough to Flynn Daly, she might be his ticket to
bringing the asshole down.

The machine finally beeped—what happened to the
good old days when answering machines cut people off
after a minute or so?—and the second message started.
Mercy, again, announcing that someone seemed to be
filching the toilet paper from the executive commode, and
she would gladly pay a real private detective to investigate if, alas, only there was one in town.

"It's a damn shame," he muttered as he hit the delete
button.

Then he listened to the third message. It was from a
voice he didn't recognize, a woman's voice so small and
mousy he was a little surprised his machine had picked it
up at all.

"Hello? Um, Mr. Tucker? This is Rhonda Bacon, Gordon Chase's secretary, and I'm calling because . . ." There
was a long pause, and in the background a man's voice
was talking. Finally there was the sound of a door clos-

ing and she was back, her voice even lower than before. "I'm calling because I have information I think you might be interested in." She cleared her throat and lowered her voice. "Information about Mr. Chase. About what he's been doing." There was the sound of a door opening. Jake thought he recognized Gordon Chase's deep, greasy tones this time, and then the line went dead. The electronic time stamp lady announced that the call had come in on Tuesday at 3:13 A.M., which was of course wrong, since it was Monday; Jake had never bothered resetting his machine after the last storm had knocked the power out. Which had been about a month ago. But based on his estimates of when Mercy would have left her messages, he figured the call came in sometime after two-thirty that afternoon, right about the time he was showing Flynn Daly into Esther's cottage.

Jake stared at the machine for a while after Rhonda's message ended, then walked over to the fridge to grab a beer. He wasn't typically a daytime drinker—wasn't much of a drinker at all, actually—but this was an occasion that called for a beer.

After all, this just might be his lucky day. How often did the secretary of your sworn enemy call you offering evidence on a silver platter? Jake was no statistics expert, but he figured not often.

He took a swig from his beer and stared at the machine, his brain getting to work on sorting out the stuff that didn't make sense. For one, why had Rhonda called him? If she knew that Chase was guilty of something, didn't it make sense to go straight to the police? Why call a disgraced—and prematurely retired—rookie cop? Even if he was still on the force, he'd be little more than a grunt with the ability to ticket people for speeding and indecent exposure. He was small potatoes any way you sliced it, so it made no sense for Rhonda to be beating down his door.

Unless maybe she was implicated. Maybe Chase had somehow gotten her to break the law without her realizing what she was doing. Jake knew precious little about Rhonda Bacon, but in the months following his termination from the Scheintown Police Department, he'd done some digging on everyone connected with Chase. From what he'd gathered about Rhonda, she was quiet and easily intimidated, and Chase was just the kind of asshole to use her as a human shield should the circumstance require it.

Jake put the beer down on the coffee table and rubbed his hands over his eyes. He could feel the build happening, the energy pooling under his feet. This was it. This was his chance. He could jump on it, try to take Chase down, and finally end this thing. It wouldn't bring his dad back. It wouldn't get him his job back. It wouldn't even make him feel better about the night he followed Elaine Placie, her rhinestone flask and her killer legs, out to the parking lot at the police station while that laptop disappeared.

But it would feel really, *really* good.

On the other hand, this was also an opportunity to heed the plaintive advice of Mercy, his three other sisters, and his mom, and just move on. Grow up. Pass Go. Collect $200. This was what his oldest sister Liv liked to call "a defining moment," a moment in which you have a choice, and you can either choose the path that leads to growth and enlightenment, or you can continue fucking everything up just like always.

Liv would be disappointed, but he wasn't that interested in growth and enlightenment. He was more interested in finding that laptop, which was impossible. It had surely been wiped clean and either tossed or sold. But that was the beauty of fantasy, no reality required, and in his, he would bring that laptop straight to Gerard Levy, dump it on his desk, and let the justice system take care of Gordon Chase. Then the town would throw a big parade, give him the key to the city, and beg him to come back to work. With a raise.

And as long as he was fantasizing, he wanted Elaine Placie back, too. Not in the sexy con artist way she'd used to tank his career, but rather in the humble, remorseful, begging-for-forgiveness way. Jake leaned back and closed his eyes, picturing her in an orange jumpsuit, blond hair scraggly, wrists manacled, mascara smudged and running, as she begged the judge not to blame Jake.

"It's not his fault," she'd say. "Do you see these legs? He was only human, Judge. And I'm so, so, so"—here, she'd turn her eyes, welling with tears, to Jake—"so sorry. I was wrong. And naughty. Very, very naughty."

That, of course, wasn't going to happen, either. Less than a week after Jake had traded his career for silky legs and a rhinestone flask, Elaine Placie had cleaned out her apartment and conveniently disappeared. Jake had looked for her for a while with some fantasy of her testimony helping to take Chase down, but the trail had gone cold before he could find her. His best guess was that she was out there somewhere, living under an assumed identity and sleeping on a mattress stuffed full with cash courtesy of Gordon Chase. The assumed identity seemed like overkill to Jake, but if she was the kind of girl who'd distract a cop on watch for money, who knew what else she had done? And an assumed identity was the only way to explain how there'd been absolutely no blip on any of the radars he'd set up to look for her. As far as the general bureaucracy of life was concerned, Elaine Placie no longer existed.

Well, he thought, raising his beer in a quiet salute to Rhonda Bacon, *who needs her, anyway?*

Chapter Three

♡ The old lady sat in the rocking chair in the corner of the room. She was rocking, but the chair was not.

Weird.

Flynn sat up in the bed, but at the same time, knew she was still asleep. She could feel the heaviness in her limbs, the steadiness in her breath. Also, it was late, the sun was definitely down, but the room was filled with a misty, orange glow.

And she was staring at a see-through old lady in a rocking chair.

Definitely a dream.

"You moved my cows," the old lady said.

Flynn stared for a moment, her brain moving in fuzzy waves as she tried to connect to what the lady was saying. Cows. She hadn't moved any—

"Oh!" she said, snapping her dream fingers. "The creamers? The ones on the shelf? Hell, yeah, I moved them. They were creeping me out."

The lady stopped rocking. "You're scared of ceramic cows?"

"Cows in general. I'm not a fan. Actually, most farm animals kinda bug me. And bugs." She shuddered through an exhale. "I don't like nature much."

The old lady chuckled, "Boy, did you ever come to the wrong place."

"Maybe." Flynn tried to formulate her next question so it wouldn't make her sound crazy, but then gave up. What the hell? It was just a dream. "Are you, um . . . are you my great-aunt Esther?"

"Is your grandmother Elizabeth Daly?"

"That was my father's mother. Yes."

"That was my sister." Ghost Lady started rocking again. "Guess that makes me your great-aunt Esther. You can just call me Esther, though."

"Oh. Okay. But you're . . . you know. Dead, right?"

Esther glanced up at her, and for the first time, Flynn noticed she was knitting an afghan in various shades of purple. Crazy dream.

"It would appear so," Esther said. "Came as quite the shock to me, too."

All right. This was not okay. It was not okay to be sitting in a strange bed in a strange place that smelled like old lady and having a conversation with a dead woman. Flynn closed her eyes and tried to wake up, but when she opened them again, the room was still all glowy.

She was still dreaming.

Shit.

"Got any Pop-Tarts?" Esther asked suddenly.

"No." Flynn swallowed. This was by far the weirdest

dream she'd ever had. And that included the one with the duck.

"Shame." Esther sighed. "I really miss Pop-Tarts. The strawberry ones with the frosting and sprinkles were my favorite."

Flynn rubbed her fingers over her eyes, but when she opened them again, Esther was still there.

"Look, not to be rude, but isn't there a white light or something you need to be going toward?"

"I think perhaps you need to examine your concept of rude. And, no, to answer your question, there isn't a white light. There isn't anything. Just me in this little house, doddering about. No Pop-Tarts." She shot a ghostly glare at Flynn over her bifocals. "I assume it has something to do with you."

Flynn felt a rush of panic go through her. "With me? Why me? We've never even met before."

"And yet, there you are, sleeping in my bed, moving my cows—"

"Look, I'm sorry about the cows, okay? Had I known it would upset the dead lady, I would have thought twice."

Esther let out a martyred sigh. "Don't worry about it. I put them back."

Flynn felt herself roll over in her sleep, and yet there she was, still on the edge of the bed, locked in an awkward silence with a dead woman.

Okay. That's enough.

"It was nice to meet you, Aunt Esther. I'm going to wake up now, and you'll just go away, right?"

Aunt Esther continued knitting. "I don't know. Why don't you give it a try?"

With a deep gasp, Flynn shot up in bed. For real this

time. She no longer felt all fuzzy, and with her hand on her chest she could feel her erratic heartbeat and uneven breathing. She reached over and flicked on the lamp, then looked at the rocking chair in the corner of the room.

It was still.

And empty.

Thank God.

She glanced at the clock. 12:34. She'd been sleeping for six hours. No wonder she was disoriented. Dreaming about dead old ladies. How ridiculous.

She tried to laugh, but it came out all wavery and weak. She felt a chill go down her spine, and shuddered as she tried to talk herself down from the panic welling in her gut.

It was just a dream.

She hopped out of the bed, grabbed her suitcase, and tossed it onto the bed.

There's no such thing as ghosts.

She unzipped the suitcase, pulled out a pair of jeans and a light sweater.

Even if she's really a ghost, she can't hurt you.

She got dressed quickly and zoomed out of the bedroom. She snatched her purse from the half-moon table and then froze as she saw something out of the corner of her eye.

She turned.

She looked.

Oh, holy Jesus.

Had she dreamed taking the ceramic cows down and putting them in the closet? She remembered all the details clearly, from the light sheen of dust on the ceramic to the old musty smell of the closet as she tucked them way in the back.

And yet, there they were on the shelf on the wall, exactly where they'd been when she'd found them.

Well, then she must have dreamed putting them away, too.

She *must* have.

"It was nice meeting you, Aunt Esther," Flynn said loudly as she pulled the front door open. "Now go away."

Jake wiped the inside of a wineglass and hooked it into the holder above the bar. Monday nights were typically dead; the locals who drank early in the week usually went to dives like the Bait and Tackle on Route 9, and guests of the Goodhouse Arms tended to be early-to-bed types. The last customers had left fifteen minutes earlier and Jake started in on closing up, taking advantage of having a few moments alone to think.

But there were really only two things on his mind: Rhonda Bacon and Flynn Daly.

Rhonda, because he needed to figure out how he was going to approach her without Gordon Chase getting wind of it. Shiny was a small place; you couldn't have a dirty thought without everyone knowing about it. Meeting with the secretary of your sworn enemy? They'd be talking about it in the preschool.

And Flynn Daly, because Jake needed to find a way to undo the damage from their meeting that afternoon and try to talk her into keeping the place before Gordon Chase swooped in and convinced her otherwise. If Flynn didn't delay her family on the sale for at least a little while, there'd be no bright, shiny objects to keep Chase distracted while Jake did his investigating on the sly. If he could just get Flynn to gum up the works for a little while . . .

Of course, he'd have to get her to trust him first. He'd thought about stopping by the cottage after work, but it was way too late for a casual social call. She'd think he was there for sex or a raise, and neither assumption would reflect well on him. The wrinkle was, Chase had certainly smelled the niece in the water by now. If Jake was a betting man, he'd put his last dollar on Chase being there first thing in the morning, which meant that in order to beat him to the punch, Jake would have to get to Flynn before eight, and he didn't have her pegged as a morning person.

So when he heard the door swing open and saw Flynn Daly push into the bar looking like a woman who needed a drink real bad, Jake's smile couldn't have been more genuine. Flynn, however, didn't look quite so happy to see him.

"What are you doing here?"

"My job." Jake flipped a bar towel over his shoulder. "I'm your bartender."

"I thought you were maintenance."

"Why would you think I'm maintenance?"

"Well . . . you said . . ." She paused for a moment, then shook her head. "I don't know."

"Okay." He leaned one elbow on the bar and pulled on the charm smile. It almost never failed. "That's a good reason."

She slumped down on a bar stool. "This is not going well."

"You think?" he said, setting a dish of pretzels out for her. "Because I'd have to disagree. My night just started looking up."

Flynn raised her head up from the bar and glared at him.

"Don't charm me, Tucker."

"Can't help it. Charm is part of a package deal. It comes with the clever and the good-looking."

"Oh, stop it. I know your type." She sneered and moved her fingers around in the air in front of his face, as though conjuring his "type" from thin air. "I wasted most of my precious college years dating your type. I . . ." She blinked, and her eyes cleared, and she shook her head. "Why am I talking about this? Jameson's neat, please."

Well, I guess making friends and gaining her trust is out, Jake thought as he set a rocks glass on the bar and filled it. *This is where a plan B would have come in handy.*

He slid the glass to her in silence. She took it and looked up at him with guilty eyes.

"I'm sorry," she grumbled finally. "I'm usually not this cranky. I'm actually, typically, kind of a fun person."

Jake perked up. Was she starting to confide in him? That could be good. He leaned forward slightly. "I think you're scads of fun."

She gave a mini eye roll, then sighed. "My family thinks I'm a loser. They sent me here because they don't think I'll ever make anything of my life on my own." She lifted her glass and snorted into it. "The kicker? They're probably right."

Jake waffled for a moment, then chose a direction. "If you think so, then they are."

Her glass froze in midair, and her eyes raised up to his. "Excuse me?"

"I have four sisters and a mother. I know a little something about familial disapproval. The secret is not to let it get to you. They love you, they're worried about you, they say hurtful things, but it's just because they want what's best for you. But only you know what's best for you, so go ahead and humor them so you can get through Thanksgiving without bloodshed, but don't believe any of it."

She stared at him in stark silence. Jake held his breath. He'd either just won her over or completely blown it, and he wouldn't know until she said something.

But she wasn't saying anything. She just held his gaze for a long moment, and then, without any change in facial expression, said, "My father has angina."

Jake broke into a deliberately confused grin. "Really? Is that possible? For a man to have—"

She huffed. "Not a *vagina. An*gina. It's a heart—"

"A heart thing," Jake said, playfully swatting at her arm with his bar towel. "I know."

Finally, she broke into a crazy, tremendous, heart-stopping smile, and it felt like all the lights in the room upped their wattage. She lowered her glass, shook her head, and laughed lightly.

Jake grinned. He hadn't blown it.

"So, your dad," he said. "He's okay?"

She lifted her head, the smile still playing on her lips. "Yeah. He's fine. And now, he's not worried about me anymore, so that should help."

"Ah," Jake said. "Taking one for the team, are you?"

She looked around the bar, assessing her surroundings. "Yeah. Guess you could say that."

The smile was almost gone. Jake wanted to see it again, see if the entire room brightening was just his imagination, but there were things to be accomplished first.

"I think you did the right thing," he said. "And let me tell you why."

"You sound like that guy from *The Music Man*," she said. "Does your reason start with a capital T, which rhymes with P, which stands for—"

"The Goodhouse Arms," Jake jumped in. "Let me tell you why I think you shouldn't sell this place."

"Oh, hell." Flynn lifted her glass and took a long swallow, but that smile played once again at the edge of her lips.

"Here's the thing," he said, leaning closer to her, creating an air of intimacy between them. "This place, it's a great place. With great people. There's history here. Did you know that George Washington actually slept here?"

"How do you know he's not *still* sleeping here?" she muttered, and took another drink.

"Well . . ." Jake chuckled, hoping she was kidding. "Because he's dead. But I find the dead to be a really depressing topic. Hey, let's talk money."

"Or, hey, let's not."

"We don't make much here."

She raised a brow at him. "*That's* your hard sell?"

"Esther liked to pay her people well, and that ate into the profit margin a bit. But you see, this place is about more than profits."

"More than profits?"

"More than profits. It's about history. And legacy. And the Goodhouse name, which may not mean much to you because you don't carry it, but it's still in your blood."

He waited, not speaking again until she smiled, which, he was glad to note, didn't take too long.

Hell. This might just work.

"Flynn, it's a great place. And we do a decent business. Esther got along just fine. So can you. Why don't you just give it a try? Stay for, say, a year. Run the place. If it doesn't work, you can always sell then."

She bolted upright. "A year? Are you kidding? I'm not staying the night."

Wow. He *really* sucked at this.

She looked at him for a long moment, then shrugged and downed the rest of the drink.

"It's been a long day," she said, sliding the glass to him to refill. "I should be sleeping right now, but I can't because, as it turns out, I've got a roommate."

Jake felt a bristle at the idea, but covered with a laugh. "Well. That was quick."

She blinked. "What?" Her eyes widened, and then she smacked at his arm. "Oh, God. No. Who could I possibly have seduced between now and when you dropped me off this afternoon?"

"I'd believe it," Jake said. Flynn met his eye.

"You say that like it's a compliment."

"It was."

Flynn opened her mouth, then closed it, then waved her hand in the air. "Okay. Whatever. Anyway. I was talking about Esther. Esther's my roommate."

"Mmmmm, don't think so," he said, smiling lightly. "We may not be up on all the latest things here in Shiny, but we have hopped on the bury-the-dead bandwagon."

"I don't mean her *body*. A body I can deal with. I'm talking about her"—she waved her hands around in the air, as if trying to conjure the word—"*spirit*." She downed another gulp of her drink, then shook her head. "I think she moved the cows."

Jake gently pulled the glass from Flynn's fingers. "You know, I think maybe we're done with this."

She whipped her eyes up to his and then narrowed them dangerously. Jake drew back in a self-protective instinct.

"Look," she said, her voice low and serious, "let's get a few things straight here. I'm not some ditzy, spoiled Daddy's girl who can't think for herself or put in a hard day's work. And I'm not crazy, either. I dreamed about Aunt Esther, and okay, *fine*, maybe she didn't move the cows, but it creeped me out, and that's a completely sane response. Now, I'm here to do a job, and I'm gonna do it, and that's that. So don't charm me, don't condescend to me, and if you value your hand—"

In a flash, she snatched her glass back; Jake was impressed that she did it without spilling a drop.

"—do not *ever* take my drink away again, okay?"

Their eyes connected, and Jake felt everything go still. Flynn Daly was just plain odd. Alternately combative and congenial, pretty and prickly. She had this weird effect of shifting gravity when she walked in a room, making him feel perpetually off balance in her presence, and there was something about her that occasionally snuck up and dope-slapped him in the back of the head.

He liked her, much more than he thought he would. Not enough to stop him from using her to get to Gordon Chase . . .

She raised her eyes to his, and a suspicious look flashed through them.

"What?" She swiped at her face. "Do I have something on my nose?"

Jake smiled and jerked his chin up toward the clock. "It's closing time. One A.M."

"I don't think so. I own the place." She took a swig from her drink and set it down on the bar. "From now on, we're open until I'm done drinking."

"Fine," he said. "But you'll have to take that up with the town board. They make the rules, and right now, we're in violation of the law."

Her eyes met his, and behind her tough expression, he could see the vulnerability there. She was scared. Somehow, though he didn't think it was possible, that made him like her even more.

He smiled and nudged the glass toward her with his finger. "Take it with you. It's your glass now anyway."

"Great. Can I get a room, too?"

"I don't know. The desk is closed."

"The desk is closed? This is a *hotel*. What if someone needs something? Like, to get a room?"

Jake shrugged. "I don't know what to tell you. The desk closes at six. And I don't know which rooms are available. Annabelle has this . . . system. It's weird. It involves tarot cards and an abacus and a trained monkey—"

"She has a *system*? What, you don't have computers?"

Jake grinned, amused that she took the joke literally. "Yeah, we have computers. But it's this weird program Annabelle's, like, uncle or cousin or something wrote. It's linked with the bookkeeping, and the last time I tried to reserve a room for someone, twelve thousand dollars went missing from the books and it was kinda bloody.

Annabelle put a password on it and she's the only one
who can get in."

Flynn stared at him. "We've got one person doing reservations for this entire inn?"

"The inn is historic, but not typically overbooked. Win-
ters, we don't even use the west wing. Most of the money
comes from the bar and restaurant, which are top quality,
highly rated, and well worth keeping to the lucky person
who inherits them."

She didn't look impressed. "So that's a long way of
saying . . . ?"

"Yes. We've got one person handling reservations for
the entire inn."

"Great." Flynn downed the last of her drink and pushed
off her bar stool. "Fine. Okay. Whatever. I'm an adult.
There's no reason I can't go back to the cottage and just
deal with my dead roommate." She looked at him, tucked
a strand of wild caramel hair behind her ear. "It *was* just
a dream, right?"

He couldn't help but smile. For some reason, the
weirder she got, the more he liked her. "Yeah. It was just
a dream."

She took a step toward the door, then turned around,
nibbling on the edge of her lip. "What if she starts talking
to me again?"

"Talk back?"

"Oh, right. What would I say? 'Bummer you're dead, I
hear the white light rocks, go find it'?"

"I don't know," he said, holding her gaze. "You could
start with the ditzy Daddy's girl thing. It's effective
material."

Flynn cocked her head to the side, as if deciding how to take that, then finally allowed a small smile.

Jake smiled back. "Give me ten minutes to close up here and I'll walk you back."

"Oh, thank you." She released her breath and her shoulders slumped in relief as she sat back on the bar stool. Jake chuckled and tossed the bar rag into the bucket of bleach water by his feet. This was working out better than he'd ever thought.

He was going to have to be careful around that smile, though. It knocked him over every time.

Chapter Four

♡Flynn rubbed the towel over her wet hair and took a deep breath of the sweet morning air coming in through the window. The bedroom, not half as creepy now as it had been last night, was aglow in the tree-filtered rays of the autumn sun, and Flynn felt much more confident than she had the day before. She gave her damp hair one final rub and tossed the towel on the rocking chair, which she'd turned around to face the corner the night before. She was pretty sure the visitation from Esther had been her imagination, but there was nothing wrong with sending a message, was there?

She turned and checked herself out in the big standing mirror in the corner. Her jeans were a bit wrinkly, but her oversized cable-knit sweater hung low enough to cover most of it, and since the professional wardrobe Freya'd ordered wasn't in yet, it would just have to do.

Flynn worked on pulling a stray piece of yarn into her sweater as she walked out into the living room. Her eyes registered the two male legs sticking off the edge of Aunt Esther's prim little love seat, but her brain took a moment to catch up. When it did, she jumped back and screamed, then put her hand over her pounding heart as she gripped the wall for support. Tucker let out a startled bellow of his own and jumped up off the sofa, landing squarely on his feet.

"Oh, my God," she said, trying to catch her breath. "How drunk was I last night?"

"Hmmm?" He looked at her blankly for a moment, then his eyes widened. "Oh. No. Not very. But . . . um." He yawned and shook his head quickly. "Yeah. Remember the whole ghost thing?"

Flynn recalled clutching the back of his jacket in her fist like it was a tether rope on a rock wall as she made him open the front door for her.

"Yeah. Little bit."

"Well, you seemed kind of freaked. I thought I'd just sit here until you fell asleep. You know. Make sure you were okay." He ran his hand through his hair. It didn't do much good. "Guess I must have passed out."

Flynn watched him standing there with his hair sticking up and couldn't help but smile. She lowered her hand from her chest and took a deep breath.

"Thank you. That was sweet."

"What can I say? I'm a sweet guy." He grimaced, rubbed his neck, and nodded to indicate the tiny sofa. "Wow. I had no idea Nazis made love seats."

Flynn laughed before she could stop herself, then tried to tighten up her expression when he looked up.

"Can I . . . uh . . . make you some coffee?"

"Yeah," he said, smiling. "That'd be nice."

His smile looked better this morning than it had yesterday. So did he, even with the rough shadow that was claiming his jawline, and the fact that he was rumpled from head to foot and his hair was shooting out in a thousand different directions. He was . . . cute.

Cute. Good God. She hadn't thought of a guy as *cute* since the ninth grade. She smiled. "I'll just go make some coffee, then."

Tucker nodded, but then waved his hand in the air to stop her. "Actually, forget it. Esther didn't have a coffeemaker."

Flynn felt a tinge of horror strike her heart. "She didn't? Oh, how sad."

"Well, it's not the last ten minutes of *Old Yeller,* but sure."

Flynn let out a little laugh, which was followed by a toe-scuffing silence. She wasn't sure how to deal with Jake Tucker. They were clearly from different worlds. He was her employee, technically, but he was also the closest thing to a friend that she had so far in Scheintown. Still, seeing him this early in the morning was strangely intimate, especially considering she'd known him for less than twenty-four hours.

So many reasons to feel awkward, she thought. *How to choose just one?*

"Well," she said, "I guess they'll have coffee at the inn, then? Maybe we could go there?"

He looked at her for a moment, then shrugged. "Well—"

"I mean," she said quickly, holding her hands up to stop him before he could misread her and think she was asking him out, "unless you want to go home and get some real sleep. Which, of course, you do because you're a bartender and this has to be crazy early for you."

"Actually," he said, the edges of his lips twitching up in a smile, "I think coffee would be nice. There's kind of something I want to talk to you about, anyway."

She watched him warily. "Does it have to do with whether or not I'm selling this place?"

"A little. Maybe." He let out a long breath, and something in him seemed to tense up. "There's this guy. Local businessman. He's probably going to contact you today, and I just wanted to warn you about him."

"Warn me?"

"Yes. He's . . . uh . . . he's not a good guy. You need to watch your step around him."

Flynn wanted to laugh, but Tucker didn't look like he was joking.

"And what exactly do you think this man is going to do to me?"

The line of his mouth went flat, and there wasn't the slightest hint of amusement in his eyes. "Just don't trust him."

For the first time since she'd met him, Jake Tucker was actually dead serious. It was a little unsettling.

"I don't understand," she said. "I just got here. What would this guy want with me?"

"It's not you he wants," Jake said. "It's the inn. He wants you to sell the inn."

Flynn allowed her annoyance to seep into her laugh. "I knew it. This is what all that 'this place is so great, don't sell it' stuff was about? It's about you wanting to stick it to this guy, right?"

"No." Tucker took a step toward her. "This is a great

place, and you shouldn't sell it. But this guy has an agenda—"

Flynn had to laugh at that. "Pot calling the kettle, sounds like."

"Look, I just . . ." He sighed heavily, and turned plaintive eyes on her. "I don't want to see you get hurt."

"Funny," she said, "because I think this actually has very little to do with me."

Tucker opened his mouth to speak, but was interrupted by a knock at the door. Flynn kept her eyes on his.

"Gee. I wonder who that is?" she said flatly.

Tucker cleared his throat nervously. "Hey, mind if I use the bathroom?"

"Sure, go right ahead," she said, but he had already disappeared through the bathroom door before the words were out.

Okaaaaay. She went to the front door and pulled it open.

"Good morning. Flynn Daly, I presume?"

The first thing she saw were the teeth, smiling at her so brightly that she swore she could hear that little *tink* sound like in the toothpaste commercials.

Next, she caught the eyes. Blue and crystalline.

Then the suit. Armani.

Finally, the hair. Black, naturally shiny, and graying just a touch at the temples.

This was possibly the most classically handsome, well-groomed man she'd ever seen in her life. How the hell did a guy like that end up in a place like Scheintown?

Or more specifically, on her doorstep in a place like Scheintown?

"Good morning," he said again, a little louder. He held

out his hand. "My name is Gordon Chase. I hope you don't mind me dropping in on you so early in the morning, but Annabelle told me you'd be out here and I wanted to introduce myself."

"Hi." Flynn shook his hand, which was big and strong and warm and softer than a baby's bottom. *He must manicure twice a day.* "I'm Flynn Daly."

His smile *tinked* at her again. "I know. It's a pleasure to finally meet you. I've heard so much."

"Really?" she said. "From whom?"

His smile faded into an expression of sincere concern, and he covered their joined hands with his free one. "I was so sorry to hear about Esther's passing. Your great-aunt was a treasure in this community, and she'll be sorely missed."

Hard to miss her if she won't go away. "Yes, she sure will."

He finally released her hands, digging his own into his pockets in an affected boyish manner, which put Flynn instantly on her guard. Anyone who'd muss an Armani line to appear boyish was not to be trusted.

"Anyway, I'm the president of the Historical Preservation Society, and I was hoping you'd let me treat you to breakfast this morning. I think we'd have so much to talk about."

Tink.

"Actually, right this minute isn't that great for me . . ." Flynn started, but was interrupted by what had to be the world's loudest toilet flushing. If there was any doubt in her mind that Gordon Chase was the man Tucker had been warning her against, it was gone.

Meanwhile, Gordon Chase's eyebrows rose an easy quarter inch.

"Oh," he said, a look of confusion washing over his face for a moment. "I see. Well." *Tink.* "Maybe some other time. Are you free for lunch, perhaps?"

"Oh, sure, why not?" Flynn said, just as an incredibly loud and unmistakably male belch emanated from her bedroom. She acted as if she hadn't heard it. "Why don't I meet you in the lobby at noon?"

Gordon's smile faltered, then widened. "Perfect. I'll see you at noon."

The second the door was shut, Tucker emerged from the bathroom, without even the slightest look of contrition on his face. He was amazing. She just wanted to sit and watch him for a while, like a zoo animal.

"Ready for that coffee?" he asked brightly.

"As soon as you tell me what that performance was all about."

He had the nerve to look surprised. "Performance? Oh, you mean the . . ." He trailed off, the picture of delicacy. "Sorry about that. Must have been the enchiladas I had for dinner last night."

Flynn watched him for a moment. "That was Gordon Chase. At the door."

Tucker nodded, and his face looked uncharacteristically tense. "I figured."

"Yeah, I figured you figured. I didn't appreciate the soundtrack, by the way."

"Hey, sorry, I was just—"

"I don't care what you were *just,*" Flynn said, advancing on him. "I don't care what your agenda is, or what Gordon Chase's agenda is. I came here to do a job, and

I'm going to do it. And I won't be target practice in whatever little pissing contest you've got going on with him.
Are we clear?"

Tucker let out a hard sigh. "I'm just trying to look out
for you."

Flynn put her hand on her forehead and sighed. "At
any point in our association have I ever asked you to look
out for me?"

He smiled smugly. "You mean, aside from last night
when you needed a bodyguard to protect you from your
dead aunt?"

Flynn clenched her teeth until they hurt, her emotions
evenly split between anger and embarrassment. Tucker
lowered his head a bit until his face was in her eye line,
his expression infuriatingly playful.

"One toke over the line, huh?"

"You know what?" She grabbed a fistful of his sleeve
and guided him toward the door. "Go."

"Because I did think about not pointing the ghost thing
out, but you really left yourself wide open."

"Good-bye, Tucker."

He shrugged out of her grip as they reached the door,
then turned to face her. "So . . . what? Rain check on the
coffee, then?"

"You still have your job," she said, trying to keep any
hint of amusement out of her voice, although it was hard
not to smile a little. "Maybe now's a good time to take
stock. Count your blessings."

"Okay. But just to let you know, firing me would be
a huge mistake," he said, leaning against the door. "I'm
very popular here. Everyone loves me. It'd be hell on
morale."

She yanked the door open, knocking him slightly off balance as she did. "I'll take that under advisement."

He sighed. "Okay. Fine. Just . . ." His eyes met hers, and once again, they were serious. "Just watch your step with Chase, okay? I'm not sure he's not dangerous."

Flynn stared at him for a moment. "What the hell does that mean?"

Tucker shrugged and looked out the door, then back at her. "It means what it means. Look, if you don't believe me, talk to Mercy. She's your chef, and she's a completely unbiased source of information."

She stared up at him, her anger and annoyance fading away under the warmth of his smile, and she was forced to admit the truth to herself. Despite her best efforts, she'd let him charm her. The only defense she had left was to make sure he didn't know it.

"Good-bye, Tucker," she said firmly, holding the door open for him. He winked at her, and she chewed the inside of her cheek to keep from smiling back, then finally he left. When she closed the door behind him, though, she allowed herself one smile.

Just one, she thought, pulling the edges of her lips firmly down again. *You're a professional.*

Jake whistled to himself as he jaunted smoothly along the path to the Arms, willfully ignoring the edgy buzzing in his limbs. This was okay. This was all right. This was workable. So, Flynn was going to lunch with Chase. It was fine. If she was anywhere near as prickly and defensive with Chase as she'd been with Jake, it would actually be perfect. Flynn going out with Chase was in The Plan. It was the crux of The Plan.

So why did the thought of it bug him so much? There'd been a moment when Jake had been sitting on the edge of Flynn's bathtub, listening to Gordon Chase getting his smarm all over her, that he hadn't wanted her anywhere near Chase. He'd almost let that protective instinct get in the way, but then he remembered The Plan. Get Flynn close to Chase, stay close to Flynn. It was still a good plan.

It just needs a little tweak, he thought as he turned on his heel and headed to the front door of the Arms. *One small tweak, and it'll be perfect.*

He pushed through the front door. Annabelle smiled when she saw him approach the desk, and he pulled on the most charming, carefree smile in his arsenal.

"Good morning, lovely Annabelle," he said, leaning one elbow on the desk.

"Hi, Jake," she said, her blond curls jiggling along with the rest of her. She was a cute girl, Annabelle, but every part of her seemed perpetually in motion, and it got a little unnerving sometimes. "What are you doing here so early?"

"Oh, just checking in, helping out, doing my part for life, liberty, and the American way." He casually straightened a pile of brochures on the counter. "Hey, have you seen the niece yet?"

Annabelle's eyes widened. "Nope. Nobody's seen her. Except you, right? You picked her up, right? What's she like? Is she beautiful, you know, like that big-city beautiful, you know, all exotic with Manolo Blahniks and Gucci? Jake?"

He blinked. Whenever he talked to Annabelle, he always felt like that dog in the cartoon, the one that only hears, "Blah blah blah Jake blah."

"Yeah, sure," he said. "She's great. Anyway, she asked me to take care of something for her. She's having lunch with Gordon Chase at noon."

Annabelle's eyes widened to tennis-ball size. *"Here?"*

"Yeah. Here." He blinked innocence. "Why not here?"

"Because he never comes here. He knows we all hate him," she said.

"Everybody in town hates him. Man's gotta eat somewhere."

Annabelle sighed. "And the last time he was here Mercy tried to kill him."

"Pffft," Jake said, waving his hand in the air dismissively. "That chef's knife slipped from her hand. Total accident. Speaking of Mercy, be sure to let her know to serve him something berry special." Jake leaned forward. "Write it down. Berry, with a *b*."

"Berry special?" Annabelle said. "Seriously?"

"It's a Tucker thing." He grinned. "And when have you ever known me not to be serious?"

Annabelle smiled and jotted *Berry Special* down on her notepad, then raised her eyes back to meet his.

"So, did Ms. Daly need anything else?"

Hmmm. *Did* Ms. Daly need anything else? The idea struck like lightning, and Jake smiled as he ran with it. "Actually, now that you mention it. Go ahead and block out the Rose Banquet Room for . . . say . . . one o'clock. She wants to hold a staff meeting."

Annabelle nodded, scribbling, then looked back up at Jake with hungry eyes. "What's the meeting about?"

Jake shrugged innocently. "I have no idea. I think it's just a get-to-know-you thing. She seemed really interested in meeting the staff. Tell everyone to bring all their questions."

She leaned forward, her chin in her hand. "Really? Because everyone's kinda freaked out about a sale. Do you think she's going to sell? Because I hear that the big chains all come in and cut salaries and then fire everyone who doesn't quit."

"Annabelle, come on. That's ridiculous. You and I both know that big chains disembowel everyone and stick the heads on pikes to stake at the four corners of the village."

Annabelle giggled and rolled her eyes. "Shut up."

"Can't. I have one more favor to ask you."

"What do you need?"

"Let that trained monkey out of its cage and block out a room for me."

Annabelle huffed and reached for her mouse, waking the screensaver on the computer, then glanced up at Jake. "Look away."

Jake turned his eyes ceilingward as Annabelle tapped in the password. "I'm personally offended that you don't trust me."

"Oh, don't take it personally. It's just that it took me a long time to find all that money last time. Okay. You can look now."

He lowered his eyes and leaned over the counter, watching her. "You know, it would be a lot easier if you'd just show the rest of us how to work the system."

"Mmmm, maybe," she said, tapping her way into the computer. For someone so . . . well, dim . . . she sure did type like lightning. "So, you need a room blocked out? For how long?"

"I don't know. Long as you can give me. It's a just-in-case thing."

Annabelle raised her eyebrows. "Planning on entertaining a lady friend?"

Jake shrugged. "I just think it's a good idea to have it around. In case someone's too drunk to drive home." *Or thinks she's being haunted by her dead aunt.* "Put the key in the bar safe for me?"

She nodded. "No problem."

"All right. I'm gonna go home and get a little sleep before the big meeting." He tapped the desk twice in goodbye and turned toward the front door.

"Wait, Jake!" Annabelle jumped up from her seat and hung over the front desk.

Jake turned again. "Yeah?"

"The niece. You didn't tell me what she's like."

Jake took a second to contemplate. *What is Flynn Daly like?*

"She's like a Disney heroine after a fifth of scotch," he said, then escaped into the daylight.

Chapter Five

♡ Flynn tucked the last of the cow creamers into the shoe box she'd found in the back of the closet, and then picked at the ragged edge on the roll of duct tape she'd found under the sink. Even though she knew, in her heart, that she had dreamed putting them away the day before, she saw no reason to take chances now.

This time, those damn cows were staying put.

After she'd attached enough duct tape to them to secure them for the rest of their unnatural lives, she tucked the shoe box into the very back of the front closet, stood up, and shut the door.

There, she thought, and stuck the duct tape on the shelf as a reminder to anyone who might need reminding of just who was embodied here.

She checked her watch. It was getting close to noon. She had planned to go to the front desk and retrieve the box of stuff Freya'd ordered for her, but the fact was, she didn't really want it. Not enough to deal with two dozen

Jake Tuckers, all there haranguing her about selling the inn. She knew she'd have to go down eventually, be a "presence" or whatever, but she wanted to get it clear in her head exactly what she would say.

It doesn't matter what you say, Freya's voice played in her head. *What matters is that they see you as an authority figure. Don't get friendly, don't get personal. Just walk around like you own the place and tell them only what they need to know. They'll all fall in line.*

At the time, it had seemed like sound advice.

Now, it seemed not specific enough. Did her bartender sacking out on her couch count as getting personal? Had she violated the "need to know" rule when she told him about being haunted by Aunt Esther? And how exactly does one "walk around like you own the place"? Flynn was pretty sure she walked the same way whether she owned a place or not.

Although, technically, she'd never owned anything before. And she didn't really own this place, either; her father did. Still, she wasn't comfortable with her task here, so secluding herself in the cottage—while perhaps not the mature choice—had been the preferable one.

She checked her watch. Five minutes to noon. She could always stand up to Gordon Chase and hide out here for the rest of the day, except that she was going to have to face the music eventually, anyway, and she was intrigued by Chase. She wondered if he was really as bad as Tucker had made him out to be, or if they were just rivals who'd fought over something stupid, like a woman. Or a pizza. She wouldn't put it past either of them, and it sure would explain a lot.

Either way, it didn't matter. She couldn't hide out here

forever. Sooner or later she'd have to deal with things, and it might as well be sooner.

She grabbed her purse off the half-moon table and headed out the door, locking it behind her. Once outside, she took a deep breath and tried to walk like she owned the place. Holding her head high, she attempted to view her surroundings as though they were hers. The trees that filtered the gorgeous fall sun into dappled patches that grazed her feet; the cobblestone walkway that led her past the east wing; the birds that chirped as she walked by, including one that almost pooped on her shoulder. All *hers*. It worked, kind of, until she found her way to the huge French doors at the front, pushed through them, and . . .

. . . *wow*.

The rich red carpeting was the first thing to grab her notice. It had obviously been there for a while, but it still looked great. The walls were covered in deep cherrywood panels up to the wainscoting, then luscious mauve wallpaper freckled with a subtle Victorian design stretched up to the corniced ceiling, which was easily twenty feet high. Above her head, a tremendous chandelier released light in glimmering droplets. The lobby stretched out to her left with a series of seating clusters—some with chairs, some with love seats, all intimate—that revolved around a fireplace so large you could easily fit a horse in it. To her right, the interior entrance to the restaurant—she'd seen the exterior entrance the night before, when trying all the outside doors until she found the bar, which was tucked away on the other side of the restaurant.

I own this place. I belong here, she affirmed internally, although the queasiness in her stomach argued the other way.

"Can I help you?"

Startled, Flynn glanced up and saw a perky young blonde smiling at her from behind the huge front desk.

Flynn swallowed, held her back straight, and tried to walk like she owned the place. She caught her toe on the carpet and flailed a bit, but managed to regain her footing and continued the rest of the way to the front desk without incident.

"Yes. Hi. I'm Flynn Daly."

The blonde grinned and held out her hand. Flynn took it.

"Oh, hi! I'm Annabelle DeCross. I'm your concierge-slash-bookkeeper-slash–Girl Friday. Anything you need, really. I'm so glad to meet you. How was your trip? I heard you took the train. Are you afraid of flying, because I'm terrified. It's totally unnatural to be thirty thousand feet in the air, don't you think, Flynn? Oh, is it okay that I call you Flynn? Or would you prefer Ms. Daly? Esther always had us call her Esther, because she was Esther, you know?"

Annabelle finally released Flynn's hand and Flynn forced a smile as she pulled it back, hoping Annabelle wouldn't be able to tell that she was kinda weirded out. Flynn had always been naturally suspicious of perky people, and Annabelle was beyond perky.

Give her a chance, Flynn thought. *People are just like this out here. Get used to it.*

"Nice to meet you, Annabelle," she said. "You can call me Flynn, that's fine. Um, did anything arrive for me today?"

Annabelle's eyes widened and she giggled. "Oh, you mean all the boxes?"

"*All* the boxes?" Exactly how much had Freya ordered, anyway? She'd known it had been expensive, but she hadn't expected more than one or two packages. "How many boxes?"

"Six. I had Herman put them in the back of the Rose Banquet Room because I didn't want to bother you if you were still sleeping, and also, he almost threw his back out working on the roof last month, so I thought maybe Clyde—he's Mercy's sous chef, have you met Mercy yet? Anyway, I thought maybe Clyde or Jake could help you, maybe after the big meeting?"

Flynn blinked, feeling like she'd just walked into the middle of an Oscar Wilde play without a script. "Uh . . . big meeting?"

"Yes." Annabelle nodded enthusiastically and Flynn was entranced by the bounciness of her hair. What shampoo did this girl use, anyway? "Jake told me all about it, so I got you the Rose Banquet Room for one o'clock and I've called everyone, even the people who don't work today, and most everybody's going to be here because we're all really excited about meeting you."

A big meeting.

Jake told her.

And everyone was coming. Plenty of witnesses to keep her from killing the bartender. Smart move. Flynn forced a tight smile. "That's great. Thank you."

"So, with all those boxes . . ." Annabelle stood up, moved closer, and lowered her voice. "I mean, with all that stuff, you must be planning on staying awhile, right? So, you're not going to sell, are you?"

"Well . . . we, uh . . . We haven't made any decisions."

Annabelle patted her hand. "It's okay. I understand, if

you want to save the announcement for the big meeting. I promise I'll keep my trap shut." Annabelle somehow managed to contain her grin long enough to mimic locking her lips and throwing away the key. Flynn stared until she realized she was staring, then forced herself to speak.

"Thank you," she finally managed, but as she spoke, Annabelle's focus went to a spot behind Flynn's shoulder and her eyes darkened considerably. Flynn was just about to turn around when she heard Gordon Chase's voice booming behind her.

"Flynn," he said, marching up to her and planting a kiss on her cheek. Flynn had to work not to recoil from him. "So good to see you again." He looked at Annabelle and didn't seem to notice the daggers she was shooting at him. "Good to see you again, Annabelle."

Annabelle stood up straight and her lips thinned to form a tight, disapproving line. "Your table is ready for you in the restaurant."

Flynn glanced at Annabelle. She couldn't remember asking for a reservation, but then again, her mind was still processing . . . well . . . Annabelle.

"Oh?" Gordon Chase's eyebrows lifted. "We're eating . . . here?"

"Um . . ." Flynn glanced at Annabelle. "Yes?"

Annabelle nodded primly and motioned toward the restaurant with her left hand.

Flynn looked back at Gordon Chase, whose eyes might have been registering a tiny bit of alarm, although it was hard to tell, because nothing seemed to faze him. So, once again, there she was, lacking even the slightest clue as to what was going on.

"Is that okay?" she asked.

Whatever it was she thought she might have seen in Chase's eyes vanished, and he smiled brightly. "It's perfect."

He pulled the heavy wood and glass door open, then stepped aside and gave a "ladies first" motion with his arm. Flynn smiled as she cut past him into the restaurant, the details of which—high-ceilinged, corniced, and gorgeous—fled past her. Mostly, she was noticing the looks.

The first one came from the hostess, a tall woman with a patrician nose whose name tag read Nancy and who refused to make eye contact with Gordon Chase. As a matter of fact, Flynn would swear that Nancy deliberately dropped the wine list hard enough to slosh his water.

The next look came from the waiter, Gregory, who smiled warmly at Flynn as she gave her order, then snatched the menu from Chase's hand so fast he gave Chase a small paper cut.

Then there was the couple in the corner. Their looks weren't actively hostile, more shamelessly intrigued. Chase had a rep about town, that was for sure.

Chase, however, seemed immune to it. As they drank their wine and waited for their salads, he seemed positively chipper. Either he hadn't noticed the seemingly intense dislike surrounding him, which Flynn thought doubtful, or he genuinely didn't care, which she found fascinating. Even Freya, for all her toughness, cared at least a little what people thought. But Chase just glanced over the menu like there was nothing interesting happening at all.

Fascinating.

"So," he said, leaning slightly forward, "how do you

like the place? It's nice, isn't it? Have you seen the rose garden?"

"Just from my window," Flynn said, taking a sip of the wine Gregory had recommended. It was good stuff. "I haven't really had much time to get acclimated yet."

"Well, it's a terrific property." Chase took a sip of his wine and gave her that strange, *tink*ing smile again. "You should see the whole area while you've got the chance."

Flynn put her wineglass down. "While I've got the chance?"

"Well, I assume it's temporary. Isn't it?" Chase raised one eyebrow casually. "I mean, a number of established companies have been interested in this property for years. I tried to encourage Esther to sell, but she never listened to a word I had to say. I could understand, I guess. She'd grown up here; it was home. But honestly, Flynn, a large company with resources like that? It would make a world of difference for these people. Updated systems, bigger paychecks." He waved around generically, indicating the staff. "Not to mention what a boon that kind of business would bring to the town."

Wow. Agendas, agendas everywhere. And for some reason, Chase's bugged her even more than Tucker's had.

"So, what?" Flynn said carefully. "You don't think I should try to run this place myself?"

Something like surprise flashed over Chase's face, but he hid it under a smile. "Are you thinking of doing that?"

Not on a bet. But she wasn't going to tell Chase that. She had a feeling it would be a good idea to play her cards close to her chest, at least until she knew what he wanted from her.

"I don't know," she said. "I'm still thinking about it. Is that so crazy?"

"Don't get me wrong," Chase said, keeping his eyes on hers lazily. Almost seductively, Flynn thought. "I don't doubt for a moment that you could succeed at anything you put your mind to. If you wanted to run this place, I bet you'd do great. But it's not really what you do, is it? Hospitality, I mean?"

"My family runs a number of hospitality properties," she said, pretty sure that was true. Her dad mostly bought properties, developed them, and then sold them to the highest bidder. Some of the properties had been hotels, so he must have run them during the process. Not that the truth mattered; at this point, she'd claim to be Paris Hilton herself if it wiped that smirk off Chase's face.

As he watched her, his eyes dancing, the smirk stayed firmly in place. "But it's not what *you* do, though, is it? And your father chose to send you. I find that very . . . telling."

He stabbed a leaf of his salad with an expression of smug satisfaction, as though he were an ancient hunter taking down a wildebeest for the tribe. *Igh,* Flynn thought, every part of her body bristling with intense dislike. While Tucker's researching her and her family had been annoying, Chase's was outright pissing her off. She sat up straighter, and decided to switch defense for offense.

With this guy, she had a feeling she was going to enjoy taking offense.

"So," she said, leaning an elbow on the table and her chin into her curled hand, "how do you do it?"

Chase gave her a confused half smile. "Do what?"

Flynn gestured toward the wait staff and the diners. "Not care. I mean, everyone here just hates the shit out of you. I can tell. I'm sensitive to those things. But it doesn't seem to bother you, not even a teensy little bit. Is it because you don't know that they despise you, or that you don't care?"

Chase took another sip of his wine. "People liking or disliking me is of no consequence. I'm a businessman, and some people are not going to like what I do sometimes. If I let it bother me, I lose my advantage." He leaned forward a bit. "And, just to let you know, I'm more popular in other places."

"So, you're saying the people here have particular reason not to like you?"

Chase eyed her for a long moment, and she sensed that he was evaluating her while forming his answer. "There's a man here who thinks I'm responsible for everything that's gone wrong in this town and in his life, and he's a very convincing guy. These people like him, so they don't like me."

Ah. Tucker. "Or maybe their disliking you has nothing to do with him, and everything to do with you." She shrugged playfully. "Just a theory."

Chase paused for a moment, his eyes twinkling with amusement. "You know, some men don't go for ballbusters, but I don't happen to be one of them. I like you."

Flynn grinned. "I've got spunk."

Chase chuckled, then picked up his wineglass and took another sip. He opened his mouth to speak again, but coughed lightly into his hand before he could get the words out. His expression went from smarmy and amused to concerned, and his skin seemed to be getting . . . blotchy.

Igh.

"Are you okay?" Flynn asked. She picked up her untouched water and handed it to him.

"I'm fine," he choked. His face was turning beet red. Flynn stood up and waved to Nancy.

"Nancy! Call 911!"

"No." Chase held up his hand and stood. "I think I'm okay. I have a little berry allergy." A dribble of sweat ran down his face. "Must have been in the wine."

"Are there berries in cabernet?"

"All I need are some antihistamines," he said, his voice strained.

"Well, let me see if Annabelle—"

Chase held up his hand. "No. No, thank you. I think I'd prefer to take care of it myself." Even with the wheezing and the sweat and the beet red face, he managed to give her one last *tink*. "Don't worry. I'm fine. Please excuse me."

Flynn nodded mutely as Chase took off. A moment later, she heard some scuffling behind her and turned to see a short, round, redheaded woman in a white chef's hat running toward her.

"Oh, no," the woman said, her face full of false alarm. "I'm too late." She snapped her fingers and slumped dramatically. "Darn it."

Flynn raised her eyebrows. "What happened?"

"I have a wineglass that I keep raspberries in," she said, her eyes overwide with blatantly faked innocence. "You know, to snack on during the day. Well, I'd finished them off but I got busy, you know, as chefs do, and I just left it sitting out." She bit her bottom lip. "I think Gregory must have somehow *accidentally* gotten a hold of that glass and used it for Mr. Chase's wine." She leaned in a bit. "He has that terrible berry allergy, you know." She leaned back, and Flynn swore she saw the edge of a smile in her eyes. "I'm so mortified. Was he okay?"

Flynn stared at her. "Gosh, you know, that was really good, but I think you overplayed the *accidental* angle a little bit." She put one hand on Mercy's shoulder and leaned in. "Here's a tip: don't overexplain. Innocent people don't need to explain themselves."

Mercy eyed her for a moment, then smiled. "Thanks."

"No problem." Flynn released her shoulder and stood up straight.

Mercy nodded toward the door Gordon Chase had fled out of. "If it's any comfort, I knew it wouldn't kill him."

"Actually, that's quite a comfort, thank you." Flynn held out her hand. "I'm Flynn Daly."

The chef wiped her hands on the towel hanging from her apron and shook. "Hi, Ms. Daly."

"Flynn. Please."

Mercy smiled. "Flynn. It's nice to meet you. I'm Mercy Glavin."

"Mercy." *Well, now things are beginning to make sense.* "Yes. Jake Tucker told me to talk to you."

"He did? What about?"

"Oh, nothing. He just wanted me to confirm something with you, but I think that's been taken care of."

"Okay." Mercy grinned. "So, you've met Jake, huh? I know I'm biased because he's my brother, but don't you think he's just the cutest thing?"

"You two are related?" Flynn crossed her arms over her stomach and stared at the chef. "Why does that not surprise me?"

Mercy glanced at her watch. "It's only five after twelve.

Why don't you come back with me? I'll show you the kitchen, get you a little something to eat before the big meeting. I make a pumpkin risotto'll pop your head right off."

Flynn smiled. Did she want to go have some pumpkin risotto made by the woman who'd poisoned her date?

Eh. Life was short, anyway. She grabbed her wineglass. "Lead the way."

Flynn tucked herself in the corner next to the stove while the kitchen staff whirled around her. She'd tried to introduce herself, but these people were busy, and they held knives, so it wasn't long before she figured that the best thing she could do was stay out of the way.

"So, here's the thing about my brother," Mercy said, sprinkling a pinch of something into the orangish glop that sizzled in the pan. "He's kind of a wise-ass."

"You don't say."

"He thinks he's funny and most of the time he is, so that just encourages him." Mercy grinned sideways at Flynn. "He's so like my dad. Never say a sincere word when a joke will do." She picked up a large metal spoon and stirred the concoction. "My mother always says she only married my dad to shut him up, and my dad used to say that's why he knocked her up with my oldest sister so fast, so that she'd be stuck."

"Wow. Your dad sounds like a lot of fun," Flynn said, trying to imagine her father ever making a joke.

Nope. Couldn't do it.

"He was." Mercy's smile turned sad. "He was a safety inspector for OSHA, and he was killed in a piano factory. A baby grand fell on him."

Flynn wasn't sure if Mercy was joking or not, and kept her expression flat. "Wow. I'm really sorry."

Mercy grinned. "It's okay to laugh. Dad would have loved the irony of it. We started making jokes about it at the funeral and we haven't stopped since. It's what Dad would have wanted." Mercy paused for a moment, then shrugged. "Well, my sisters and my mom and I joke about it. Jake never does."

There was a long silence as Flynn struggled over what to say. She couldn't make light of it, but Mercy would obviously brook no sympathy. So finally she said the only thing she could say.

"Your brother seems like a really nice guy." She mostly meant it, and it was worth throwing a compliment Tucker's way to get out of the awkward conversational spot.

Mercy's eyes lit up. "He is, isn't he? I know he's my baby brother and everything, but I just think he's the greatest guy." She grabbed a spoon from a can full of them, dipped, and tasted. She closed her eyes for a moment, inhaled through her nose, and then smiled at Flynn.

"It's perfect," she announced, then grabbed a ladle and poured some into a bowl. Flynn took it, along with a clean spoon from the can. She eyed Mercy sideways.

"You were kidding when you said it would pop my head off, right?"

Mercy leaned against the counter, crossing her arms over her chest. "All I'm gonna say is I take no responsibility for what happens to you."

Flynn laughed and dipped her spoon in, taking a bite. It was warm and sweet and rich and spicy and . . .

"Oh, my *Goooooooooooodddddd*," she said, going in for another spoonful. "This is amazing."

"Told you," Mercy said smugly. She cocked her head to the side and looked at Flynn. "Would it be inappropriate for me to say that you and my brother would have the most adorable babies?"

Flynn froze midchew, then swallowed. "Yeah. Kinda."

Mercy smiled and patted Flynn lightly on the shoulder. "Just an observation."

Jake leaned against the stack of boxes in the corner of the Rose Banquet Room and smiled to himself. The shipping labels read "Flynn Daly, c/o The Goodhouse Arms."

Ha! He *knew* she had more luggage than that one bag.

It was almost one o'clock and the room was packed. He did a visual head count and estimated that, aside from a few key restaurant personnel, everyone was here, even people who weren't on the schedule for today. Proof once again that there was absolutely no one better for spreading news than Annabelle.

". . . got beet red and ran out . . . face all sweaty and gross," he heard a woman's voice saying. He glanced through the crowd and located the source of the voice; Lucy from housekeeping. She was talking closely with another girl he recognized but couldn't name, and they were giggling happily about Chase's berry special Goodhouse Arms lunch.

Good ol' Mercy, he thought.

A small niggle of guilt—on Flynn's behalf, not

Chase's—poked at him, but he ignored it. Giving her lunch date a case of the berry sweats was all in good fun, but dumping a surprise staff meeting on her was a total dick move. Unfortunately, it was necessary. How Flynn reacted to this thing was going to tell him a lot more about her intentions than he'd ever learn by bugging her over Jameson's neats at the bar. If she told them all flat-out that she was going to sell, then he'd know his chances of getting her to string Chase along for a while were nil. If she hemmed and hawed, he had a shot. Plus, putting someone in front of a firing squad and seeing which way they duck is always a great form of entertainment.

The door opened, and Flynn walked in, with Mercy trailing close behind. They shared a grin—interesting—and Mercy dove into the crowd as Flynn made her way up to the front. Something was different about Flynn, though; she wasn't walking like a little girl in her mother's heels anymore.

Guess she's not feeling too bad about poor Chase and his hives.

Jake smiled to himself.

Flynn stepped up behind the podium set up at the front of the room, and the chatter quieted down. She smoothed her hair behind her ears and smiled her crazy, wide smile and Jake wondered if everyone else was as mesmerized by that grin as he'd been. He glanced around, saw that the ratio of happy faces to suspicious ones was pretty much in a dead heat. She didn't have everyone in her corner yet, but considering the circumstances, Flynn was doing pretty damn good.

"Good afternoon," Flynn said, and the buzz in the

room died down. She glanced at the back of the room and spoke louder. "Can everyone hear me?"

A chorus to the affirmative came up from the back of the room, but Flynn caught Jake's eye and held it until he nodded yes.

"Good. Thank you for coming to this meeting this afternoon. I'm glad this meeting was called"— she gave Jake a sharp look—"because I . . . uh . . . really wanted to introduce myself to you all. Um, as most of you probably already know, my name is Flynn Daly. Esther Goodhouse was my great-aunt, and when she died, she left the Goodhouse Arms to my family."

There was a long, awkward pause as Flynn stared out into the sea of faces. Jake pushed up from the boxes and stepped a little closer.

"Um, okay then," she said, letting go with a nervous laugh. "That's pretty much it. If you don't have any questions—"

"Do you have any experience in running a hotel?"

Jake glanced toward the voice, which had come from Olivia, the head of housekeeping and one of the more skeptical faces.

"You mean, me personally?" Flynn cleared her throat. "Well, my family has been in real estate development for a long time, and over the years we've owned a number of hospitality businesses."

"My dad was a mechanic," someone to Jake's left grumbled. "Doesn't make me a car."

"Esther gave us raises on the anniversaries of our hire dates," Selah, one of the bar waitresses, called out. "My anniversary is in October. So am I just shit outta luck or what?"

Selah wasn't known for her delicate nature.

"I, uh . . ." Flynn blinked a few times. "I haven't had time to review Aunt Esther's financial policies, but—"

A hand waved in the air, and relief flashed across Flynn's face as she pointed to Annabelle. "Yes, Annabelle?"

Annabelle stood up. "I think what people want to know is, you know, if you're going to sell to a big chain or something? Because, I mean, we know they don't, like, disembowel people and put their heads on pikes—"

Jake dropped his face into his hand and laughed.

"—but, you know, they do sometimes come in and kinda clean house and we all really like it here and like this place the way it is."

Flynn's eyebrows knit and she seemed frozen while trying to unweave the delicate strands of Annabelle's logic. "Um . . . was there a question in there . . . somewhere?"

"Yeah. She's asking if you're going to sell us out." Oscar, one of the landscaping guys, took a step forward from where he was standing at the back. "Because if you are, we need to know so we can find other jobs."

"Well . . ." Flynn's eyebrows were practically meeting above her nose. "I mean . . . even if we did sell, you'd keep your jobs."

Oscar folded his arms over his chest. "Can you promise that? Can you put that in writing?"

Flynn looked like she'd been slapped, and Jake felt a knot of anger rise in his gut. Despite the fact that he had no one to blame but himself, he really wanted to take Oscar outside and pummel his fat head.

"In writing?" Flynn said. "No, I can't. But if someone

takes over this place, someone who . . . who . . . who knows what they're doing . . . I mean, why wouldn't they keep you?"

"Because we get paid decent," Selah said.

Oscar nodded. "Esther valued us, and she paid us like she valued us. You think a big chain is going to do that, sweetheart? Think again."

Flynn blinked. "I . . . uh . . . well . . . I . . ."

Jake had expected this to happen. Watching how Flynn responded to the situation was a big part of getting to know who he was dealing with. It was *his* response that was throwing him for a loop. He hadn't anticipated how impossible it would be for him to simply stand back and watch her swing.

He took a step forward.

"I was wondering," he said, noting the completely reasonable expression of alarm in Flynn's eyes as he walked up the aisle toward her, "what you thought of the place?"

He stopped, mid-aisle. There was a pause while Flynn seemed to be waiting for the sucker punch, but when it didn't come, she allowed a small smile.

"I think it's . . ." She paused for a moment, seeming to fight within herself until one side won. Her face relaxed a bit, and an almost smile played on her lips. "I think it's incredible. The grounds are gorgeous, and so well kept. And the lobby is . . . oh, if I could move into that lobby, I would, I'm telling you." There was a mild smattering of appreciative laughter. Flynn motioned out to the area where Mercy had taken a seat. "The pumpkin risotto is a dream come true."

"So it's safe to say you're impressed, right?" Jake kept his eyes on her.

She met his gaze and nodded. "Yes."

"Well, considering you haven't even been here for twenty-four hours yet, I think that's pretty much all we can ask."

"Bullshit," Oscar said. "We can ask about the sale."

The room went starkly quiet. Jake turned toward Oscar, wanting to pummel him now more than ever.

"She just got here, man," he said in a low voice. "Back off."

"No."

"It's okay."

Jake raised his head to find Flynn moving her focus over the crowd, connecting with as many people as possible. "It's a fair question. It deserves a fair answer. The truth is, I don't know. The decisions haven't been made, and I honestly don't know yet what I'm going to do. If you feel that you want to look for employment elsewhere, I certainly wouldn't fault you. But I think this place is very special, and I hope those of you who think so too will stay."

Flynn gave one quick, decisive nod to the crowd and left the podium. She walked gracefully down the aisle, but Jake could see her hands shaking as she passed him by. He stood where he was, watching the doorway through which she'd disappeared, until he felt a faint tug on his sleeve.

"Oh, hey, Annabelle," he said, glancing down at her quickly before returning his stare to the doorway.

"Um, Flynn had those boxes come in for her, and Herman almost put his back out—what do you think she has in them? A dead body? Anyway, I thought maybe you could—"

"Have Clyde do it," he said quietly, pulling his focus away from the door and turning a forced smile on Annabelle. "I'm the last person Flynn wants to see right now."

"Oh, I'm sure that's not true," Annabelle said. "She seems really nice."

"She is really nice," Jake said, still staring at the doorway.

Too bad I'm a total asshole, he thought.

Chapter Six

♡Oh, God," Flynn groaned, sitting up in her bed. "You again?"

The room was golden. Aunt Esther was sitting in the corner, rocking on her phantom rocking chair, not caring that the real one was backward and her face was passing back and forth through the wooden slats that supported the headrest. Flynn made a mental note to turn it back around in the morning; this was infinitely creepier than the first time.

Esther set the purple afghan in her lap and looked at Flynn. "I've come to a decision."

Flynn closed her eyes, inhaled deeply, and tried to alter her dream through sheer force of will.

Okay. Sunny beach. A drink with an umbrella, delivered by a faceless yet handsome man wearing only a wink and a smile.

"Ahem."

Lady, stop screwing up my concentration. Okay. Ocean

breezes. Warm sand. Fully loaded drink. Faceless Yet Handsome wearing a wink and a smile . . . *and* a mysterious tattoo right above his—

"*Ahem.*"

Flynn opened her eyes. "You don't like me very much, do you? Because you know this is just mean, right?"

Esther picked up her afghan and continued knitting. "It's not a matter of whether I like you or not. It would appear we're stuck with each other. And it occurs to me that the white light of which you speak so fondly may not be available to me until we figure out whatever it is we're supposed to be doing." She raised her eyes to Flynn's, yanked out a loop of yarn, and wrapped it militantly around the tip of the needle.

"What *we're* supposed to be doing? *We* are not supposed to be doing anything. I'm supposed to be sleeping, and you're supposed to be dead." She sniffed. "And why does this place always smell like peppermint? Is that like a special ghost thing? I've had the windows wide open for two days—"

Esther stopped rocking and focused her ghostly eyes on Flynn. "I need you to do something for me."

"Do exorcisms only work on demons? Couldn't a good priest just"—she wiggled her fingers toward the apparition—"cast you out?"

Esther rolled her eyes. "You really are a prickly little thing, aren't you?"

"Sometimes. Maybe." Flynn swallowed. "Can you blame me? You're really creeping me out."

Esther sighed. "I can see how you're Elizabeth's granddaughter. Same contentious nature."

"Gee, I wonder if I'd be less contentious on a full night's sleep. Let's try it, shall we?"

Whoosh. Suddenly Flynn wasn't in her bed anymore. She was in the corner of the Rose Banquet Room, watching herself staring down at Tucker from behind the podium. Tucker was standing in the aisle, smirking up at her with that smirky little smirk. After throwing her up there like a piece of raw meat in front of a pack of wolves, he had the nerve to stand in that aisle and come to her defense with that smirk?

Whatever.

"So it's safe to say you're impressed, right?" His words were soft and fuzzy, echoing through her memory.

She watched her own face, looking stricken and confused and very much *not* like she owned the place. "Yes."

Tucker was still locking eyes with Flynn's podium self, and this time, she saw something she hadn't seen in the moment, when her whole being had been focused on the fantasy visual of throttling his neck.

This time, she saw what might possibly be a hint of regret.

"Well," he said, "considering you haven't even been here for twenty-four hours yet, I think that's pretty much all we can ask."

Then his eyes drifted over to the corner, connecting with Flynn's dream self. The rest of the room faded, but Tucker stayed still, watching her from where he stood.

"I'm sorry," he said, his lips not moving.

Another *whoosh,* and Flynn shot up in her bed. The room was dark and empty. No fuzziness. No orange glow. No dead aunt.

Well. That was a good start.

Flynn leaned forward and put her face in her hands. This whole thing was a big mistake. Obviously, her mental state was taking serious hits from coming here, and she wasn't even doing a good job. Her lunch date had been poisoned, she'd completely hosed the staff meeting, and the one person she'd trusted had betrayed her. After her public humiliation, she'd retreated back to the cottage, unpacked the boxes from Freya (exactly how many clothes did Freya think she'd need, anyway?), and curled up on the bed like a scared little girl.

Add to all that the fact that her subconscious was torturing her in the form of a dead aunt she'd never met, and Flynn felt secure in her assessment that things were not going well.

She tossed her legs over the side of the bed, grabbed her jeans up off the floor, and stuck her feet in. Camisole, sweater, sneakers, and she was ready to get out of that creepy cottage. She wished she'd had the presence of mind to ask Annabelle for a room, but in her rush to escape, she'd forgotten.

Tomorrow, she was getting a room. Maybe her subconscious would settle down in a different environment. Maybe she'd dream about being haunted by George Washington, or Eleanor Roosevelt.

Pretty much anyone would be an improvement on Esther.

She stepped outside, and the chilled air woke her up immediately. The moon was full, and a light mist lay over the ground. The faint scent of roses hit her, and she turned toward the back of the courtyard. Pebbles crunched under her feet as she followed the path, the dappled moonlight

giving her just enough illumination to keep her from trip-
ping over the three stone steps that led through an arch-
way covered with roses, and then . . .

"Oh, wow," she breathed as she took it all in.

It was beautiful. The garden was laid out in a circle,
with pebbled paths cutting through the rosebushes like
spokes on a wheel, all leading to the gazebo in the center. Flynn wandered down the first spoke, sniffing the
roses as she went. She didn't know anything about roses,
but she could tell that each bush had a different variety.
Some were red, some pink, some yellow. Some blossoms
were huge, petals wide open to the world, and others
were dainty little bulbs. They all had their own take on
the basic scent of rose, some smelling more fruity, others
going the more traditional floral route. By the time she'd
wandered through all the pebbled lanes and found her
way back to the gazebo, the creepy feeling she'd had in
the cottage was gone, replaced with a flush of excitement.
She sat down on the gazebo bench and inhaled deeply,
closing her eyes. The fragrance that surrounded her was
more soothing than any bubble bath she'd ever taken, and
the moonlight was making the place seem magical, and
hers alone.

Maybe nature's not always a bad thing, she thought
as she leaned over to lie down on the gazebo bench. She
closed her eyes and took in another deep breath, feeling
snug in her big sweater and comfortable in her skin.

And then her mind went blissfully blank.

"Um. Flynn?"

There was a nudge at Flynn's shoulder and her eyes

shot open. Sunlight was breaking through the roof of the gazebo, and she sat up.

"Are you okay?" Annabelle asked, sitting down next to her, putting her hand on Flynn's shoulder. "A guest told me there was a homeless woman sleeping in the gazebo and I thought it would be crazy Jeanne, but . . ." Annabelle looked at her with concern. "Are you okay?"

"I'm fine," Flynn said, allowing a little yawn. How had she slept out there all night and not even noticed? The wooden benches were comfortable, but they were still wooden benches. "I just . . . was having trouble sleeping, so I went for a walk and . . ." She sighed and rubbed her hands over her face. "I must have fallen asleep."

"Oh. Okay." Annabelle nodded, her face the picture of support. "It's beautiful out here, isn't it?"

"Yes. It is." Flynn rubbed at her eyes. "Um, what time is it?"

"Eight-fifteen."

"Wow." Flynn smiled at Annabelle. "You're here early."

Annabelle smiled. "I try to get here about seven or so, you know, so I can get a jump on the bookkeeping before things get too busy."

"So, you're the bookkeeper, the concierge . . . everything? Isn't that a bit much for one person?"

Annabelle shook her head, curls bouncing around her grinning face. "Oh, no. Not for me. I like to keep busy."

"Okay." Flynn stretched. "Okay, then. Hey, I'm gonna go take a shower, and I'll see you in the office in about an hour. You think you can get me up to speed on this place?"

"Sure, but there really isn't that much for you to do.

Esther left most of it to me. You know, she was elderly and everything."

Flynn stood up, expecting her back to be bothering her from the hard wooden bench, but she actually felt better rested than she had in a long time. "Well, I'm not. You've got a big load on your shoulders, Annabelle, and you shouldn't have to do it all alone. I'm not trying to impose on your territory. I just want to see how things work so that I can . . ."

She trailed off. She wasn't sure exactly what it was she was supposed to be doing, but she needed to do something while she was here besides fight with her dead aunt. Getting involved in the day-to-day seemed like as good a place to start as any.

Annabelle nodded, then nibbled her lip. "Are you sure you're okay?"

"Yeah. I'm fine."

"Because if you're having trouble sleeping, you could maybe try some of that Tylenol PM. I was having a bit of insomnia this spring, and I'll tell you, one of those at night, and you're out like a light."

Flynn shrugged, wondering how Tylenol PM would stand up to dead Aunt Esther. She gave it comparable odds to an Olsen twin going up against Godzilla, but smiled anyway.

"Maybe I'll give it a try," she said. "Thanks, Annabelle."

Annabelle nodded, turned, and bounced her way back toward the inn. Flynn wrapped her arms around herself and followed the path back to the cottage, taking the time to sniff a few roses along the way.

*   *   *

The Poughkeepsie dive where Jake had set up his appointment with Rhonda Bacon was dark and smelled vaguely like feet and peanuts. Jake stared down into his drink, which he hadn't touched. It was barely noon, and if the clientele in this place were any indication, drinking during the day was the gateway to a sad, sad place. But in his experience, people tended to let their guard down more around people they perceived to be weaker than themselves, and he was going to have to be pretty damn pathetic for a mousy girl like Rhonda to perceive herself as the stronger person.

He checked his watch. It was barely noon. He took a small sip of scotch. Yep. Just the right amount of pathetic.

"Mr. Tucker?"

He'd caught Rhonda coming into the bar in the mirror, but he started at his name for effect, anyway.

"Ms. Bacon," he said coolly, motioning to the seat next to him. "Thanks for coming all the way out here to meet me. Shiny's a small town. Didn't want to take the chance of anyone seeing us." Which was true enough.

"Oh. Yes. Of course." Rhonda sat down, tucking her skirt nervously around her knees. She was an odd duck, Rhonda. She was maybe thirty-five years old, but dressed like she had one foot in the grave and the other behind a librarian's desk. She had thick glasses and seriously kinked brown hair that, if red, would be eerily reminiscent of Bozo the Clown. She wore a matching sweater set with a long gray wool skirt and a pair of Keds, and she had a squirrelly look in her eyes that gave away the fact that she'd been working for a total dickhead for the past five years.

"I'm sorry I'm late," Rhonda said. "There was traffic." She pushed her glasses up on her nose and gave a tentative wave to the bartender, who passed by her like she was invisible. Jake waved his hand, and the bartender nodded and gave a *just a minute* motion with his hand.

"So, you gonna tell me what your message was about, or am I going to be forced to make small talk?" Jake twirled his glass lightly under his fingers. "Because if that's the case, I'm gonna need another one of these."

Rhonda squirmed in her seat. "I just wanted you to know that you were right," she said quietly, then lowered her voice even further. "I think Mr. Chase has been taking money from somewhere. You know." The whisper got hoarse. "Embezzling."

Jake worked up a look of mild surprise. "And I would care about that because . . . why?"

Rhonda's eyes widened a bit. "Because . . ." She shifted on her seat. "Because he's breaking the law."

"In which case, it's my understanding that the appropriate thing to do is go to the police."

"I can't go to the police," she said.

He angled his head to look at her. "Why not?"

She sighed. "It's complicated."

"Breaking the law tends to get that way."

"I was in Mr. Chase's office last week, and I noticed that the safe door was open a crack. I was surprised, because it's not like Mr. Chase to ever leave the safe open, so I went to shut it and I saw a laptop. The thing is, Mr. Chase? He does all his work at the office, on his tower computer. I've never seen him with a laptop before. So then I . . ." She wrung her hands and glanced downward. "I did something I'm not very proud of. I snooped."

"Really? I gotta admit, I hadn't pegged you for the type, Rhonda."

She continued, staring off into the distance, talking as if Jake wasn't even there. "I don't know why I did it. It's just that I handle all the books, and Mr. Chase isn't the kind of man to take work home, so I just wondered what it was for. I found some . . . accounts. A subsidiary company I've never heard of. Transactions that just don't make sense." She turned her eyes on Jake. "You know Mr. Chase is the president of the Historical Preservation Society." She lowered her voice, leaned sideways toward Jake, and talked out of the side of her mouth. "I think Mr. Chase has been siphoning money from those funds. You know. The government restoration grants?"

Jake leaned to his side, too. When in Rome. "You *think* he's embezzling? Or you *know*? Do you have evidence?"

Rhonda straightened up. "That's just it. Mr. Chase came back in so I shut the laptop and put it back in the safe. I don't think he knew what I was doing. But I don't have the combination to the safe, so I can't get back in there."

Jake stared at her. "And again, I'm failing to see where I fit in here."

She paused, waged an obvious internal war, and then continued. "There was a large cash withdrawal from the account about six months ago."

The bartender wandered over and put a napkin down in front of Rhonda.

"A seltzer with lime, please," Rhonda said, so quietly that the bartender had to ask her to repeat it. Jake waited to speak again until she had her drink, partially because the silence would put her on edge, and partially because he was too stunned at his dumb luck.

"Six months ago, huh?"

She smoothed her hands over her skirt nervously. "The withdrawal is dated March twenty-sixth."

March 26. The week after the evidence went missing and Jake's life went to hell. Right about the time that Elaine Placie ran off. *Well, hellooooo kitty.*

"So, what exactly are you saying, Rhonda?"

Rhonda took a sip through the tiny stirring straw. "I'm saying that there's something strange going on. And after connecting some of the dots, I thought that maybe you might want to know about it."

Interesting. Jake shook his head. "I just realized you never answered my question before. If you think your boss is such a bad guy, why not just go straight to the police?"

Rhonda held his eye for a long moment, then her lower lip started to tremble and silent tears slid down her cheeks. Jake reached forward, grabbed a fresh napkin off the pile behind the bar, and handed it to her. She dabbed at her face and took a deep breath.

"I know he's not perfect," she said. "Trust me, I know that better than anyone."

Jake stared at her for a while, his brain momentarily resisting the obvious because it was just too weird.

"You're in love with him," he said, trying to keep the surprise out of his voice. Although he guessed, on some plane, it made sense. *Mousy librarian type + handsome albeit slimy boss = seriously sick love connection.*

Actually, he was surprised he hadn't thought of it before.

Rhonda sighed heavily and her eyes grew moist again. "He's going to need someone standing beside him when all this comes out. If I go to the police, I can't be that person. But I can't know about all of this, either, and not do anything." She turned pleading eyes on Jake. "I know it'll be hard on him, but his only chance of ever being a truly good man—the man I know he can be—is if all this comes out. He'll spend a little time in jail, and when he gets out, I'll be there, waiting. He can start over. *We* can start over." For the first time in his memory, Jake saw Rhonda Bacon smile. Hell, she wasn't just smiling; she was glowing from within.

Okay, this chick has watched way too many Lifetime movies-of-the-week.

"So," Jake said, twirling his glass slowly on its napkin. "You came to me so I could take him down, leaving you free and clear to pick up his broken pieces. Am I getting that right?"

Rhonda nodded.

Jake shook his head. "I'm gonna need more. You've gotta give me account numbers, dates, something solid to go on."

"I can't," Rhonda said. "I mean, I won't. I'll give you a nudge in the right direction, but I won't betray him any more than that. You're a police officer, Mr. Tucker, surely you can—"

"Correction." He lifted his glass and met her eyes, allowing his anger to show through. "I *was* a police officer, until your boss had me taken out of the game. What I am now is a bartender who likes to mind his own damn business."

Rhonda pushed her drink away and clutched her bag

primly in her hands. She stared at a point on the wall behind Jake for a while, then sighed and stepped up off the bar stool. Just as Jake thought she was about to leave, she put her hand on his shoulder.

"It's not fair, what he did to you, Mr. Tucker," she said. "Hiring that woman to distract you while he took that evidence. I know it might be hard to understand how I could love a man like Gordon, a man who steals and lies and doesn't have a strong sense of morality. I know it must look . . . strange . . . to you. But the thing is, when you love someone, nothing makes sense. If you decide not to follow up on this, that will just have to be your choice. I'll know that I did what I could to help Gordon, and if he and I are not meant to be, then . . ." She sniffed. "Then I'll just have to accept that, I guess."

Jake looked up at her. It wasn't hard to pick out liars. They didn't make eye contact, they tended to look up and to the left, they fidgeted. What was hard was when someone didn't do any of those things, like Rhonda Bacon. It didn't necessarily mean they were telling the truth; it could just mean they're sociopaths. With those people, you had to go on pure gut instinct alone, and Jake's gut said Rhonda Bacon was telling the truth. Somehow, despite natural law and common sense and the fact that Gordon Chase was way below her, she really loved him, and she really thought the only way she could have him was by surreptitiously sending him to jail. Jake had had one or two tangles with love that had made him nuts, but he had a deep suspicion that, in this case, love-crazy was being piled on top of standard-issue-crazy.

And that was one dangerous combination.

"I'm not making any promises," he said.

Rhonda cocked her head to the side, studied his face for a while. "I believe you're a good man, Mr. Tucker. I trust you to do what you think is best."

She pulled an envelope out of her bag and placed it on the bar. "This is as far as I'm willing to take things. The rest is up to you."

Jake grabbed the envelope and opened it. At first it seemed empty, but when he shook it, a single key fell into his hand.

Looked a helluva lot like an office key. He chuckled and turned it over in his hand. Rhonda laid one hand on the bar in a quick good-bye, then turned and started out.

"Rhonda," Jake called after her. She turned and raised her eyebrows at him expectantly.

"That laptop you found. Was it by any chance a Dell, with a little splash of red nail polish on the cover?"

A look of confusion crossed Rhonda's face, but then, slowly, she nodded. Jake waved at her. She watched him for a few moments longer, then turned and retreated.

So, Chase had wiped the laptop, then kept it and used it to track his latest nefarious activities. He was either the stupidest guy on the planet or he had an ego like nobody's business.

Or a little bit of both, Jake thought. He tossed twenty bucks on the bar next to his full glass and told the bartender to keep the change.

He was feeling lucky.

Flynn threw her feet up over the edge of the tremendous oak desk that had been Esther's, and was now hers. She concluded that fairies themselves must have built the leather office chair she was sitting in, because she couldn't remember the last time she'd been that comfortable sitting up. The carpet below her was a deep green, and the walls an antique white. Two large, glass-paned French doors faced out into the courtyard, with an unobscured view of the fountain in the center. As she tucked her cell phone between her ear and shoulder, she wondered if she could bring the desk and chair back with her to Boston.

"Freya Daly." Even at a spa in Tucson, Freya could not get the business out of her voice.

"Just checking in, boss," Flynn said. "So far this morning I have taken a detailed tour of the grounds, had four cups of coffee, a wonderful lunch of grilled Alaskan salmon with a side of the creamiest saffron mashed potatoes known to man. I'm sitting here in my office with my feet on the desk, and doing absolutely no work."

"Oh, my God," Freya said, her voice rising in a fake cry. "Did you just say 'my office'?" She sniffled dramatically. "You're going to have to give me a moment."

Flynn pulled her feet off the desk. "What am I even doing here? There's nothing for me to do. Apparently, Aunt Esther did nothing but sit here and look pretty, and everything's running just fine without me lifting a finger. The concierge practically bit my hand off when I tried to get a look at the reservations system."

Freya released a sigh. "Honey. You're not there to work. You're there to be a *presence*. And the staff is gonna be territorial. Change freaks people out. Your purpose there is to keep them from freaking out. Leave the damn reservations system alone."

"So . . . what?" Flynn pulled out the mammoth file drawer on the left side of the desk. It was empty. "I'm supposed to just . . . what? Exist?"

"Pretty much. Enjoy it. I promise, I'll have plenty of real work waiting for you when you get home."

Flynn stood up and walked over to the French doors looking out over the courtyard and leaned her head against the frame. "I can't just exist here, Freya. This place is freaking me out. There's nature everywhere."

"You know, you would have made a horrible cave-woman," Freya said.

"And the front desk girl? Totally perky. You know how I feel about perky people."

"Well. No wonder you're freaked."

"Exactly. I need something to do. Something to distract me. I think hard work is the answer. I think if I can apply myself to something, then maybe . . ." *Maybe the lambs will stop screaming.* "Plus," she went on quickly, "these people already don't like me. I thought maybe if I pitched in, proved myself, I could get their respect, you know?"

"You get their respect by paying their salaries," Freya said. "Don't get all romantic about it. Look, if you don't like sitting around, then don't. Hit the town. Pick some apples, tip some cows, do whatever the locals do. Find a good-looking man and have inappropriate sex. Just make sure he doesn't work for us." She paused. "Trust me. Bad idea."

Flynn touched the window glass with one finger, and a flash of Jake Tucker's face went through her mind. "Oh, God, Fray. I would never. That would just be . . ." *Kinda nice maybe.* ". . . wrong."

"I can't believe you're calling me to complain about not having enough work. Most people would love this, you know."

"Most people aren't being haunted by their dead aunts," Flynn muttered.

Freya snorted. "Sorry, what?"

Flynn hesitated, then closed her eyes tight and said it out loud. "Aunt Esther. She's been haunting me every night."

"Darling, Aunt Esther is dead, and there's no such thing as haunting. Dead is dead. Dead is gone."

"I know. I'm not saying she's *really* haunting me. But that cottage is creepy. It's full of old lady stuff. It smells like peppermint. Don't they say that ghosts all have a particular smell?"

"I'm sure some crazy people have said that before. But sane people know that ghosts don't exist, hence they lack a scent. And if her cottage creeps you out so much, move into one of the rooms."

Flynn sighed. "You're right. I know. It's just stress, I think. I just . . . I don't belong here, Fray."

"Sweetie, you know I wouldn't have sent you there if I didn't think you could do this, right?"

No. "Right."

"So don't worry about it. Get out. See a movie. Wander around the grounds twice a day looking like you know what you're doing and then go get a mani-pedi." There was a shuffle on the phone and Freya seemed to be talking to someone, then she was back. "Look, babe, I'm about to get a very nice massage from a man so beautiful you should have to prick a hole in a piece of paper just to look at him. Relax, you'll be fine. Love you."

"You, too," Flynn said, then flipped the phone shut and closed her eyes.

Relax, she thought. *Think of city streets. Museums. The sounds of traffic. The T. Civilization.*

She opened her eyes, feeling just as tense as ever. She turned and stared at the desk. There had to be something she could do. Esther must have done *something.* She sat in the leather chair and pulled at the drawer on the right.

It was full of Pop-Tarts. Strawberry frosted.

With sprinkles.

Flynn's heart started booming in her chest. Pop-Tarts. Pop-Tarts. Something about Pop—

I really miss Pop-Tarts. The strawberry ones with the frosting and sprinkles were my favorite, Esther's voice said in her head.

Flynn shot up out of her office and scrambled down the hall to the front desk.

"Oh, hi, Flynn," Annabelle said, her grin fading as she took in Flynn's expression. "Is everything okay?"

"No," Flynn said. "What's up with all the Pop-Tarts?"

Annabelle blinked. "What Pop-Tarts?"

"In Esther's—in my desk. There's Pop-Tarts." Flynn felt a bead of cold sweat run down the back of her neck. Her heart started to race.

It wasn't possible. They were just dreams.

It wasn't possible.

"Ohhhhh." Annabelle giggled. "Those are Esther's. She had a thing for Pop-Tarts, would eat them all day long if I didn't make her have something healthy."

"Get them out." Flynn pulled on a tight smile. "Please."

Annabelle's face fell. "I'm sorry. I do remember seeing them in there when I cleaned out her desk. I must have forgotten to take them out. If I thought they would upset you, I would have. You're a little pale. Are you okay?"

"No." Flynn glanced at her watch. It was almost two. She'd put in enough of a presence for the day, right? Five hours including a lunch break. It would have to do. "Look, I've got something I need to take care of right now. What was that stuff you were talking about? The stuff that would knock me out? The stuff that you don't dream with?"

"Oh, Tylenol PM?" Annabelle nodded. "It'll knock you out. I don't know about dreams. I didn't have any when I used it, but I don't tend to dream much. If you want, I can ask Herman to make a run down to Hannaford's and—"

"Yes," Flynn said. "Please. I'll be in the cottage. Can you have him bring them there?"

"Sure." Annabelle picked up the desk phone and dialed, then raised her eyes up to Flynn. "Is there anything else I can help you with?"

"Actually, yeah." Flynn smiled. "Is there a Catholic church within walking distance?"

Chapter Seven

♡ Jake sat in his sister's Honda Accord and stared across the street into Gordon Chase's dark office window. If looks could laser, he'd already be inside. As it was, he was waiting patiently to make his move until the last of Chase's business park neighbors, a lawyer by the name of Finola Scott, finally cleared out of her office. The last thing he needed was anyone tipping off Chase that they'd seen him lurking around; still, the key Rhonda Bacon had given him was practically burning a hole in his palm, and he was anxious to use it. He knew that anything he found wouldn't be admissible in court, but if he knew it was there, he could give Gerard Levy a nudge in the right direction, let the department take it from there. Then he would have fixed what he'd broken, and he could move on from it. Finally forget the whole damn thing. All he had to do was be sure the evidence was really there first, and in order for him to do that, Finola Scott had to go the hell home.

He glanced at the clock glowing green in front of him, watched as 8:52 switched silently to 8:53. Jake thumped his head back against the headrest. This was going to be the longest night of his life. He could feel it.

The cell phone in his shirt pocket vibrated. Glancing back at Finola Scott's window—light still on, he could see her riffling through the filing cabinet, her and her damn work ethic—he glanced down at the caller ID: *The Goodhouse Arms.* He flipped the phone open and smiled.

"I didn't steal your car, Mercy. I borrowed it without permission. Totally different thing."

"Jake?"

Even with only one syllable, her voice bounced. "Hey, Annabelle. What's up?"

He leaned forward in his seat as he caught some movement behind Finola Scott's window; was she finally putting on her coat?

"I know it's your night off and everything," Annabelle said, "and I really wouldn't call you if it wasn't important, you know that, right?"

"Yeah. Of course."

"Oh, good, because I would hate it if you thought I'd just bother you for any old thing, but I didn't know . . ."

Yes, Finola Scott had definitely put on her coat. And now she was pulling her keys out of her purse.

About damn time.

". . . and the music is really loud and she won't answer the phone, and all the shades are drawn and I don't think there's been any movement . . ."

Jake shook his head and tried to latch on to something in Annabelle's conversational meandering that made any sense.

The light in Finola Scott's office went off.

"Look, Annabelle, I've kinda got a thing going on. You wanna cut to the chase?"

"It's Flynn," she said, her voice taut with worry. "I'm probably overreacting, so I don't want to call the police, but—"

"Wait, what?" Jake blinked, glanced away from Finola Scott's window, and tried to focus. "Why would you have to call the police?"

"Because of the *sleeping pills*," Annabelle said, frustration deep in her voice.

Jake's hands tightened around the steering wheel. "What sleeping pills?"

"I *told* you, Flynn had Herman deliver her a bottle of Tylenol PM this afternoon. Weren't you listening?"

Jake relaxed. "Tylenol PM are not sleeping pills. They're glorified antihistamines."

"Not when mixed with a liter of peppermint schnapps," Annabelle hissed. "I'm really worried about her. She was acting kinda weird today."

"And that's different from every other day how?"

"I'm serious, Jake. She found a bunch of Pop-Tarts in Esther's desk and got really upset. It was weird. I think she might be . . . you know . . . unstable."

Jake shrugged. "Again. We've covered this ground."

"But then she asked me to have Herman deliver a bottle of Tylenol PM. When Herman dropped it off, he saw Esther's old rocking chair just sitting on the porch, and there was an empty bottle of peppermint schnapps on it."

"I'm sure it's all fine. If she was alive and well enough to dump the rocker on the porch—"

"That was *five hours* ago. Music has been blaring from

the cottage since three o'clock this afternoon. She's not answering phone calls. She's not answering the door."

Tendrils of alarm began to vibrate within him, and Jake sat up straighter. He didn't figure Flynn Daly for the suicidal type, but if he'd learned anything while he was a cop, it was that everyone had a surprise or two up their sleeve.

A chill went down his spine. Flynn had just had lunch with Chase. Had she obstinately told Chase she *wasn't* going to sell just to be a pain in the ass, to prove to him that she wouldn't be played? It seemed in her character to do something like that, and people who ended up being a pain in Chase's ass usually ended up neutralized one way or another.

But Chase wouldn't hurt her. He had no reason to hurt her.

Unless he had a reason Jake just didn't know about.

"Christ." Jake tossed Chase's office key on the passenger seat and started up the car. "I'm on my way. Go on in there and make sure she's okay."

"My key won't work," Annabelle said. "Esther never locked up, so I haven't ever had to try it, but it doesn't work. And what if . . ."

Jake screeched out of his spot on the street, cutting off Finola Scott's BMW as he did.

"Jake," Annabelle said, anxiety thick in her voice. "What if she's dead? I don't like dead bodies, Jake. They make me very tense."

"I'll be there in two minutes," he said, running the red light in the center of town. "You go out there and bang on the window, try to peek through the shades. If she doesn't answer, or you can see she isn't moving, you call the police whether I'm there yet or not, okay?"

He flipped the phone shut and tossed it down, unconcerned about where it landed, certain even as his heart pounded in his chest that this was a nothing situation. Flynn Daly was the last person in the world who would commit suicide . . .

On purpose. But chasing over-the-counter meds with booze without thinking first? She seems exactly the type.

. . . and it was a hell of a stretch to think that Chase would do anything to her . . .

Although Esther got in his way, too, and look where she is now.

A vision flashed in his mind: Flynn, lying on the bed where they'd found Esther, body limp, dead eyes staring blankly out into the world. He pounded the accelerator. He had no idea why he was so panicked, she was probably fine, but reason wasn't a player at the moment. He had to get to that cottage, had to see for himself that Flynn was okay even though he knew in his gut that she was.

He ran a stop sign.

He'd worry about how that made sense later.

Flynn sat cross-legged on the bed in her golden aura'd bedroom, smiling smugly at Aunt Esther, who rocked on the ghostly chair in the corner. As one of the many anti-Esther tactics she'd employed that afternoon, Flynn had dumped the real rocking chair on the porch. She'd also doused the room with holy water, which turned out to be more emotionally comforting than technically effective. In a case of true serendipity, when she was out in the garden shed looking for wood she could fashion a cross from, she'd found a CD player with AC/DC's *Back in Black* in a garden shed and been hit by inspiration. Blaring the music hadn't prevented Esther from visiting, but the obvious annoyance on the old lady's face as she tried to shout over the music was oddly gratifying. Flynn put her hand to her ear and shook her head at her aunt's ghost.

"Sorry?" she yelled. "I can't seem to hear you, lady. Maybe you'd better just go find that white light, because I'm of no use to you if you can't communicate with me, right?"

Aunt Esther merely rolled her eyes and wound another piece of purple yarn around the tip of one knitting needle.

Okay, fine. So maybe the blaring music wasn't working as far as the general haunting went, but it sure was shutting up Aunt Esther. That was a good thing. That was progress.

BOOM! Flynn gasped and jerked as a loud banging sound came from the living room. What the . . . ? She turned wide eyes on Esther.

"Was that you?"

Esther put her hand to her ear, shrugged, and pointed at the stereo.

Flynn narrowed her eyes. "No one likes a smart-ass, lady."

THWACK! The bedroom door burst open and suddenly Tucker was in the room, his eyes all wide and crazy. Behind him, Annabelle flew in and ran to the CD player, which she shut off. The quiet was so marked, it felt loud. On the bed, Tucker was shaking Flynn's sleeping body, and Flynn could feel the pull of his will on her.

"Flynn!" Her teeth rattled as he shook her shoulders. "Flynn! Wake up, goddamnit!"

As Flynn felt herself being yanked back, she caught one last glimpse of Esther grinning, and heard the old lady's parting shot: "We'll talk later, dear."

With an almost audible pop, Flynn's eyes opened and she looked up to see Tucker's face just inches from her own. His cheeks were red, his eyes crazy, his breath ragged and coming down over her in rough, angry waves. His right hand came up from her shoulder to touch her face, and she could see his Adam's apple jump as he swallowed hard.

"Flynn," he said, his voice oddly soft, "what the hell did you—"

But then Annabelle pushed herself between them, pulling Flynn into a tight, bouncy hug.

"Oh, my God, Flynn. I was so worried!" Annabelle's bony arms wrapped around Flynn, and it kinda hurt, but Flynn fought the urge to recoil. Instead, she glanced up to see Tucker stepping back from the bed, running his hand through his hair. He turned his back to her, so she couldn't see his face, but based on the tension in his stance, she guessed he was at least a little pissed off. Which didn't make any sense. She was the one who'd been woken up like a crackhead on an episode of *COPS*.

". . . and the music was playing and I couldn't see through the shades and my key doesn't work so we had to break the door down and . . ."

Annabelle was chattering away, her hands grasping at Flynn's as she spoke.

". . . but whatever it is, it's not worth your life. Life is so precious, Flynn. *So precious*, and you have to know that you're so much better than—"

Flynn held up her hand to shush Annabelle.

"Wait. What? You guys think I tried to kill myself?"

Tucker motioned toward the bottle of Tylenol PM on the nightstand by her bed, his eyes blazing with accusation. When he spoke, however, his voice was calm and controlled. "Between this and the empty bottle of booze sitting on the porch, what did you expect us to think? You're out here for hours, music blaring, no sign of life . . ."

"Oh, for Pete's sake." Flynn leaned against the wall and motioned toward the pill bottle. "Open it. Go ahead."

A shimmer of surprise flashed over Tucker's expression, then he grabbed the bottle, popping the top off. He stared at it for a long moment before handing it to Annabelle, who blushed hard as she saw the unbroken silver safety seal.

"The booze was Esther's. It was leaking, stinking up the place. I found it in the bed. Literally, *in* the bed. She actually cut a hole in the box spring to hide it."

Annabelle's eyes widened. "Oh, my God." She turned and looked up at Tucker. "That's my fault. I used to take her bottles sometimes." She turned her pleading eyes on Flynn. "I didn't mean to drive her to hiding it. Isn't that a sign of alcoholism?"

"No, that's drinking until you pass out," Flynn said, right as Tucker said, "Not if you can't find the bottle." Flynn raised her eyes to his and allowed a quick, involuntary smile until she remembered she was still kind of pissed off at him.

"Anyway," Flynn said, directing her focus to Annabelle. "Personally, I'm not a schnapps kind of girl, so I emptied what was left of it into the sink and tossed it on the porch with the rocker." She took a deep sniff, and could still detect the sticky peppermint. "I think I'm going to have to burn this box spring, though."

Annabelle silently took the plastic cap from Tucker's hand, then snapped it back onto the Tylenol and returned it to its spot on the nightstand. She glanced up at Flynn, eyes guilty as she nibbled at her lower lip. "Am I fired? I mean, between the pills and the booze and the music and the not answering—"

"No, you're not fired. I can't fire anyone for four more days."

A look of confusion flashed over Annabelle's smile. "Okay. Well. I guess we'll just be—"

"You go on ahead," Tucker said, his voice quiet. Annabelle glanced at him, then back at Flynn, and Flynn could see the hurt on her face. Tucker, however, seemed oblivious. How was it possible he didn't know Annabelle had a huge thing for him?

He's a man.

"Um, okay." Annabelle squeezed Flynn's hand one final time. "I'm so glad you're all right. Sorry about the door."

"It's no problem, Annabelle," Flynn said. "Thank you for looking out for me."

Annabelle nodded and pushed up off the bed. Tucker didn't speak until the front door closed with a soft click, but when he did, his voice was heavy with accusation. "So, what the hell was that?"

Flynn pushed herself up off the bed. Now that they were alone, she felt awkward being with him in her bedroom.

"It was me, trying to get some damn sleep." She headed into the living room, Tucker tight on her heels.

"With the doors locked? Shades drawn? Blaring music like that? What the hell, Flynn?"

"Fine!" Flynn turned on him, her index finger bearing down on his chest as she nudged him back against the wall. "I was trying to get rid of her, okay? Every time I go to sleep, there she is, on that stupid rocker, knitting her stupid little purple afghan, talking to me about Pop-Tarts. My life is complicated enough without my dead aunt seeing me as her own personal Jennifer Love Hewitt. All I want to do is sleep like a normal person, and I can't do that when she's there all the time!"

To her horror, tears of exhaustion filled her eyes. She glanced upward to spread them out, keep them from falling.

Not in front of him. Anywhere but in front of him.

"I'm not crazy," she said finally, her eyes focusing on the wall over his right shoulder.

"I never said you were. Not to your face, anyway." His voice was kind, and soft, and full of humor. She raised her eyes to his in search of his typical sarcasm, derision, and cockiness. But none of that was there. He just looked down at her, his gaze trailing down from her hair, over her forehead, down her nose, to her mouth. She wondered if he thought her lips were too full, her smile too big, her eyes too wide apart, and then she wondered why she was wondering. Finally, he smiled, setting a flock of butterflies loose in her stomach.

Stop that.

"So," he said, his voice thick with amusement, "you thought blaring music was the way to get rid of her?"

Flynn blinked away the last of the moisture in her eyes and shrugged. "It was a theory. It did shut her up. I couldn't hear her. But she was still there." She glanced toward the front porch. "Maybe if I burn the rocker . . ."

"Maybe if you *listened* to her . . ."

She turned her attention back to him. "What?"

"Pardon me for pointing out the obvious, but if she's trying to tell you something, maybe you should just listen to her. What have you got to lose?"

"Sleep, for one."

"Which you're losing anyway, so that argument doesn't hold water."

"Then there's my sanity."

He grinned. "Can't lose something you don't have."

"Hey!" She thwacked him on the shoulder. "Just because you come busting into my room to save my life—which was never in danger, by the way—does not mean you get to be all chummy with me. I still haven't forgiven you for that stunt you pulled the other day."

He sighed, and the grin abated. "Ah, yes. That."

"Yes. *That.* It was a lousy thing to do."

"It was."

"I don't know what your game is here, but I don't like being played."

"No one with half a brain would." He paused, dipping his head so he could smile directly into her eye line. "For what it's worth, I'm sorry."

She had expected him to fight back, and the lack of anticipated resistance made her feel a little off balance.

"Okay." She crossed her arms over her stomach. "As long as all parties understand who the big jerk is here . . ."

He held her eyes for way longer than absolutely necessary. "All parties, I think, are in complete agreement."

His smile faded and Flynn felt the mood downshift a
bit. He was looking at her in *that way* again, and they
were standing closer than was absolutely necessary. Her
skin began to tingle, and she thought . . . maybe . . .

But that would be bad, fooling around with the bartender. On a lot of levels, not the least of which was that
Freya would never let her live it down.

"I don't believe in this, you know," she said quietly.

Tucker's eyebrows quirked in question, but he didn't
say anything.

"In ghosts," she continued. "I don't believe in them."

"You don't believe in life after death?"

"I don't believe in *chatting* after death, no," she said
quickly. "Do you?"

"I don't know. But there's a lot I don't know. I still
can't figure out how they get that automatic foaming soap
to automatically foam. It's completely beyond me. So on
matters of ghosts and spiritual whatsis, I try to keep an
open mind."

"My dead aunt Esther is *not* talking to me, okay?"
Flynn rubbed her arms to ward off the goose bumps
forming on her skin. "It's my subconscious. I'm torturing myself because of some deep-seated psychological
issues. Or something like that. That's the only reasonable
explanation."

He smiled, and the butterflies inside took flight once
again.

Enough, already.

"Okay," he said. "Let's say it is your subconscious. If
it's appearing to you, in whatever form, it obviously has

something to say. It stands to reason that the only way to make it stop is to listen to it."

He was right, of course. And Flynn knew it. The only admission she allowed, however, was the slight shrug of one shoulder.

Tucker smiled, recognizing her minor acquiescence. "I'm just saying it's worth a shot. So, tell me, what has your subconscious in the form of Esther been telling you?"

Flynn thought back on her interactions with Esther. "Well, mostly, she doesn't like me much and she misses Pop-Tarts."

Tucker gave a scandalized gasp. "There are no Pop-Tarts in heaven? I have to say, that comes as a surprise."

"She's not in heaven yet. She's kind of . . . caught. I think. I don't know. She thinks that since I'm the only one who can see her, that it's my responsibility to help her move on."

"I guess that makes sense." He smiled down at her, and once again Flynn became acutely aware of how close they were standing. There was a whole living room, and yet she was just a few inches from him. How had that happened without her noticing?

"What else did she say?" Tucker asked.

She took a step back. "What does it matter? It's my *subconscious*. It doesn't mean anything. It's like when you dream about a train going into a tunnel."

"Well, that's obvious sex imagery."

"No, water is sex. A train in a tunnel is just . . . Hitchcockian."

Tucker chuckled. "You said *cock*."

She tried not to laugh, but failed. "Oh, my God! What are you, twelve?"

"On occasion." Their eyes connected again, and Flynn felt a little dizzy.

"Look, all I'm saying is that I don't think it means anything," she said, her voice thick with lack of conviction.

"Fair enough." Tucker took a step back and nodded toward the bedroom. "Now, go pack an overnight bag."

Flynn stayed where she was. "And where, exactly, do you think I might be going overnight?"

"Well, you shouldn't stay here, not with a front door that won't lock." He motioned toward the door, and Flynn noticed that the wooden doorjamb was completely splintered where the dead bolt had been. "Herman can probably fix it tomorrow. In the meantime . . ." Tucker reached into his pocket and pulled out a key, then handed it to her. It was old, like the one that opened the cottage, the key chain an oval of silver with *Thank you for choosing The Goodhouse Arms* engraved on one side and *Rm. 213* engraved on the other. She looked up at him.

"You keep room keys in your pocket?" She gave him her most skeptical look. "How convenient."

"I got it yesterday. You know. In case someone might need it."

His eyes met hers, and she realized that he'd gotten this room specifically for her. She looked down at her hand and tightened her fingers around the key.

"Thank you, Tucker."

"It's no big deal." He reached out and touched her arm gently with his fingertips. "Go pack. I'll walk you up there and get you settled. Maybe Esther will leave you alone there, maybe not. But it's worth a shot, right?"

Flynn nodded. "Right."

She kept her eyes on Tucker as she started toward her bedroom, then turned away and focused on the task at hand, trying to ignore the residual tingle she felt where his hand had grazed her arm.

Here we go. The one-two punch of butterflies and tingles was more than even she could ignore—she officially had a thing for the bartender. Which was okay. He was cute, she was human. It wasn't like she was going to *act* on it; she'd learned her lesson about workplace romances. So, it was okay. A little crush. No big deal.

She opened the armoire and surveyed her nightwear options, her eyes instantly locking on to a lovely pair of cream-colored silk pajamas that Freya had ordered for her . . .

Flynn closed her eyes.

Having a crush is okay. Acting on it is not. Do. Not. Act.

She released the breath, opened her eyes, and pulled a thick, decidedly unsexy BU sweatshirt on over her cotton camisole and ratty flannel lounge pants. She glanced at herself in the full-length mirror. If he hit on her while she looked like this, there was no hope for either of them.

Jake opened the door for Flynn, poking his head in the room and turning on the light before stepping back to allow her passage.

"All clear," he said. "No dead Esthers."

Flynn made a show of rolling her eyes before stepping in, but he caught the small smile she let slip when she thought he couldn't see her. For a moment he considered just shoving her in and hurrying back to Gordon Chase's business park, but he realized now that it would be rude. Inhospitable. And how long would it take to show her around?

"So, you can see, the king-size bed," he said, walking around behind her and turning on the light by the bedside. "Dial 109 on the phone to put on a Do Not Disturb; it'll go right to voice mail. Although I'm the only one who knows you're here, so . . ." Their eyes met and held. Jake cleared his throat and motioned toward the bathroom. "The bathroom is fully stocked with your basic toiletries, and the armoire has extra blankets if you need any."

Flynn nodded, then sat down on the edge of the bed.

"Nice," she said, bouncing a bit.

Jake's mouth went dry. "Yeah. Well. You get some sleep. I'm just gonna . . ."

He motioned behind him toward the door, but he couldn't turn away. Flynn sat on the bed, looking up at him with that wild hair falling around her shoulders, and all he wanted was to strip that sweatshirt off of her, to know what it would feel like to bury his fingers in that hair . . .

He felt a familiar stirring down below. Time to go, or Flynn would soon know exactly what kind of pull she was having on him. For the gazillionth time in his life, he envied women the fact that their bodies allowed for a little mystery.

"So, good night," he said, his voice tight. His hand was on the doorknob when she called out, "Tucker?" behind him.

He closed his eyes for a second. *Dead kittens. Physics textbooks. Queen Elizabeth II.* He opened them again and turned to face her. "Yeah?"

"If you have a few minutes, I'd like to know what the deal is with you and Gordon Chase."

Well, that certainly did the trick. Jake leaned his back against the door. "Why do you want to know?"

"Because you two both seem intent on marking me as your personal territory. I think as the object in the middle of your competing urine streams, I'm owed an explanation. I know I'll never get a straight answer from Chase, so I'm going direct to the source: you."

She stared at him, her eyes sharp and intent on their target. Jake swallowed, trying not to smile as the words *I know I'll never get a straight answer from Chase* vibrated in his head. She'd seen right through Chase, charm, smarm, and barrel. It only confirmed what Jake already knew, that Flynn Daly was smarter than your average bear, but still. Knowing she'd seen past Chase's money and good looks only warmed him in places that didn't need warming at the moment.

"It's a long story," he said finally. "And I know you want to get some sleep, so I'll just—"

"I've been sleeping all day," she said. "Kind of. And as soon as I go to sleep, Esther's gonna be there, nagging at me. I'm happy to put that off for a while." She played with a frayed edge of her sweatshirt, then sighed and rolled her eyes. "Just humor me, okay? Distract me with your sordid tale of testosterone gone stupid." She nibbled one corner of her lip, scuffed the toe of one Ked on the floor, then raised her eyes to his, her hair hanging loosely over one shoulder as she cocked her head to the side. "Please?"

That hair. There was so much of it. He could reach out and touch . . .

Oh, man. *Dead kittens.*

"Look," he said. "I need to . . . I've got a . . . Um." He motioned toward the door. *Harvey Fierstein. Carol Channing. Gramma Tucker.* "I'm gonna get us something from the bar. If you really want me to give you the whole story, it's gonna be a long night."

Flynn's face lit up. "Jameson's?"

Wow. Had she been that pretty when she first got off the train? He knew she'd been pretty, but he didn't remember her being *that* pretty.

"Yeah. Sure. I'll be right back."

He ducked out and shut the door behind him, leaning against the door and staring up at the ceiling. On a scale of one to ten, he wondered how bad an idea it would be to tell her everything; he placed it at about a three. It wasn't like he was going to continue dangling her in front of Chase, anyway. He'd made that decision when he ran that last stoplight on the way to the Arms, when he thought that all his games might have gotten her hurt, or worse. He could find another way to distract Chase, and if Flynn knew how dangerous he was, then maybe she'd agree to stay away from him. Of course, there was the risk that if he told her about Chase, she'd run off and tell Chase what he was up to, but at least then Jake wouldn't have her getting hurt on his conscience.

Then, it would be her own damn fault.

Oddly, that didn't make him feel any better about that possibility. Since seeing Flynn passed out on the bed in Esther's cottage, his entire being had been buzzing with a strange, stupid, and inappropriate need to touch her, to protect her, to not let anyone near her who wasn't him.

Although, unable to shake the vision of her bouncing

on the edge of the bed in the hotel room, his desire to touch her had hit number one with a bullet.

He pushed away from the door and headed down the hall, untucking his shirt and working hard to drum up images of dead kittens.

"So . . ." Flynn sat cross-legged on the bed, leaning back against the headboard, her mind whirling with all the new information Tucker had been telling her over the last hour. "Wow."

"Yeah." Tucker twirled his glass in his hands. "That pretty much brings you up-to-date."

"I'm really sorry about your dad."

Tucker shrugged it off. "Yeah, me, too. But it was a long time ago."

Flynn watched him, remembering what Mercy had said about their father's death being so hard on Tucker. Considering the fact that his dad wouldn't have even been at that factory if it wasn't for Gordon Chase's greed, it all made sense. Suddenly the piano falling on the safety inspector didn't seem even remotely funny anymore.

"So," she said, shifting conversational gears. "You really think Gordon Chase killed Esther?"

Tucker shifted in the antique tub chair he'd pulled up next to the bed. His feet rested on the far edge of the nightstand, which was being used as a temporary cocktail table. "No. I don't know. Something's off. Esther was old, and she had a heart condition . . ." He shrugged and took a sip from his glass. "But something's still not sitting right with me."

"It's that cop's intuition," Flynn said, feeling as though it was a new Tucker sitting before her. A Tucker who'd been a cop. A Tucker who cared about more than he let on. A Tucker whose eyes . . .

She blinked and sat up straighter. She must be drunk, thinking about eyes. She set her glass on the nightstand and then edged it a little farther away with her index finger. Just to be safe.

"So, anyway. That's what all that Gordon Chase stuff is about." He smiled lightly. "By the way, feel free to light into me at any time for putting you in the middle of that. I'm waiting for that other shoe to drop."

"Oh, forget it. I'd have done the exact same thing." She waved her hand in the air and attempted a casual laugh, but it came out in an awkward snort. Tucker chuckled. *This is what happens when you start thinking about eyes,* she admonished internally. She cleared her throat and asked, "So, how are we going to nab him?"

Tucker raised an eyebrow. "Did I miss a memo? When did the 'we' happen?"

"Well, you were using me to get to him anyway—"

"Hey, there's that shoe."

"I'm not dropping a shoe. I'm just saying, I don't think it was all that bad a plan. I can totally string him along while you investigate. And I won't even have to be all that dishonest about it. I mean, we *haven't* made any final decisions yet about this place." Which was true enough; Freya said it would be at least two weeks before Dad chose a buyer.

Tucker focused on his glass and ran his index finger along the rim. "Really? You're thinking about staying?"

Flynn shrugged and felt a small shot of excitement ride through her at the thought. Maybe it was the booze, maybe it was the sleep deprivation, but she was starting to feel kinda . . . warmly toward the place. Her eyes trailed over the room, with the canopy bed and tub chairs and antique writing desk. The roses on the wallpaper. The tall windows. Her gaze landed on Tucker sitting next to her bed, watching her with an inscrutable expression.

The bartender.

"What?" she said, rubbing self-consciously at her nose.

"You're thinking about staying." It was a statement this time, as though he'd just read her mind and was merely saying it out loud for the record.

"No," she said, using the petulant tone of a twelve-year-old denying a crush on her science lab partner. She worked up the nerve to meet his eye, allowing the big humming ball of strange and awkward energy to intensify between them before losing the game of chicken and looking away first.

"You know how many jobs I've had in the past eight years?" Flynn angled her head to look at him. Tucker shook his head. "Fourteen. I have been, in no particular order, a nanny; a cashier at a bakery; a database administrator; a slime line worker in an Alaskan fish cannery; a prostitute at a Renaissance Faire . . ." She trailed off and smiled gently at him. "I mean, I *played* a prostitute."

He whistled and shook his head. "Now you've gone and spoiled the fantasy."

She laughed, turned her eyes back to the ceiling. "I like animals, so I was a veterinarian's assistant for a while, until I discovered I really only like healthy, fluffy animals. I've done everything, pretty much, at least once, but I never found it. You know, the one thing I really wanted to do for the rest of my life." She spread out her arms and breathed in deep, then lowered her eyes to Tucker's and, for reasons she didn't quite understand, said, "My mother was a dancer. She taught ballet to little girls." Just as she was working up the energy to explain what that meant, he nodded his head and said, "I get it."

She blinked in surprise. "You do?"

"Yeah. Dancing isn't the kind of thing you do to pay the bills. It's the kind of thing you do because you love it. Because you can't *not* do it. That's what you were looking for."

Flynn lowered her eyes, feeling suddenly overwhelmed. "So, I mean, yeah, the thought has crossed my mind that if I'm not gonna find it at the Renaissance Faire, I might as well not find it . . ."

". . . here," he finished for her. Their eyes met again, and Flynn knew that the heat in her face had nothing to do with the booze, although if asked, she would have sworn otherwise.

"Look," she said, "even if my father keeps this place, there's no way he'd ever let me run it. I have no experience. No idea what I'm even doing here. He'll put someone in here who knows what they're doing, and I'll go back to some desk job in Boston."

"I guess that makes sense."

She leaned forward, hugging her knees to her chest. "So let me help you."

Tucker laughed. "You're gonna give a guy whiplash, you keep taking corners like that."

"This thing with Gordon Chase, it could be my last chance to . . . I don't know. Do something that matters, I guess. And you know, I've got a stake in this, too. If Chase did kill Esther, then that's probably why she's haunting me."

He stared at her in silence, his eyes narrowing in thought, and she was sure he could see her heart pounding even through the bulky sweatshirt. She waited for him to say something, but he just watched her with an intent gaze.

"Okay," he said finally.

"Okay? Okay, what?"

"Okay. You can help." He held up an index finger. "But we've gotta have ground rules. Number one is, you don't so much as look at Chase without me knowing about it. If he calls you or contacts you in any way, you let me know before jumping into anything."

Flynn sat forward, practically bouncing in excitement. "Okay. Deal."

"I'm not done. You don't tell anyone about anything. If Chase did get to Esther, he might have someone here on the inside helping him, so keep quiet about it."

"You think someone here would harm Esther? It seems like everyone loved her."

"All it takes is one person who didn't," he said. "And I haven't really wrapped my head around a solid theory yet, so, just keep it all under your hat for the time being, okay?"

"Okay. Fine." A sudden yawn hit her like a truck. She indulged it, then blinked away the moisture in her eyes. "So what do I do?"

Tucker chuckled, sat forward, and put his glass down on the nightstand. "You get some sleep. We'll talk about it tomorrow."

He shifted, about to get up, and Flynn was surprised by

how powerfully she wanted him to stay. It was the smell of his skin, or maybe the kindness in his smile, or the amused tones in his voice—something about him was so innately comforting to her that she hadn't even noticed until he made the move to leave, threatening to take her comfort away.

"I don't want you to go." The words were out before she'd even had time to think them, let alone to stop herself.

He let out a rough sigh. "You know I can't stay."

She stared at him for a long time, not sure what to say. She hadn't intended to hit on him, exactly. It wasn't that she wanted to sleep with him—although her stomach did take flight at the thought—she just wanted him to stay. Something about him seemed to fill cracks inside her she didn't know she had, and now that they were filled, she didn't want to go back.

"You can stay for a little while," she said quietly, hoping she didn't sound as pathetic as she felt.

"I can't, Flynn." There was regret in his smile, which was only a small comfort. "You've been drinking. There are rules."

"I'm not saying . . . We don't have to . . . That's not what I'm asking for. I just don't want you to go. Not yet. I . . ."

She groaned and put her hand over her eyes. She was the lonely, horny innkeeper, hitting on the bartender. She was a cliché, a tired joke, a sexual harasser.

She heard him get up, and her whole body froze as she prayed that he'd just leave and then she could keep her hand like this, covering her eyes, for the rest of her time here. It wouldn't be easy, but it would be doable, she was sure.

She felt the mattress shift as his weight settled next to her on the bed. Warm fingers circled her wrist, pulling her hand away from her face. His smile was gentle, and his eyes were kind, and even his tousled, unkempt hair was making her stomach tighten.

He opened his mouth to say something, then closed it again. One of his hands rested next to her hip, his body crossing hers, blocking her from jumping up and running to the bathroom for sanctuary. His other hand still held her wrist, one thumb absently tracing the tendons under her skin. With every second of silence, her heart beat harder, and she was sure her face was practically radioactive with heat by now. He released her wrist and reached up to touch her face, his fingers grazing her cheek, making her skin tingle.

Okay. That's enough. She pushed her back up against the headboard, putting only maybe an inch or two of extra space between them, but it was space she suddenly needed.

"Tucker—"

"We're in bed together. I think you can call me Jake now."

"I can't." She swallowed.

A slow smile spread over his face, and he laughed. "Stubborn, thy name is Flynn."

She could feel heat from his body, hovering so near, not technically touching her but still effecting an intense visceral reaction. This had to stop. He either had to get in that bed for real or leave.

"Jake . . ." she said quietly, hoping he'd understand his

choice without her having to lay it out for him. Avoiding that humiliation was worth the concession of using his first name.

He nodded. He understood, and she could tell by the look of resignation on his face that she'd be alone in just another minute. Still, he leaned forward, one hand cupping the back of her head in his hand, and his lips landed softly on hers, at first gentle, but then the energy between them started to crackle and he dove in deeper.

Oh, this is good. This is goooood. Her entire body hummed with the feel of him as he leaned over her. Sensations came at her in bits and pieces; the softness of his hair under her fingers, the strength of his arm as it pulled her up to him, the harmonizing heart-pounding rhythms that reverberated through them both like primal drumbeats. Her fun parts were just getting into the swing of things when he put his hands on her shoulders and pulled back, his eyes heavy-lidded and, she thought with satisfaction, not entirely able to focus.

"Well," he said. "That was . . ."

She let out a sharp breath. "Yeah. It was."

"Okay." He released her shoulders, then ran one hand through his hair. "Okay." He hopped up off the bed, took a few steps toward the door, then turned back to face her, gesturing over his shoulder toward the door. "I'm gonna go."

"Fine." She heard the petulant strain in her voice, but there was nothing to be done about it. She gave him a stiff wave. "See ya."

A confused look flashed over his face, and he took a step closer. Good God. Was he *trying* to torture her? Why didn't he just *leave* already?

He squinted at her a bit, his expression unsure. "Are you mad?"

"Mad? No. Why would I be mad?"

"I don't know. I just—"

"I mean, just because you kiss me like that and then run off like it's Superbowl Sunday. Who would possibly be offended by that?"

"Oh, Christ." He took another step toward her, looked at her like she was the crazy one here. "Flynn, I'm leaving *because* I just kissed you like that. I . . ." He shook his head and let out a long breath. "There are rules."

"Since when do men care if a girl's been drinking a little? I thought most guys used Jim Beam for their wingman."

"Well," he said, his eyes locked on hers, "I'm not most guys."

"So . . . what, then? Are you gay or something?"

His head reeled back in shock. "Am I . . . ? You think I'm *gay?*"

"Look, I would have stopped you." *Probably.* "But you didn't even go for the sex. That means gay, married, living with Mother, or crazy. None of which bode well for you."

Anger flashed over his face. "Or, maybe, I was raised by a family of women who beat it into my brain that there are certain things you don't do when a girl is—"

He stopped suddenly. Flynn threw her legs over the side of the bed and stood up, advancing on him as she spoke. "When a girl is *what?* Weird? Undesirable? From Boston? What?"

"*Special.*" He raised both hands, his fingers raking the air in frustration. "When a girl is *special,* you take her on a date first. You shower beforehand. With soap. You buy her flowers or candy, both if she's really making you nuts. You follow steps, you stick to the rules. God! I'm killing myself to do the right thing here, and you assume I'm *gay*? What, were you raised by wolves?"

Flynn softened, chose to ignore the raised by wolves comment, and smiled.

"You think I'm special?"

He let loose with a frustrated chuckle. "There are many definitions of *special*."

"You think I'm special," she said in a teasing singsong voice as she took a step closer to him.

He smiled and shook his head. "You thought I was gay?"

"If it helps, I hoped you were just living with Mother." She wrinkled her nose. "You don't live with Mother, do you?"

"Oh, hell." He threw his arms up and headed toward the door. "Good night, Flynn."

"Good night," she said softly to his back. His hand touched the doorknob, then he froze where he was. She was just about to say something when he turned suddenly and grabbed her, pulling her to him so fast she thought she might get whiplash. She closed her eyes and fell into the kiss with him, allowing the feel and scent of him to finally silence her internal chatter. Every movement sent off sparks in different parts of her body, and if she had been able to think anything, it would have only been, *Don't stop.*

But he did, and they pulled back from each other a bit, both of them breathless and flushed.

"Okay," she said. "I take back the gay thing."

He laughed, put his hand on her face, and traced her lower lip with his thumb, making the muscles in her legs tremble. She let out a little moan and his eyes fluttered a bit, but then his face cleared and he released her.

"Do something for me?" he asked softly.

"Yeah?"

He let out a rough breath. "On another night, when the time is right, if you're so inclined and you haven't been drinking . . ." He smiled and kissed the tip of her nose. "Ask me again."

She made some kind of guttural sound that she hoped would pass for, "Sure."

He let out a soft laugh. "Good night, Flynn."

"Night."

He shook his head, chuckled lightly to himself, and then let himself out, leaving her alone, dizzy, and unsure. She leaned forward slowly and let her forehead rest against the dark wood of the door. She saw his face when she closed her eyes, and it wasn't hard work to recall the feel of his arms around her, the earthy scent of his skin, the . . .

"Hoo boy," she said, releasing a breath as she pulled herself away from the door. She walked to the bathroom, turned the shower on, and stared at herself in the mirror.

"This is a prime example of poor decision-making," she told herself. "Bad news. Do not get all gooey over the bartender."

As her reflection smiled back at her, she heard the retort clear as a bell in her head.

Too late.

Chapter Eight

♡ Something was buzzing. Rattling against wood. Something was . . .

Flynn opened one eye just as her cell phone vibrated itself right off the nightstand and clanked perfectly into a glass with about a half inch of Irish whiskey. She'd moved it to the floor in the middle of the night because the smell was bothering her, but she'd lacked the motivation to carry it all the way to the bathroom sink.

"Oh, shit," she said, reaching in, glancing around, then finally wiping it on the bedspread. The Arms was a nice place, but it was still a hotel. Surely the bed had suffered worse indignities. She flipped the phone open.

"Yeah?"

"Flynn." Her father's voice came through the line. Taut and businesslike, the way it always was, even on birthdays and Christmas. She sat up straight in a Pavlovian response.

"Hey. Dad. Wow. What time is it?"

There was a slight pause. "Nine thirty. Are you in your office?"

She glanced at the half-empty bottle of Jameson's on the floor. "Yep."

"Good I'll need an update on the situation with the financials. I have some preliminary reports here, but they're only current as of the end of the second quarter. I'll need everything up to and including the end of the third quarter."

"Mmm-hmmm. You bet. I'll get right on it." First, of course, she'd have to ask someone what a quarter was. It sounded like a football thing, but somehow Flynn doubted that was the case. "Anything else?"

There was a hint of surprise in his voice when he answered, as though he'd been expecting the football question. "Uh, yes, actually. There's a local contact down there I'd like you to take a meeting with." There was a slight pause. "I just want you to make initial contact, establish a relationship."

"Dad. You know I'm not that kind of girl."

He didn't laugh. "I'm talking about a business relationship."

"Yeah. I know. You see, it was funny because—"

"You're the face of the company out there, Flynn. Take him to lunch, dinner, coffee. It really doesn't matter. If he asks you a question you don't know how to answer, just tell him you don't know and you'll get back to him."

She shrugged her shoulders to release the tightness there. "So anything other than 'What's your favorite color?' then?"

Another joke, landing like a brick. "I've got my team working on things here, but apparently this guy can help

us work through the local red tape, which is always help-
ful in little places like Scheintown. They're notorious for
making things hard on outsiders, and I'd like to get this
off my plate quickly. The guy's name is . . ."

She listened as her father ruffled through his notes, and
then said the name in unison with him: "Gordon Chase."

Her father paused. "Has he contacted you already?"

She thought on this for a moment. "His name has . . .
come up."

She decided to leave it at that. If she started talking
about embezzlement, suspected murder, and poisoning by
berry, Dad would pull Freya out of Tucson in a heartbeat.
And then likely put Flynn in a treatment program. What
was it Freya had said? Only tell people what they need to
know?

Good advice, she thought, then realized her father was
still talking.

". . . three meetings in New York on Tuesday, then . . ."

She sat up straighter. "Three meetings? In New York?
Dad, shouldn't you be . . . I don't know. Slowing down a
bit? Can't that wait for Freya to come back?"

There was a long silence. "Why should I slow down?"

Flynn sighed. "Dad. Freya told me. About the
angina."

"What angina?"

"Your angina."

"I don't know what Freya told you, but I don't have
angina. I'm fine, Flynn. You must have misheard her."

Flynn snorted. "Well, there's only one other thing that
sounds like angina, and I know you don't have that."

Crickets. Good God, what did it take to break that
man?

"Dad," she said, more seriously. "Freya said—"

"I don't know what Freya told you, Flynn, but I assure you, I'm fine. I had a full checkup in August and my doctor gave me a clean bill of health. I can have him fax over an official statement if you'd like."

"No," Flynn said slowly. "That's not necessary."

I might need a good lawyer for when I kill Freya, though.

He cleared his throat. "Can we get back to business?"

Flynn threw one hand up in the air, but kept the frustration out of her voice. "You bet."

"Good. I should have a decision on a buyer by the end of next week, so you won't have to be there much longer."

A buyer. The words struck a surprisingly uncomfortable chord in her gut.

"Dad? Have you thought at all about maybe keeping the place? It's really beautiful, and the people are amazing. The chef makes this incredible pumpkin—"

"Don't get attached, Flynn. It's the first rule."

She rolled her eyes. Stupid men and their stupid rules. "But it turns a profit. Okay, not a *big* profit, but not losing money is a good thing, right? And what if some big chain buys it and replaces the rose garden with a waterslide? Or fires everyone and then no one will know which room George Washington slept in? What if they put onion blossoms on the menu? Have you thought about that?"

There was a long silence, then, "I want the numbers by tomorrow morning, Flynn."

She released a heavy sigh. "Okay. You'll have them."

"Thank you. I'll be in touch."

Click. She made a face at her phone and tossed it down

on the bed. Her father was a good man, she knew. He was fair and moral and hygienically irreproachable. The only niggle she had about him was that he didn't seem to possess a soul, or at least not one anyone could see.

His heart, though, was fine. Apparently. Flynn picked up the phone again and thought about dialing her sister and demanding an explanation, but rejected the idea. She didn't have the energy to confront Freya right now. Right now, she had bigger things on her mind.

Like waterslides and onion blossoms.

She sighed and looked around; when, exactly, had this place gotten under her skin? She should hate it, what with all the nature and nothing within walking distance and the cottage that was quite literally making her insane. But the rose garden had charmed her, and the rooms were gorgeous, and then there was the bartender . . .

Tucker.

She sucked in a breath and a flash of panic ran through her as she remembered the events of the previous night.

"Oh, God," she said, dropping her face into her hands. Had she really thrown herself at the bartender?

Yes. Yes, she had. It had been late. She had been drinking. And he had those warm brown eyes that made her go all gooey inside. The eyes were really at fault. If he just hadn't *looked* at her that way . . .

Oh, God.

She'd called him *Jake.*

She'd *kissed* him.

She'd told him about the Renaissance Faire prostitute thing.

"Ugh," she groaned. And now she was going to have to work with him on this Chase thing, which at first had seemed fun and exciting and oddly necessary, but now didn't really seem to stand up to the humiliation of facing him again.

"You are a big bottle of stupid," she said, leaning over and picking up the Jameson's and glasses from the floor. "No more stupid for me."

She had just finished rinsing out the glasses when there was a knock on the door. Her back stiffened.

Tucker. He was the only one who knew she was here. She peeked in the mirror, touching her hair briefly before deciding not to bother. She needed a full rehaul, and there just wasn't time.

"Just a minute!" She squeezed a dollop of toothpaste on her finger, swished it around her mouth, and rinsed. She walked across the room and pulled the door open, ready to launch into a big speech about how she'd been so drunk the night before she couldn't remember *a thing* when she heard a high voice say, "Oh!"

It was Annabelle. Flynn relaxed and smiled. "Hey, Annabelle."

"Um." Annabelle stepped back, glanced at the door, and then looked back at Flynn, confusion on her face. "This is 213."

"Yep."

"But that's . . . that's Jake's room. I mean, the room I gave to Jake for any bar patrons that couldn't drive home. But Jake wasn't working last night. How . . . ?" Annabelle stopped talking and her eyes widened. "Oh."

"No!" Flynn put one hand on Annabelle's arm. "No, it's not like that. He just . . ." She scrambled internally, wanting to say something, anything, to take that heart-broken look off sweet Annabelle's face. "Because of the door. Last night. He kicked it down. It's broken. The lock, I mean. So Jake brought me here and then"—*skipping three or four hours*—"he left."

She sounded guilty as hell even to her own ears, but Annabelle didn't seem to catch it. She smiled brightly and nodded. "Oh, that's right. I'm sorry. I'll have Herman fix that for you today."

Flynn released a breath, and the tension drained from her shoulders. How could Jake not see how Annabelle felt about him? Was he really that clueless?

Well. He *was* a man.

"Anyway, I'm sorry to have bothered you," Annabelle said. "It's just that one of the housekeeping staff said she saw the Do Not Disturb sign on the door, and I was all, 'No, I don't think we have a guest there, that's Jake's room, and he wasn't working last night,' and so I came in to check just in case and when I saw you here . . ." Annabelle stopped and lowered her eyes. "I'll have Herman fix that lock."

"Thank you," Flynn said. She was about to shut the door when she suddenly remembered the conversation with her father. She poked her head out into the hall.

"Annabelle?"

Annabelle turned around. "Yes?"

"Please don't tell anyone I had to ask you this, but what's a quarter?"

Annabelle blinked. "What do you mean? Like, the money?"

Flynn smiled. "I don't think so. My father called. He wants all the financials for the third quarter. Whatever that means."

Annabelle nodded. "Yeah. The third quarter just ended last Friday."

Oh. So it was a calendar thing. *Gotcha.* "Okay. Well, can you get some reports together for me? Profit and loss or . . . whatever?"

She smiled. She knew she probably sounded like an idiot, but she trusted Annabelle to pretend that wasn't the case.

Annabelle's face, however, was unusually stiff. "Um. Sure. It might take a few days."

Flynn sighed, leaned against the doorjamb, and gave Annabelle a comrades-in-pain expression. "He wants it tomorrow morning. Is there anything I can do to help?"

"No." Annabelle's voice was unusually high, even for her. "No. No. I can . . ." She pulled on a bright smile. "Sure. I can do that."

"Thank you. I'll be down in the office in a little bit."

Annabelle gave a little wave and disappeared into the stairwell. Flynn stared down the empty hallway for a long moment, her mind traipsing back to the night before with Tucker. A smile spread across her face and she shook it away, going inside to get changed and start her day.

It promised to be a long one.

Jake lay sprawled across his couch, one arm resting on his forehead, and stared at the ceiling. He'd been in that position for most of the morning. Then all of the afternoon. Now, his shift was going to start in an hour, and still he hadn't come to any conclusions, except that the water stain on his ceiling looked a little like Vladimir Putin.

He glanced at his watch again. Five minutes after five. It was still possible he'd receive the perfect stroke of brilliance on exactly how to convince Flynn that she didn't want to help him on this Gordon Chase thing. So far, all he had was that investigations involved long, boring nights of sitting in cars drinking stale coffee. They required you to sift through other people's trash.

They got you in the path of guys like Gordon Chase.

Which, when it came down to it, was the real reason he didn't want Flynn involved. He didn't want her getting hurt, and he damn sure didn't want to be the reason she got hurt. But the truth was the hardest to defend, because it was based on emotion, not logic. So . . .

Focus on the trash.

He released a breath. He couldn't blame his stupidity on the booze; he'd had less than half a glass of Jameson's over the course of three hours. Still, he'd managed to make a promise he really didn't want to keep, and it had bugged him all night. He'd slept fitfully, his brain unable to process her into a dream, but still unwilling to release her. Why had he told her she could help him investigate Chase? Anything that really needed doing, he could do himself, and for more reasons than one she'd be best off staying as far away from it as possible. What had he been thinking?

Of course, he knew that was just it; he hadn't been thinking. He'd been looking at her plaintive eyes, that wild hair grazing the creamy expanse of her neck, and he couldn't find it within himself to deny her anything she wanted. If she'd asked for the head of a unicorn, he'd have gone out looking for an ax.

Well, today he was going to have to tell her no. Although maybe it was better done over the phone. Over the phone, it would be easier. No eyes, no hair, no flowery shampoo smell to worm its way into his head and make him stupid.

As if on cue, his phone rang. He glanced at the caller ID: Goodhouse Arms. He raised his eyes Godward.

"I would have gotten to it," he grumbled, then picked up the phone and hit the talk button.

"Yeah," he said gruffly, trying to sound as though he wasn't excited to hear her voice. It was more work than he'd expected.

"Jake? Turn on your TV."

He released a breath as a mix of relief and disappointment flowed through him. "Mercy?"

"Channel Four. Right now. Turn it on!"

"Okay. Jesus. Just a minute." He threw his legs over the side of the bed and hitched up his boxers as he padded out into his living room. "What's going on?"

"Oh, crapola. It's gone. Well, they'll run it again. Turn it on anyway."

He grabbed the remote and pointed it at the television. "You want to tell me what's going on?"

"The news," she hissed into the phone, as though she was trying not to be heard by anyone else. "It's my saucier!"

He rubbed his eyes and tried to focus on the images. Some woman in a suit behind a desk, talking. Nothing too interesting there.

"Merce, whatever's going on, can it wait until I get in to . . . ?" He trailed off as the screen cut to images of the Hudson River, and what looked like a team pulling a body out of the water.

"There it is!" Mercy said, right as the video cut to a

dented silver pan with what looked like a bungee cord knotted around the handle.

". . . weighted down with bricks and what looks to be some sort of pan, possibly the murder weapon. Authorities ask that anyone with any . . ."

Mercy's voice toppled over the anchor's. "Pan! It's not a pan. It's an All-Clad copper core saucier, you brainless wench. And it's *mine*!"

"Wait a minute, Merce. How could you possibly know it's yours?"

"How many people in this area do you think use All-Clad copper core sauciers?"

"If I knew what you were talking about, I'd venture a guess."

"Ohhhh," she groaned. "It's *dented*! Do you know how much those things cost? It was one thing when I thought someone had stolen it to sell on the black market—"

He wandered into the kitchen. "There's a black market for sauciers? In Shiny?"

Mercy released an aggravated sigh. "I tried to get you to look into it. But oh noooooo. You're too good to investigate my missing, three-hundred-dollar saucier."

He snorted. "You paid three hundred dollars for a pan?"

"It's not a *pan,* goddamnit! It's an All-Clad copper core saucier, and that's not the point. Someone killed someone with my saucier!"

Jake grabbed a mug from the cabinet and filled it with water. "All right. Calm down. Are you sure it's yours?"

There was the sound of careful breathing for a few moments, followed by a long sigh, and when Mercy returned, her voice was calm. "Factor it, Jake. It's a three-hundred dollar saucier, exactly like the one that went missing. What are the chances that it's *not* mine? Besides, I just *know*. I felt it, as soon as I saw it."

Jake had learned a long time ago not to argue with women's intuition. Not only did it piss the woman in question off, which never worked in his favor, the plain fact was that more often than not she was right. He put the mug in the microwave and reached for the instant coffee.

"Okay. So it's yours. When did it go missing?"

"Last spring. Remember? I told you about it, and you ignored me."

"I remember the radishes."

Mercy released a harsh sigh of frustration. "This was before that. Although I did bring it up again on the night with the radishes and you ignored me—again. God, Jake. Do you ever listen to me?"

Jake decided that was a question best left unanswered. "Look. Call the police and tell them it's yours. Tell them when it went missing, as many details as you can remember."

"But, Jake . . ." There was a long pause. "It was taken from my kitchen. *My* kitchen. No one has access except employees, and sometimes friends or whatever, but it's not Main Street." Her voice lowered into a whisper. "What if someone here is a murderer?"

"You're jumping to conclusions, Mercy. I mean, it's possible that someone stole it, sold it, and then it got into the hands of the murderer. Someone at the Arms is a thief, but not necessarily a murderer." Even as he said the words, something niggled at the back of his brain. If he included Esther's death, then that made two potentially suspicious expirations linked with the Arms. It was a little too coincidental for comfort, but there was no need to say that to Mercy. She was freaked out enough as it was.

He pulled the mug out of the microwave while Mercy rattled on about the saucier and how it had always been her favorite, letting it slide that there had been a person on the business end of that pan who probably felt less affection for it. He pretended to listen, adding an encouraging, "Mmm-hmmm," here and there while his mind wandered over the new terrain. It wasn't until the anchor returned to the hot story, rerunning the footage, that something in the background of the saucier shot caught his attention.

It was a plastic evidence bag, which held a flask. Jake grabbed his remote and rewound live TV, thanking God and his cable company for TiVo. He paused the video on the frame and released a breath.

The flask had something shiny around the cap. Something that looked a lot like rhinestones. He quickly calculated the facts.

The saucier went missing last spring. So did Elaine Placie. As for rhinestone flasks, he could only remember ever seeing one, and it had belonged to Elaine. Not to mention that women like Elaine Placie had a tendency toward making enemies . . .

"Crap," he muttered.

"Jake? Are you listening to me?" Mercy hissed through the phone.

"Gotta go," he said, and disconnected the call. He tossed the handset on the couch and stared at the screen, his mind oddly calmed as it processed the new information.

Elaine Placie hadn't skipped town, after all. Although someone had put a fair amount of elbow grease into making it seem that way. And Jake had a strong feeling he knew exactly who.

He headed for the shower. He wanted to be calm, clean, and in control when he told Flynn that there was no way in hell he was letting her get within a country mile of Gordon Chase.

Also, if he got caught breaking into Chase's office that night, he figured the least he could do for his mother was to look well groomed in his mug shot. It's those small touches that mean so much.

"Flynn? You in there?" Jake stepped back as he heard some movement inside the cottage and looked around. The porch was cleared of the rocker from the day before, and two brand new locks gleamed at him against the freshly replaced and painted doorjamb. Unfortunately, he didn't hear either of them turn before Flynn opened the door.

"You know, locks are much more effective if you actually lock . . ."

He trailed off at the sight of her. Flynn smiled, tilting her head as she attached a long, dangling silver earring to her right earlobe. It matched the silver necklace that decorated the space between her breasts, a space that was bared to bursting because the little black dress she was wearing was big on the *little* part.

"Hi." Flynn stepped aside to let him in. "What are you doing here?"

He swallowed, raised his focus up to her eyes. "I needed to talk to you about . . . Are you going somewhere?"

"Yes," she said, grinning. "I have a date."

He stared at her, his mind going blank for a moment. "Did we have plans?"

"No. *I* have plans." She turned her back to him, heading for the bedroom. Jake waited for a long minute, then followed her in to find her inspecting her reflection in a standing mirror in the corner. "I know I promised you I'd talk to you first, but it all happened so fast that I just went with it. Gordon showed up at the office about a half hour ago and asked me out for tonight, so I thought it'd be a perfect chance for you to use that key. I called in Carole to cover your shift tonight, and Gordon will be here in about twenty minutes, so you really should get going."

Smooth, calculated curls of hair fell about the back of her neck and shoulders, but the rest of her typically wild mop was pulled up, held in a loose knot at the back of her head with what looked like two ornate chopsticks. She pumped her lips and swiped her pinkie lightly along one edge of her mouth. For a brief moment, Jake lost his place in the conversation, but then he remembered that she was primping for Chase, and he took a step toward her.

"Call him. Tell him you're not going."

She looked at him like he was crazy. "What? Why? This is a perfect chance for you to get into that office. I thought you'd be happy."

Jake pulled out his cell phone, flipped it open, and punched Chase's number in.

"Tucker, what are you doing?"

Jake put the phone in her hand. "Just hit the green button. When he answers, tell him you're not going out with him. Ever."

Flynn took the phone, flipped it shut, and handed it back. "No. My father asked me to take a meeting with him, and you need him out of the way for a while. Two birds, one stone. You should be gone when he gets here, though. It's not very stealthy if he sees us together."

Jake flipped the phone open again. "He's not going to see me here, because he's not coming to pick you up, because you're canceling."

He started punching the numbers into the phone, but Flynn put her hand over his to stop him.

"Tucker, what's going on? Last night you were fine with this."

He raised his eyes to hers. "Last night I thought Elaine Placie was still alive."

Flynn stared at him for a long moment, then pulled her hand off of his. "Who's Elaine Placie?"

"The girl with the rhinestone flask."

Flynn's eyes widened. "The one who helped Chase get that laptop?"

Jake nodded. "They pulled her body out of the river last night. They haven't identified her yet, but it's her." He continued dialing Chase's number and handed the phone to Flynn. "So. Call."

Flynn took the phone in her hand and stared down at it, then flipped it shut again and handed it back to Jake, her expression confident and determined. "I don't think it was him."

Jake stared at her. "Wow. If pulling the dead conwoman out of my sleeve fails to impress you, keeping this relationship exciting is going to be a challenge."

"Think about it, Tucker. He hires Elaine Placie to help him steal the laptop. He pays her off. So why would he kill her? Even if she demanded more money or threatened to go to the police, he's a reputable businessman and she was a small-time con artist. Her word against his, and he had all the power. Murder seems unmotivated. Plus, I just can't see it. Chase doesn't have an ethical bone in his body, fine, but do you really think he's a murderer? I mean, really?"

He knew she was making sense. He'd had the same thoughts himself, but had been so intent on removing Flynn from the situation that he hadn't entertained them for long. He could think clearly later; now, he had just one goal in mind. He handed her the phone. "I can do this all night, you know."

"Don't think I haven't heard *that* one before." She took the phone from him, flipped it shut, and tossed it over her shoulder, where it flew over the top of the armoire, hit the wall, fell to the floor, and skittered under the bed.

They stared each other down. Jake felt his body go still, tight with tension in the face of her blunt determination.

"So, what are you saying?" he asked finally. "Chase is a decent guy now? Just another eligible prospect?"

She crossed her arms over her chest and cocked her head to the side. "Oh, my God. You're jealous? Of Chase?"

"No," he said, his voice harsher than he intended. He took a breath and started again. "No. It's not that. But Elaine Placie's murder just upped the stakes here, and I want you as far away from this as possible."

She tucked a lipstick into her purse and snapped it shut, then looked at Jake. "Do I look helpless to you?"

He shook his head. "Don't twist this around, Flynn. It's not about that and you know it."

"I took self-defense classes for three years. I have a

cell phone and a Mace key chain. Being a woman doesn't mean I can't think or defend myself."

"The sexism card doesn't work on me. I've got four sisters and a mother, none of whom I'd want to come up against in a dark alley. It's not about that. It's about—"

He trailed off, releasing his breath. It was about the fact that he wouldn't be able to think knowing she was out there with Chase, especially not now that he had the visual of her in that dress. It was about keeping her safe. It was about keeping her his. It was about a million things he couldn't name, most of which he didn't want to. He was trying to think of a way to express this without actually expressing it when she advanced on him, hooked one leg around the back of his knee, and tried to knock him off balance, which she almost did. Jake recovered quickly, gaining his footing and grabbing her arm. He whipped her arm up behind her as he twirled her around, then hooked his free arm around her neck. She huffed loudly and a strand of hair flew up from her face.

"Crap," she said. "That always worked in class."

He leaned his head forward, his lips next to her ear. "Of course it did. But this is the real world."

He could hear the disappointment in her voice as she shifted under his grip. "So what are you saying? In the real world, I'd be dead now?"

He took a deep breath, trying not to let the smell of her distract him too much. "Depends on what the guy who has you wants."

He relaxed his grip and she turned slowly in his arms. His hands rested on her waist and she pulled her lower lip in with her top teeth. He reached one hand up and touched her face. It was impossible, how soft her skin was. Unnatural, almost.

"Tucker," she said, little more than a whisper.

He was about to lean in and kiss her when she stuffed her Mace key chain in his face.

"Spritz spritz. You're disabled, and I'm safe. So there. Nyah."

He pulled his hands away from her waist. "Gotta hand it to you, Flynn. You sure know how to kill a mood."

She shrugged smugly and put the Mace back in her bag. "If you want control of a scene, you give the other character what they most want, or show them what they most fear. I learned it in an improv class the Renaissance Faire people made me take. Works in real life, too."

"So, how'd you know what I wanted?" he asked quietly.

She lowered her eyes and shrugged. "You're a man. It was either food or sex and I didn't have a turkey leg handy."

Jake chuckled, then went silent. His heart was still beating erratically from holding her so close, and he knew anything he said now would be pointless. She had her mind set, and short of dragging her out by her hair— which, admittedly, was tempting—nothing he said was going to matter anyway. She took a step toward him, angling her head to the side in a conciliatory pose, exposing the long, creamy expanse of her neck.

"Just for the record," she said, her eyes lighting playfully as she looked up at him, "Gordon Chase is not eligible for anything with me."

Jake was a little disturbed by how good it felt to hear

that. "Yeah? He's rich and good-looking. A lot of girls in town think he's quite the catch."

"Well," she said softly, "I'm not a lot of girls."

Jake smiled and Flynn touched his arm.

"Look. Gordon Chase would be a big jerk even if he didn't set you up. But he did, and for that, I want him to pay. Whether he killed Elaine Placie or not, he's definitely connected to her, and I'm giving you a chance to find out how. So you can choose to be the overprotective alpha male and shove yourself in between us when he gets here, or you can trust me to handle myself and go get that laptop."

There was a knock at the door. Jake didn't move. Neither did Flynn.

"It's an hour to the restaurant and an hour back, I can stretch dinner out for two hours. That should give you enough time." He felt her fingers graze over his. "I have to spend four hours being nice to this jerk. Go make it worth my while."

Her hand fell from his arm, and then she was gone. Jake listened as she opened the door, barely able to keep himself from rushing into the living room and throwing a big wrench in her plans to play Nancy Drew.

But he didn't. He listened as she greeted Chase at the door, her voice happy and playful and innocent. He heard Chase's smarmy, self-satisfied tones, and a few painful moments later, the door shut behind them. Jake released a breath, sat down on the bed, and rested his head in his hands.

Realistically, he knew that the risk was minimal. Even if it was Chase who had taken out Elaine Placie and Esther, he'd publicly come to the Arms to make plans with

Flynn, and was picking her up here where everyone could see them together. If he was going to come after Flynn, it wouldn't be tonight. She would be all right. She was tough. She was smart. She was . . .

She was amazing.

He chuckled lightly to himself as the realization hit him full force. She'd gotten to him. When had that happened? He hadn't noticed it, but as he thought about her going out with Chase tonight in that dress, there it was, grating at him.

Huh. Must have been the hair.

Jake reached into his pocket and pulled out the key Rhonda Bacon had given him, staring at it as he flipped it over between his fingers. He knew he didn't have much time. He just hoped that whatever was on that laptop was worth it.

It would have to be.

Chapter Nine

♡ Chase emptied the last of the wine into Flynn's glass and made a casual finger motion in the air for the waiter to bring another. His smile didn't *tink* so much in the candlelight, which was a nice break, but an hour of feigning interest in golf and mutual funds was taking its toll. She glanced at her watch; she only needed to kill another forty-five minutes. She hoped that Tucker would be able to find everything he needed in that time, because that was all he was getting.

"So, we've been talking about me all night," Chase said, dumping his napkin by his plate. "I want to know about you."

"Well," Flynn said, "it'll be a short conversation. There isn't much to know about me."

"I don't believe that," he said. "You seem like a fascinating woman."

I seem like a woman who's standing between you and your commission.

"Not really. I'm just your average girl. I'm all about shoes, shopping, and a weekly mani-pedi." She picked up her wineglass. "The only people less interesting than me are dead. Trust me."

"Don't be modest. I know you used to act. Let's start there. Why'd you stop?"

She put her glass down. "When did I tell you about that?"

"You didn't. I did some looking into you. You are a fascinating woman, Flynn Daly. Don't tell me you didn't know."

"Nope. Sure didn't." Tucker had been right about a small town with an Internet connection being a dangerous thing.

Chase waved one hand dismissively. "I like you, Flynn. I think we're kindred souls. And when I like someone, I like to know more about them."

Flynn let the kindred souls thing go, diving in on what she felt was the more important point. "So you did a background check. How romantic."

"You make it sound so intrusive," he said, chuckling. "I just hired a private detective, who called your friends and family and asked a few questions. It's how I knew that you loved Italian food. Red wine. Blizzards from Dairy Queen." He winked. "It's all completely aboveboard."

Flynn forced a smile and gripped a handful of the tablecloth in her fist under the table to keep herself from throwing a dinner roll at his head. "I think we might have different definitions of 'aboveboard.'"

"Oh, come on, Flynn. Everybody does that sort of thing nowadays. At least I'm up front about it. And it's not like I pulled up your credit report or your criminal history. I just wanted to know about your likes and dislikes. I wanted to know about the things that mattered to you."

"And you couldn't ask me directly because . . . ?"

He grinned. "Because it would ruin the surprise." He leaned to one side and pulled a small, golden box out of his pocket. It was wrapped in ornate metallic ribbon, which culminated in a big ribbon puff on the top that looked like shimmery ganglia.

"Ugh," Flynn breathed.

"Go ahead," Chase said, making an encouraging gesture with his hands. "Open it."

Flynn went to the job of separating the ribbon from the box. Chase simply watched her, eyes twinkling. He'd done this before, Flynn could feel it. And based on the self-satisfied expression on his face, it had actually worked.

Good-looking and rich, she thought as she struggled with the gift. *The thinking girl's kryptonite.*

Finally she gave up on being delicate, picked up her steak knife, and sawed through it, then popped the top off the box.

"Oh, my God," she said, staring down into the box. It was a silver necklace with a pendant of two ballet shoes, each with a simple pink diamond at the toe. It looked like the kind of thing you'd give a little girl after her confirmation.

Chase leaned forward, his finger lazily indicating the gift.

"Your friend from college . . . what was her name? Alesia?"

"I don't have a friend from college named Alesia," Flynn said flatly, placing the box down on the table.

His eyebrows knit. "Whitney?"

Flynn shook her head.

He pulled an index card out of his coat pocket, then snapped his fingers and returned it. "Michelle. Anyway, she said how much you loved ballet slippers, that you had them everywhere in your dorm room. So . . ." He raised his eyebrows proudly, knowing the answer to his question before he even posed it. "Do you like it?"

"Do I like it?"

It was true; in college, she *had* been slightly obsessed with ballet slippers. Then during her mid-twenties crisis she and her therapist had spent ten months discovering that the ballet slipper thing was just a symbol of something she felt she'd never be able to attain, a promise she'd never be able to keep, and she had cleared out all her ballet slipper things, put them in a box, and stored them in the attic of her father's house. To get this gift now, mere days after having finally abandoned her mother's dream for her, felt a lot like being punched in the stomach.

And there was Chase, all big and smug, thinking he'd just made all her dreams come true.

Do I like it? What she'd like would be to wedge it up his left nostril with a rubber mallet. But that would be unladylike and ungracious.

And it wouldn't kill the forty minutes she had left.

"You know what?" Flynn said, standing up quickly. "I'll be right back."

She dumped her napkin onto her seat and took off for the bathroom.

Aboveboard, my ass, she thought as she locked the door on the stall.

Can't believe he actually investigated *me,* she thought as she washed her hands.

Longest night of my freakin' life, she thought as she tossed the paper towel into the bin. She glanced in the mirror and stared at herself.

"No jury in the land would convict me," she said out loud, then caught the reflection of something golden behind her in the mirror and her heart jumped.

"I'm sorry, I thought I was—" she said as she turned around.

But there was no one behind her. Her heart began to pound, and she felt a sheen of sweat form on the back of her neck. She put her hand over her chest and glanced in the mirror again, breathing deeply through her nose, exhaling through her mouth. She laughed at herself, but even to her own ears, the laugh sounded fake and shrill. She closed her eyes, inhaled again . . .

That was when it hit her. That smell . . . She opened her eyes wide and her heart started to pound erratically. Slowly, she breathed in again, and there it was, a light floral scent that brought with it a rush of memories and emotions so powerful and vibrant that she had to hold on to the sink to keep her balance.

Mom's closet. A memory hit her, herself at the age of twelve, crawling into her mother's closet, closing the door, drawing the dresses in her arms until they approximated the bulk of a person, hugging them, breathing in the light floral scent that came from the sachets her mother kept in the closet. At twelve, she'd understood the cancer and what it would bring, but it was the smell and feel of her mother's empty dresses that conveyed what she felt—the sudden absence, the consuming grief, the aching void of loss.

Flynn opened her eyes. There were tears on her cheeks,

but she couldn't remember crying them. How long had she been there, holding on to that sink? How long . . . ?

But it hadn't been more than a few seconds. It had been powerful, but brief. The smell was gone, but the feeling . . . the ache. The loss. That was still there.

The golden glow. That was what she had seen. The glow. The same glow that she saw when Esther—

"Mom?" she whispered, feeling a lump forming in her throat. There was nothing. No glow, no sachet scent. Whatever it had been, it was gone.

"It's just me, losing my mind in a bathroom." She took another deep breath, staring at herself as she pulled her compact out from her purse. Her hand was shaking too much to use it, though. She leaned both hands on the sink again and closed her eyes.

Think about Tucker. Think about all the evidence he's going to get on Chase. Think about Chase being the cell block cabana boy. Think about . . .

And then, there it was. Tucker's face, smiling down at her, those soft brown eyes warming her to her core. She imagined his strong arms around her, and her heart returned to its natural rhythm. When she opened her eyes, she picked up her compact and pulled it open, hands steady. As she fixed her makeup, she deliberately chose not to think about what it meant that she was envisioning the bartender's face to get herself through a trying moment. At the very least, it meant he was much more than just the bartender.

But she didn't want to think about that now.

"There you are," Chase said when she returned, half rising from his chair until she took her seat. "I was beginning to think you'd crawled out the window."

Oh, trust me, I considered it, Flynn thought, smiling brightly at him.

"No, I just don't believe in rushing things," she said, settling into her chair. "So. Dessert?"

"Actually . . ." He leaned forward and reached for her hand. She let him hold it and resisted the urge to flick him in the forehead with her free hand. "I was thinking about maybe getting out of here. I've got something I'd like to show you."

Oh, God. The last time she'd fallen for that line had been with Timmy Newton in the eighth grade, and she didn't need a repeat of that.

"I was actually thinking dessert," she said, extracting her hand from his and reaching for the dessert menu.

"I'm sorry," he said, getting up. "I already paid the check. But I'll tell you what. I'll drive you through a Dairy Queen on the way back. We'll get a Blizzard. It'll be fun."

He put his hand on the back of her chair and she had no choice but to get up. Which was okay; if his plan was to show her something that wasn't in his pants, she could milk thirty minutes out of it. If otherwise, then his lengthy hospital stay would keep him out of his office even longer.

Win-win, she thought, starting toward the door.

"Wait now, aren't you forgetting something?" he asked, motioning toward the table, where the little golden box sat amid the ganglia of ribbon.

"Oh, yes." She turned around and grabbed it, then motioned for him to lead the way. As she followed behind him, she dropped the stupid thing to the ground and kicked it under a table. It was a small gesture, but powerfully satisfying.

Jake dropped his head down on Chase's desk, letting it fall on the hard surface with a resounding clunk that reverberated throughout the office, lit only by the sharp beam of his Mini Mag. He'd been in there for two hours—after sitting in the parking lot for an hour and a half waiting for Finola Scott to leave the office next door—and still hadn't figured out the combination to Chase's safe. He'd tried every combination he could think of from the date Chase graduated college to the first six digits of Pi.

Nothing had worked.

Finally, Jake had turned to things in the office. He'd gone through the filing cabinets, Chase's desk, and Rhonda's desk and had tried everything from serial numbers on the computer towers to the model number on the coffeemaker. Nothing worked. The safe also didn't respond to kicks or insults about its mother. This was unsurprising, but Jake felt it was only appropriate to be thorough.

I have to spend four hours being nice to this jerk. Make it worth my while. Flynn's voice chimed in his head, and Jake glanced at his watch. He'd planned to be waiting at the Arms when Chase brought Flynn home. Not in an obsessive, jealous way, but in a casual, hey-dig-how-guilty-this-asshole-is kind of way. At this rate, though, he doubted he'd be out of there much before Christmas, let alone before Flynn got back, which Jake estimated to be about another fifteen minutes or so.

Unless they stayed out late.

Or Chase tried to take her back to his place. A wave of futile fury rushed through him at the thought, and he took a moment to calm himself down. Flynn would never let that happen. She was too smart for that. Still, Jake wanted to be out of there before the date ended. He didn't want to run the risk of Chase stopping by the office to pick something up and finding Jake there, which meant that time was running out.

"Okay," he said, pattering his fingers on the desk blotter in front of him. "I'm Chase. I need to put a combination on a safe that I won't forget. I'm arrogant, I'm cocky, I think I'm smarter than everyone else. What's my combination?"

He paused, his fingers still tapping on the blotter, which shifted and knocked into the phone. As Jake reached forward to reset the blotter back, he stared at the phone. More specifically, the little piece of paper under the clear plastic rectangle that sported the direct line to his office. Jake shook his head. No one's *that* cocky.

Still, it was worth a shot. Jake spun out of Chase's office chair and went to the safe, carefully dialing in the first six digits of the direct line in pairs, and then the final digit on its own. The safe clicked and the door creaked open obediently.

"You've gotta be kidding me," Jake muttered as he shut off the Mini Mag and tucked it into his back pocket. Carefully, he pulled the laptop out and slid it into the messenger bag that was slung over his shoulder. He shut the safe, set the office chair back where it was, and almost had his hand on the doorknob of the outer office when he heard a woman's loud laugh and froze. Someone was outside the door. The venetian blinds were drawn on the windows, so he couldn't see who it was, but he knew that laugh.

Flynn.

"Oh, I'm sorry, am I being loud?" she nearly yelled. "It must be the wine. I get a little loopy."

Then she laughed again.

A key turned in the lock, and Jake barely had time to throw himself under Rhonda's desk before the door opened and the lights flipped on.

"You can make all the noise you want," Chase said. "I like noise."

Jake's fist clenched on instinct. Flynn giggled again, but he could hear a slight bit of tension in the sigh she released afterward. Jake closed his eyes.

"So . . . what was it you wanted to show me?"

"Oh, just a little something . . ."

There were the sounds of Chase opening a filing cabinet and riffling through the files. Jake could see Flynn's feet shuffle slightly, as though she was looking around for Jake. Finally, she leaned against the desk, and he pinched her heel gently to let her know where he was.

"Oh!" she squeaked.

"You okay?" Chase's voice was moving closer. Jake guessed he found what he was looking for.

"Fly. Saw a fly. I'm freaked out by flies. By nature, actually. And, also, offices. Offices freak me out. I'm very odd that way. Maybe we should go?"

"In a minute." Chase's feet came into view, facing Flynn's in such a way as to indicate a definite violation of personal space. Jake hoped she was reaching for her key chain. It'd be worth being discovered there if he got to witness her Macing Gordon Chase. "I wanted to show you this."

There was a moment of silence and then Flynn said, "Wow. That's really something."

Jake tensed under the desk, his imagination soaring with a thousand guesses at what Chase was showing Flynn, each of them making him want to kill Chase more than the last.

"Construction's almost finished," Chase said, and Jake relaxed a bit. "And it looks more expensive than it really is. You'd be amazed at how cheaply you can build a mansion in Costa Rica."

Jake could hear the tension in Flynn's voice as she said, "Well, taking advantage of economic desperation in impoverished countries is really the way to go," but based on Chase's chuckle of agreement, he figured her real meaning had been lost on its target.

"Well, it's getting late," Flynn said. "Why don't we just . . . ?"

Chase's feet moved toward Flynn's, and then suddenly Flynn's flew upward and out of sight. A second later, there was a thump over Jake's head.

"Gordon," Flynn said. "What are you . . . ?"

Chase's toes nearly touched Jake's leg as he moved forward. Things were quiet for a moment, and Jake shifted himself to hear better.

"Gordon," Flynn said finally. "I really think you should take me home."

"Are you sure that's what you want?"

Jake tensed, ready to spring out from under the desk and pummel Chase, but not until he was sure Flynn didn't have control of the situation. She had self-defense. She had Mace. And if that failed, she had Jake.

She was going to be fine. Chase, however, was one half-inch from being Maced. Jake held his breath, waiting for the spritz and the screaming. There was neither, though, just a protracted silence. Chase's feet shuffled a little more as he moved in closer, and Jake realized why everything was so quiet.

They were *kissing*. She was *kissing* him. She was . . .

Giving him what he wants. Getting control.

Jake clenched his fist again, and was just about to slam it into the desk when she let loose with the loudest, most unfeminine belch he'd ever heard. Chase's feet shot backward.

"Oh, I'm sorry," she said, sounding flustered, but Jake caught the thread of victory in her tone. "I have this . . . gastrointestinal thing. It's so embarrassing."

A wave of relief rushed through Jake, and he had to fight not to laugh. *That's my girl.*

Undeterred, Chase's feet approached again.

"I don't mind," he said, although Jake noticed he wasn't moving quite as close this time. He was still near enough to prevent her from jumping off the desk, though.

"Um, you know . . ." she said, her voice tense. "I really should get back. I have this medicine I have to take, and if I don't take it soon, well . . . I don't want to be indelicate but it's gastro*intestinal*. You know. Like, out both ends—"

Jake wanted nothing more than to crawl out from under the desk and kiss her right then, but he stayed put. This was Flynn's game, and he was going to let her play it.

"I really . . . I think I need to . . ."

Chase's feet moved back and once again Flynn's stilettos hit the ground.

"I think you should take me home," she said. "If history serves, things are about to get really ugly."

"Oh," Chase said. "Of course. Absolutely. Let's go."

Both pairs of feet moved toward the door, Chase's moving a little faster once Flynn let go with another burp. Jake sat tucked under the desk for another few moments, smiling.

She was a hell of a girl, that Flynn.

He listened until he heard the car leave the parking lot and moved to get up, overestimating the height of the desk and banging his head on the underside. As he reached up to feel for it, his hand landed on . . . *duct tape?* He pulled out his Mini Mag to expose a manila folder stuck to the underside of Rhonda's desk.

"Curiouser and curiouser," Jake muttered, then tucked the Mini Mag between his teeth and went to work peeling the folder off the bottom of the desk.

Thank you, Freya, Flynn thought as she waved good-bye to Chase from her front door. Freya had come up with the whole gastrointestinal bit in college, and it had saved both of them from more than one bad date. It had been a little surprising that it took three more belches and a dry heave to finally get Chase to leave, but at least it had worked and he was gone, hopefully never to ask her out again.

Flynn closed the door and leaned her back against it, shrugging her shoulders against the tension there. The night had been overwhelming, to say the least. Between Chase's obnoxious smarm, the stupid ballet slippers, and the horrible experience of making out with him on the desk while Tucker hid underneath, she wasn't sure what was bothering her the most. She tried to keep her focus on these things, though, because underneath them lay her odd experience in the restaurant bathroom, and she wasn't ready to think about that. Not yet, anyway. All she wanted to do was make some tea, go to bed, sleep unhaunted, and wake to a new day.

But then there was a knock on the door, and she had no doubt who it was.

"Go away," she said through the door.

"No," Tucker said back.

She sighed, turned around, and opened the door. "I don't want to hear it."

Tucker smiled at her. "Hear what?"

"About showing up at the office. Trust me, that was not my idea. I did the best I could, and let me tell you something: You. So. Owe. Me."

She braced herself against him yelling at her for screwing everything up, but instead he just reached up and touched her face.

"You handled it great," he said. "That gastrointestinal thing was brilliant. I just wish I could have seen his face."

Oh. Okay. "So you're not mad?"

He shrugged. "No. You saved my ass." He lifted up the messenger bag and pulled out a manila folder with duct tape around the edges. "And if you hadn't come in when you did, we never would have gotten this."

Flynn blinked, staring at the folder. "What's that?"

"I have no idea." He shoved it back into his bag.

"I thought you went in for the laptop."

"Yeah, I got that, too, because I'm really, really good." He grinned, his eyes twinkling at her. "I found the folder while I was killing time under Rhonda's desk. I'll take a look at it tomorrow. Right now, I just wanted you to know your hard work wasn't for nothing."

He wasn't upset at all that she had kissed Chase. Not

that she wanted him to be upset, but part of her could have used a little contention to lean against, to distract her from the smell of her mother's closet, which lingered in her memory as if it was still fresh on each inhale.

She forced a smile. "Okay. Great. I'm gonna go make some tea."

She pushed past him toward the kitchen. She hadn't spent much time in there and had no idea where the tea or the kettle was. She opened the first cabinet to her left.

Pop-Tarts. Of course.

She closed it.

The kitchen door opened behind her and she ignored it, going into the next cabinet. Some plates, some small teacups. She wanted big. She wanted a big mug of tea, an overstuffed couch, a Cary Grant movie marathon, and Freya talking over all the good parts. She wanted comfort, and normalcy, and no dead people violating the rules of her universe. Was that too much to ask?

"Flynn?" Tucker's voice trailed in from behind her. "Are you okay?"

"I'm fine," she said. "Just making some tea. You can see yourself out. Good night."

She opened the next cabinet. *Bingo*. Teakettle. She pulled it out and walked over to the sink, but just as she reached to turn the water on, Tucker's hand clamped down over hers. He pulled her to face him, took the kettle from her hands, and set it in the sink. He reached up and touched her face, making her look at him.

"What happened?" His eyes dug into hers, and she could see the anger in them.

Finally. Thank you. Let's fight.

His anger, though, was clearly not directed at her. "Did

he do something to you? It sounded like you were in control of the situation from where I was. Flynn, if I thought for a second that he was hurting you—"

"Oh, God, no. That was fine. I mean, it wasn't *fine,* it was gross, but that's not what's bothering me."

He watched her with a severe expression for a moment longer, then softened. "Okay. So if it's not Chase, what is it?"

"It's nothing," she said. "I'm just tired, and I want some damn tea."

He nodded, released her hands, and reached for the teakettle.

"You go get changed, get comfortable. I'll make the tea for you."

"Tucker, you don't have to—"

He angled his head to look at her and smiled, but his eyes were determined. "I'm going to. Arguing with me is only going to make it take longer. Go get comfortable."

She sighed and left, trying to shake the tension as she washed off her makeup, let down her hair, brushed her teeth, and changed into her pajamas—not the silk ones Freya had bought her, but the roomy, flannel, and decidedly unsexy ones she'd packed for herself. She couldn't think about the *whatever* that was developing between her and Tucker. She couldn't think about anything; her nerves felt jangly and ready to pop, and she knew that if she started thinking about anything other than tea or sleep, she'd unravel.

There was a gentle knock at her bedroom door, and then Tucker poked his head in, carrying a teapot and a mug on a large silver tray. He settled it on the floor next to the bed.

"I hope you like peppermint," he said. "Seems Esther was a fan."

"That's great." Flynn nodded and crossed her arms over her stomach. She felt oddly cold, and her nerves were still on alert. "Thank you."

Tucker took a step toward her and touched her arm. "Do you want to tell me what happened?"

"No," she said quickly, and she didn't, but when she raised her eyes to meet Tucker's, she could see his disappointment, and she was too tired to hold up that much weight. "I saw my mother tonight."

Tucker's eyebrows knit. "Your mother was at the restaurant?"

"She died when I was twelve."

Jake's eyes widened. "Oh."

She let out a heavy breath. "I went into the bathroom, and I saw this glow. It's the same thing I see when Esther"—she searched her brain, was unable to come up with the word she was looking for, and settled—"visits. Then, I smelled my mom's clothes. She used to use these sachets. They were unique. Kind of lavenderish, but with a hint of vanilla, and a little spicy. I don't know." She clenched her jaw and blinked her eyes against the emotion. "I'd just . . . I'd forgotten how much I miss her."

Her face went hot and tears splashed down her face as the emotion took over. A moment later Jake's arms were around her and she leaned into him, absorbing the comfort as he ran his hands down her back and made shooshing sounds into her hair. Finally, the jangliness in her nerves gave way to calm, and she stepped away from him, swiping at her eyes.

"I swear, I never saw a dead person before coming

here." She sniffed, swiped at her eyes. "You must think I'm insane."

"Well, yeah," he said, smiling at her. "But if it's any comfort, I find insanity very sexy."

She reached out to smack him playfully on the shoulder, but he ducked and grabbed her hand, leading her toward the bed.

"Now, I know how this looks," he said, "but I'm just going to put you in bed and get you settled. Then I'm out of here."

Flynn snorted. "What, is there a rule about crying women, too?"

Tucker released her hand and pulled the covers back on the bed. "As a matter of fact . . ."

"You're kidding," Flynn said, crawling gratefully into the bed.

He pulled the covers around her, sat on the bed next to her, and reached down to get her mug of tea. "Drunk women. Crying women. Women within three months of a breakup or one year of a death or divorce." He handed her the mug with a smile. "Lucky for you, there's no rule against cute brunette ghost magnets."

She chuckled and sipped her tea. "I'm sorry. It's just been a weird night. And then I had to put up with Chase— who has completely ruined Dairy Queen for me, by the way—and I thought you'd be mad at me for screwing up your investigation." She inhaled with a stutter and was surprised to feel her eyes filling up again. Jesus. She was a case tonight.

"Hey, you didn't screw up my investigation." He reached for her hand and held her fingers gently in his. "You did great. You took one for the team. I'll tell you, if it came down to it, I don't know if I'd kiss Gordon Chase for you."

She laughed. He lifted her fingers and touched them to his lips.

"Get some sleep. I'll drop by your office tomorrow, we can go through the evidence and see where we are, okay?"

She tightened her hold on his fingers. "Don't go. And I don't mean for you to"—she stammered a bit, then smiled—"break any rules, I just . . ." She sighed, unable to drum up enough pride or common sense to stop herself from being honest. "You make me feel better. And I want you to stay. Just . . . stay. I mean, I'll understand if you don't want to. I know it's asking a lot."

"No, it's not."

Gratitude overwhelmed her, and she swiped at her eyes. "Really?"

He smiled as he kicked off his shoes, then crawled over her on top of the covers. He arranged pillows against the wall and sat up back against them, putting his arm out. She curled into him, resting her head against his shoulder,
    ng from the mug in her hand. Jake kissed the top of
    ad and for the first time that night, she felt com-
    y at peace.

"I gotta warn you, though," he said. "Rules or no rules, I'm still a guy. Chances are fair to middlin' that I'm gonna try to cop a feel at some point during the night."

Flynn laughed and snuggled deeper against him. "I'd expect nothing less."

Chapter Ten

♡ Flynn sat on the edge of her bed, legs crossed under her yoga style. Behind her, she could see her physical body, curled up under the covers, with Tucker on top of the bedspread, spooning her from behind. Even though her consciousness, her spiritual body, whatever it was, was on the edge of the bed, she could still feel his warmth and strength seeping into her from behind.

It was nice.

"Well, I have to say I didn't figure you for the type," Esther said as she rocked in her ghostly chair as the real one, which Flynn had returned to its original place in defeat, sat still as stone.

"What type?" Flynn asked.

"I had you pegged for uptight. A little prudish." Esther raised her eyebrows toward Tucker's sleeping form. "But you've made pretty fast work of my friend Jake there. I hope your intentions are good."

"It's not what it looks like," Flynn said. "He's a friend."

"Pffft," Esther snorted. "Exactly what does 'born yesterday' look like to you? Because I can guarantee I'm not a match."

"No, you certainly are not," Flynn said.

Esther stopped rocking, an expression of mild approval on her face. "Okay, then."

"Look," Flynn said, "Tucker told me that if I wanted you to go away, and I really do, that I should listen to you and seeing as that's the only thing I haven't tried then—" She gestured toward Esther with one hand. "Go ahead. Talk."

Esther leaned forward. "You want me to talk?"

"Yes."

"All right. I think you're a very abrasive young woman. I would never have spoken to my elders the way you do. Your hair is hopelessly wild, your tone is unfriendly to say the least, and you seem to be forgetting that *you* are the interloper here, not me. This is my house. *My* hotel. *My* home."

Esther sat back in a huff and picked up her knitting, clinking the ghostly needles together with angered force. Flynn waited for a few moments, then said, "Is that it?"

Esther froze. "What do you mean, is that it?"

"I mean, is that it? You don't like me, fine. I already knew that. Not for nothing, but I'm not terribly fond of you, either. What I need is something I can act on. Something I can do to open you up to the white light, to get you to move on. Because, while I appreciate that being dead is no joyride for you, it is what it is, lady. You have to deal with it sometime, and I'd rather you did it before you drive me completely around the bend."

Esther glared at Flynn for a while, but then her expression softened, and she started to rock slowly in her chair.

"Well," she said finally, "there is one thing you can do."

"Great. Let's get to it. What do you need?"

Esther stopped rocking and leaned forward in her chair. "Put my damn cows back."

The golden light snapped off, like someone had hit a switch, and Flynn felt a whoosh as she was pulled back into her body. She gasped and felt Jake's arm instantly respond by tightening around her, his hand moving protectively around her waist.

"You okay?" he mumbled. His eyes were still closed, and his breathing even. She rolled onto her back and stared at his sleeping face.

"Mmmm-hmmm," she responded softly, watching his face, the features outlined in the soft white glow of the moonlight creeping in through the windows. His face had a perma-smile, as though good cheer was his default setting. His jawline was rough with stubble, and his hair was hopelessly awry, as usual. She smiled as she looked at him, wondering how it was possible to feel so comfortable with someone she'd only known for a few days.

She took one last look at him, then rolled over onto her side, snuggling back into the spoon. His hand traveled up from her waist to her shoulder, rubbing her arm dreamily.

"You okay?" he mumbled again.

She thought about things. She was haunted by a dead aunt, would soon be sent off to rot in a cubicle for the rest of her working days, and was lying in the arms of a bartender with an uncanny ability to make everything feel all right anyway.

"Mmmmm," she said. "I'm just fine."

And she was.

Jake inhaled deeply as consciousness returned. The space next to him was empty, and at some point, Flynn had flipped the top blanket back over him. He smiled lazily as he looked down at it, his mind lost in a jumble of thoughts. Usually, this was about the point in a relationship where he found himself caught between the vague notion that the relationship was going somewhere and the sharp terror that the girl would ask him where, exactly. The truth was, as usual, he had no idea.

But he knew he didn't want her to sell. He didn't want her to leave. As a matter of fact, if he could worm his way in, he wanted to sleep in whatever space was next to her every night for the foreseeable future.

And he'd only known her for five days. Had to be some kind of record.

He hopped off the bed and stuck his head under it to retrieve his cell phone, smiling as he remembered the determined look on Flynn's face when she'd tossed it over her shoulder the night before. He pulled the phone out and tucked it in his back pocket, then stood up and laid the covers neatly on the bed, smoothing them over the space where she'd slept.

It was happening. Somewhere between picking her up at the train station and crawling into bed next to her the night before, he'd gotten tangled up in her but good. Now, no matter what direction he moved in, if history served, chances were pretty damn good he was going to fall flat on his face.

He ran his hands through his hair and walked out into the living room to see Flynn dressed in a blue business suit, pulling cow creamers from a shoe box sporting tendrils of crinkled duct tape, and arranging them on a shelf in front of her. Jake leaned against the doorjamb and watched her, smiling. One by one, she put the cows up, then stood back and surveyed her work. When she turned and saw him watching her, she shrugged and rolled her eyes.

"I listened," she said, dumping the empty box on the floor and kicking it through the open closet door. "Esther told me to put her stupid cows back. I am officially my dead aunt's bitch."

Jake laughed, walked over to her, took her hands in his, and leaned down to kiss one cheek.

"I quit," he said.

She blinked. "Wow. Most guys would open with 'Good morning.' Let me commend you on a brave and unusual choice."

"There's a guy named Kevin who subs in for us sometimes. He might be a good place to start looking for my replacement. In the meantime, Carole's usually happy to pick up extra shifts." Jake reached up and moved a strand of hair away from her face. "I want to be able to focus on this Chase thing for the next few days, and after that . . ." He shook his head and smiled. "I don't know. I haven't really planned that far yet."

"Oh. Um, okay." Flynn blinked rapidly and gave him a 'huh?' look. "What the hell are you talking about?"

"I think things might be less complicated if I don't work for you."

She groaned. "Oh, tell me you're not quitting your job because of me. Do I look stable enough to handle that kind of pressure? Because I'm really not."

He held up one hand to quiet her. "It's just a job. I don't like it that much to be honest. The hours suck. My boss is insane." She smiled, and Jake felt himself relax. "And, you know, I'm thinking about what you said. About loving what you do. I've got enough savings to think about it for"—he glanced upward, doing the math in his head, and returned his gaze to her—"three more weeks, give or take. I want to think about it for a while."

"Oh, God." She put her hand to her head. "Now I know how Freya felt."

"Another thing. I know we've only known each other for a few days, but I'd really like to know you for a few more. And, if that goes well, maybe a few more after that."

A sideways smile spread over her face. "Yeah?"

He reached for her waist and pulled her closer. "Yeah. And that means I should probably ask you out on a real date. Flynn, would you go out on a real date with me?"

Flynn nibbled her lip and looked up at him, her expression dripping with overplayed consternation. "Gee, I don't know. I have this rule, you see. I don't date unemployed men."

"What, you couldn't have told me that five minutes ago?"

She put one hand flat on his chest, right over his heart. He liked it there.

"Lucky for you, I'm not as much of a stickler for rules as you are."

"Good." He leaned forward and kissed her on the nose. "Six o'clock. I'll pick you up here."

He released her, grabbed his messenger bag from where he'd left it by the door, and pulled the door open, but stopped as his foot hit something on his way out. He looked down and picked up the newspaper, staring down at the front page. He could hear Flynn's footsteps coming up behind him.

"Oh, is that the local paper? I asked Annabelle to have it delivered. I like to keep up."

"Yep," Jake said as he scanned the lead story. "This is the local paper."

Flynn poked her head over his shoulder, and went quiet. "Oh, my God. Is that . . . ?"

She pointed to the headline: RIVER BODY IDENTIFIED.

"Yep." Jake handed her the paper and waited patiently for the question he knew would come once Flynn finished reading the first paragraph.

"Oh, but wait. This says it's some woman named Eileen Dietz. You were wrong."

"I would think so, too," he said, pointing to the mug shot they'd used, "if it weren't for the fact that this picture is definitely Elaine Placie."

Flynn stepped back and looked up at him. "So, what? Elaine Placie was living under an assumed identity?"

Jake nodded. "I've only had a few seconds to develop it, but that's my working theory."

"But it says here that—" She read from the paper. " 'Dietz was released last fall from the Tennessee Women's Correctional Facility in Nashville, where she'd served three years for fraud.' She's an ex-con."

"Looks that way."

"Do you think Chase knew who she really was?"

"If not, I bet he will soon."

She hugged the paper to her chest and nibbled at her lip, her eyebrows knitting, creating cute little creases in her forehead. "So, what do we do?"

"You are going to work. I'm gonna go home, find out what's on that laptop and maybe do some digging on the enigmatic Eileen Dietz." He smiled. "And then I'll pick you up at six."

Flynn looked surprised. "We're still going out?"

"Can you think of a good reason why we shouldn't?"

"Oh, gee. I don't know. The Eileen Dietz thing. A laptop full of illegal activities. Not to mention the manila folder—"

"Which probably contains Rhonda's secret recipe for Hungarian meatball soup." He took the newspaper from her grip and tucked it under his arm. "Life goes on. I'm picking you up at six."

Flynn stared at him for a moment, then smiled. "Okay. Sounds like a plan."

"Great." He headed down the steps, then shot over his shoulder, "Dress casual. I don't have Chase's budget."

"Freya, where the hell are you?" Flynn stared down at the phone on Esther's desk, waiting for Freya to answer her stupid cell. Flynn knew the phone was on, because when it was off, it went direct to voice mail. So whatever Freya was doing, she just didn't want to stop doing it to answer the phone.

Hi, you've reached the voice mail of Freya Daly. I'm sorry I can't—

Flynn reached across the front desk, hit the disconnect button, and dialed again. This would be her fifth call. Surely, this time Freya would—

"Oh, for the love of all that is holy— WHAT?!?"

Bingo.

"Freya. I need to talk to you."

"Are you bleeding? Are you on fire? Has Dad fallen over dead while he was bleeding and on fire?"

"No. My bookkeeper was supposed to have the third quarter reports waiting for me to fax to Dad."

"There was nothing in that sentence about blood or fire."

"And she's not here. And neither are the reports."

"So?"

"So . . . Dad wanted the third quarter financials by this morning. I need your help, Fray."

Freya groaned. "Do you even know what time it is in Tucson?"

"Annabelle has this strange computer system and it's got a password on it and I can't get into it and Dad—"

"It's six forty-seven. In the morning."

"—wants these end of quarter reports and I don't—"

"On my last day. My *last day* to sleep in. Do you know what that means?"

"—know how to pull the reports—"

"Oh, for Christ's sake!"

Flynn could hear the sound of bedding being thrown and she quieted, waiting for Freya's instructions.

"You can't call this Tinkerbell at home and get the password?"

"Annabelle. And no, there's no answer at her home number. I think she might have called in sick, because the voice mail light is blinking, but I don't know how to get the voice mail messages."

"And no one else there has access to this system? You have *one person* in *complete ownership* of an entire system? Is this what you're telling me?"

"Pretty much. And I can't take reservations, either, because the reservations system is part of the bookkeeping system. I guess. At least, that's the way I understand it."

"Jesus. You have one person in complete ownership of *two systems*? What kind of place are you running there, Flynn?"

"Don't blame me. This is how Esther had it. I'll give her a healthy ration of shit for it later, but right now—"

Freya cut her off. "Please tell me you didn't say you were going to give our dead aunt a healthy ration of shit. I don't care if that's what you said. Just say you didn't say it."

Flynn rolled her eyes. "I didn't say it. What I need right now is to get these reports to Dad. He said he wanted them by this morning, and—"

"Tell him no. Tell him he'll get them when you're damn good and ready to get them to him, and not a moment sooner. He's got the financials from the second quarter, and all the quarters before that back to roughly 1776, so that's good enough to work a sale from. He's just testing you. Call him back, tell him to bite your ass, and you pass the test."

Flynn sat back in her chair and took the opening. "Won't that upset his angina?"

There was a short pause. "Hmmm. What?"

"His heart. I mean, if I don't get him these reports,

he'll get upset. Stressed out. Isn't that the whole reason I'm here in the first place?"

A longer pause. "No."

Wow. That was easy. "I see."

"No, you don't see, and I don't have time to make you see. We'll talk about it later. The point is, don't let him push you around. Just call him, tell him it's not happening, and go have a cigarette."

"I don't smoke."

"Then start. You're working for Dad now. Welcome to the world of unhealthy coping addictions."

Flynn sighed. "Fray? What's going on? Are you okay?"

There was a long pause, and just as Flynn was going to check and make sure Freya was still on the line, she said, "I was worried about you."

"What? Why?"

"That neighborhood wasn't safe. I've been bugging you to move for years, but you wouldn't, and it was keeping me up nights, so I lied. Okay?"

Flynn sat back, stunned. "Um. Okay."

"Okay. So what's up with you?"

"Nothing. I'm fine."

"Then why is your voice going all high when you say you're fine? Don't lie to me. You woke me up. I'm cranky. What's going on?"

Flynn rubbed at the tension in her neck. "Aunt Esther made me put her cows back up. Oh, and they just pulled a body from the Hudson that may or may not have been killed by someone in my immediate acquaintance. And I think I'm falling for the bartender. Except he quit. So . . . I don't know. I guess it's okay."

There was a long pause, then, "So, this bartender. Is he cute?"

"He's . . ." Flynn tried to think of a word to describe Tucker. Something that encompassed his kindness, his humor, the way his smile warmed places inside her she didn't know had gone cold, what his slightest touch did to her fun parts. "He's . . ."

"Oh, holy hell," Freya said. "You've got to be kidding me."

Through the phone, Flynn heard the distinctive sound of a lighter igniting, followed by Freya's deep inhale.

"They have smoking rooms at the spa?" Flynn asked.

"No." Exhale. "Look, honey. Call Dad. Tell him he can bite your ass for the stupid reports. Take the incoming reservations on paper, and when your little Annawhatsis comes back, you put the fear of God into her. I'm serious. Threaten her job outright, don't bother with subtlety. Tell her to start researching hospitality software and get someone else trained on the system you've got *immediately*. Then, go find your bartender and have him make you the biggest margarita allowed by state law."

"Wow. You're a fun boss."

Freya snorted. "Don't come to any conclusions till we're back home."

Flynn felt herself go tense. *Back home.* Well, that was the plan. And it was what she wanted. Museums. The T. Not a ceramic cow creamer anywhere to be found.

No rose gardens.

No Mercy's pumpkin risotto.

No Tucker.

"Look, babe, I gotta go," Freya said. "You got it under control?"

Flynn forced a smile and tried to inject some enthusiasm into her voice. "You bet."

She set the phone down on the cradle, and stared at it for a long time. Something was up with Freya, but she knew she wasn't going to find out until Freya was damn good and ready to tell her. If she was ever damn good and ready to tell her. That's just the way it was with Freya.

So she might as well deal with her other family member. When she'd called earlier, Dad's secretary had said he was in a meeting and would be back at his desk around ten. She raised her eyes back to the blinking cursor in the password box. That gave her a little more than an hour to try and get those reports in. She knew Freya was probably right about how to handle things with Dad, but how could she expect Flynn to toss away thirty years of dysfunctional family dynamic just like that? It wasn't reasonable.

And it wouldn't hurt to *try* to get those reports, right?

She tapped her fingernails on the desk as she thought. She'd done all the obvious passwords—Annabelle, De-Cross, various combinations thereof, the phone number for the front desk, Annabelle's birth date, which was in two weeks; Flynn remembered seeing the date circled on the calendar in the break room. There was only one thing left that she thought might work, but it was so juvenile, she was almost embarrassed to have thought of it. She glanced around, then reached for the keyboard and typed in "AD+JT4Ever" and hit enter.

The screen flashed quickly, and then the box came back up. Flynn rolled her eyes at herself for even thinking the password would be such a thing. She decided that she was done, it was over . . . but then something occurred to her. She put her hands back on the keyboard and typed.

"JT+AD4Ever."

The screen flashed again and then went completely black for a moment. At first Flynn thought she'd tanked the entire system—she and computers didn't have a friendly history—but then, to her shock, the software popped up on the screen.

"Oh, you've gotta be kidding me," she muttered. She pushed herself away from the desk to go get some coffee. It was going to be a long day of trying to figure out how to pull reports while trying to forget that Annabelle was, apparently, mentally fourteen years old.

As was Flynn. Apparently.

It was going to be a long day.

Jake pushed through the swinging doors of the Arms' kitchen, and was instantly yanked into the walk-in freezer by Mercy.

"Oh, my God, Jake," she said. "I've been trying to call you all morning. Where have you been?"

"At the cabin. What's up?"

"What cabin? Dad's old cabin? What are you doing at the cabin?"

"Cleaning it out. Which brings me to a favor. I need—"

Mercy smacked his arm. "A favor? No time for favors, Jake. That body they pulled from the river?" Her voice raised into a hysterical whisper. *"That was Elaine Placie!"*

"I know," Jake said, rubbing his arms for warmth.

"Only she's not really Elaine Placie," Mercy continued. "It's some other woman whose name I can't remember."

"Eileen Dietz. I know."

Mercy blinked. "You know? You read the paper?"

Jake tried to work up an offended look. "I get the paper."

Mercy lifted one eyebrow. "Since when?"

"Fine. Flynn gets the paper. I saw it this morning at Flynn's. Speaking of which, I need you to make me a nice dinner for two that can sit at the cabin for a while. You know, something that doesn't necessarily need to be hot, but will still impress the hell out of her."

Mercy crossed her arms over her chest. "This morning? At *Flynn's*?"

"Like, you know, a picnic. But a nice one. With a bottle of wine. Maybe some cheese. Those tiny little sandwiches you girls like so much. Oh, and I need it by four. You think you can do that?"

"It's food. I'm the food miracle worker. I can do anything. Let's get back to this morning at Flynn's. Are you sleeping with our boss?"

"Depends on your definition of 'sleeping with,' and she's not my boss anymore. I quit."

Mercy stared at him blankly for a long moment. "I don't even know what to say."

"Hey, that's something new and different. Just put something together for me, okay? I'll be by to pick it up at four. Oh, and I need your house keys."

He held out one palm. She glanced down at it, then looked back up at him. "Are you kidding me with this?"

"No. I have a date. With Flynn. We're going to the cabin for a nice dinner, but first I have a laptop I need to print some documents from, and I need your printer. Come on, Merce. I wouldn't ask if it wasn't important."

Mercy reached into her pocket and held the keys up, just out of his reach.

"I'll do it. On one condition."

Jake sighed. He knew what was coming. "Fine. Sunday dinner."

"Not just you. Bring Flynn, too."

Jake pulled his hand away. "No. No way am I subjecting her to the five of you and your insane little girlfriend trial."

"It's not a trial. It's an attempt to get to know the girl. Make sure she's worthy. We don't tar and feather them, we just ask questions."

Jake clenched his teeth. "Okay. Sunday night. We come, we eat, we leave. One hour."

He reached for the keys, but Mercy pulled them back. "Three hours. You stay for dessert."

"Two hours. No dessert. And no questions even grazing the subjects of weddings or babies."

Mercy sighed, dropped the keys into Jake's open palm.

"Fine. Come back at four and your picnic will be waiting for you."

Jake grinned, kissed Mercy on the cheek, and headed for the door, stopping only when she called his name. He turned to see her watching him, a look of concern on her face.

"Someone killed Elaine Placie with a pan from my kitchen," she said.

Jake nodded. "I know."

"She totally screwed you over."

"Yep. She did."

"That gives you motive and means," she said. "And probably opportunity."

"You watch too much *CSI*, Merce."

"So, what are you going to do?"

He pulled on the most confident expression in his arsenal. "I'm going to find out who really killed her before the police have time to put it all together and consider me a suspect."

He hoped the plan was as good as it sounded, because for the moment, it was the only one he had. Mercy stared at him for a long time, then nodded.

"Be careful."

He grinned and put his hand on the lever that opened the freezer door. "I'll see you later, Merce. And for God's sake, do something about this place. It's like a meat locker in here."

Mercy didn't smile. "I love you."

He touched his fingers to his lips and tossed her a kiss. "You, too. And don't worry. It's all going to turn out fine."

He pulled the lever and headed out, ignoring the questioning looks on the kitchen staff and hoping to God that everything would turn out fine.

He really hated being wrong about this kind of thing.

Chapter Eleven

♡So, where exactly are we going again?" Flynn asked, leaning forward to look into the darkening October sky through the dusty window of the pickup truck. Based on the windy road, the farmland flanking them on either side, and the widely spaced streetlights, she sensed they were officially in the middle of freakin' nowhere.

"It's a surprise," Tucker said. "Now, tell me about your day again."

Flynn waved a hand at him. "No. We've already talked about that."

"But you like talking about it."

"Yeah, I do." Flynn turned toward him, amazed at how big and comfortable the seats were in that clunky old pickup. "So, I got off the phone with Freya and I was totally screwed, right? But then I think really hard, what could the password be? And suddenly, I get it! So I start typing—"

"What *is* the password, anyway?" Tucker asked.

"Oh. You know. Just something silly." She cleared her throat. She still hadn't decided if she should tell Tucker about Annabelle's crush. On the one hand, it was none of her business. On the other hand, maybe Tucker should know. Flynn guessed that if Annabelle had a say, she'd side with none of Flynn's business, so Flynn decided to let that be the tiebreaker.

"Anyway. I type it in and blammo! Everything opens up. So then I get some coffee, and I figure it's gonna take me from here to eternity to figure out this system and pull those reports, but I get back and two hours later, everything's all set and ready to go. I put off my father by telling him the fax machine was broken—"

"A brilliant move, by the way."

"Thank you. I thought so." She leaned back, allowing herself to get all pruny in her pride. "So, I figured it out all by myself. I made it happen. I contributed. I'm not a total loser."

"Please tell me you already knew that," he said, throwing a glance her way.

"I mean, I know I'm not a *total* loser. I pay my own bills. I vote. But . . . when it comes to being a productive member of society, to doing things that make a difference, things that really matter . . ." She shrugged. "It's a very short résumé."

Tucker turned the wheel and they ambled onto a dirt road.

"Where exactly are we going?" Flynn asked, glancing around them at the farmland, slightly pungent with the smell of cows and nature. Ick.

Tucker pulled the truck to the edge of the road and put it in park, then turned to face Flynn.

"Why do you do that?"

"Do what?" she asked, a little worried about this sudden change in demeanor. "Ask where we're going? Is curiosity a big character flaw with you, because if that's the case—"

"When you got off the train that day, I thought you were beautiful, which—whatever. Pretty women are a dime a dozen, and typically overpriced at that."

"Is this an attempt at sweet talk? Because, not for nothin', it could use some fine-tuning."

"Then you spoke." Tucker chuckled and shook his head. "And you were snappy and insecure and tough and fragile and weird—"

She hardened her stare. "Perhaps you could memorize a sonnet or two. Lots of girls go for that crap."

"You're . . ." He stared at her for a moment, then chuckled and shook his head. "You're funny, and you're sharp, and you're strange in really . . . great ways. I mean, what kind of girl admits that she's having chats with her dead aunt? Or puts herself on the line for some random guy she hardly even knows? You have no guile. You don't pretend to be what you're not. You're just Flynn, and you don't apologize for that. Do you have any idea how sexy that is?"

Flynn held her breath, her heart pumping erratically in her chest. "Um . . . no."

Tucker watched her for a moment, then turned his head to stare straight out at the horizon. "You're right. I'm not good at this."

"No," Flynn said, her voice high and soft even to her own ears. "No, you were getting somewhere there."

"I don't know any sonnets. I'm not that kind of guy. To

be honest, until now, I didn't think I was the kind of guy who would pack a special picnic and bring a girl out to a cabin in the country with no ulterior motive other than just getting to know her better." He chuckled and shook his head, then turned to look at her, his smile light and bemused. "I used to make fun of that guy. And now I am that guy. And I'm fine with it. For the first time in my life, the most important thing is not getting revenge on Gordon fucking Chase, and that's because of you, so if you could stop with this crap about never doing anything that matters, I'd appreciate it."

Flynn opened her mouth, but couldn't think of what to say. She'd been quoted sonnets before—which, in real life, turned out to be a lot hokier than it sounded. One guy had even stood outside her dorm window and serenaded her with a regrettable rendition of "Islands in the Stream." Also overrated. But no one had ever made the butterflies inside her freak out the way Tucker just did.

She liked it.

"You're quiet," Tucker said after a while. "That can't be good. Did I already blow it? Because the food alone will be worth giving me a second chance, I swear."

She reached out and put her hand over his. "You didn't blow it. You did the opposite of blow it."

He turned to face her, his eyes locking with hers. "Good."

She turned toward him in what she hoped was an encouraging pose, but found it challenging to strike an encouraging pose in a bucket seat. The silence intensified, the dying sunset bathed them in a dim pinkish glow; the moment couldn't have been more perfect. She licked her lower lip—if that wasn't encouraging, then she was out of the game.

Which, apparently, she was, because Tucker chose that moment to turn away and hop out of the truck.

"What the . . . ?" Flynn muttered to herself as she watched him walk around to her side and open the passenger door.

"Are you kidding with this?" she asked.

"Get out."

"I'm sorry?"

He held out his hand to her. "This is your first driving lesson."

She didn't take his hand. "What are you, crazy? I can't drive. I don't even have a permit."

"It's okay," he said, smiling. "You're on Tucker property now. We've only got about a mile to go down this road here." He raised his hand closer. "Come on."

Flynn took his hand and let him help her down. "You're serious?"

He set her on her feet and put his hands on her waist. "When have you ever known me not to be serious?"

"With the exception of thirty seconds ago? You really want the answer to that question?"

He reached up and touched her hair. "Well, I'm serious now. I wanted to take you on a date you wouldn't forget. I think this is a pretty good idea, if I do say so myself. Which I do." He grinned. "Now get moving."

She considered and rejected the idea of telling him she wouldn't likely forget it anyway, and nodded. "Okay."

He leaned down and grazed his lips lightly over hers, making her legs tremble a bit with anticipation of what might come next. But instead, he pulled back, cleared his throat, and led her to the other side of the truck. After strapping her into the seat belt and showing her where the gearshift, brake, and accelerator were, he shut her door, walked around, and climbed into the passenger seat.

"Go ahead," he said. "Put it in drive and lightly touch the accelerator. Put your hands at ten and two on the wheel, and keep the road between them. You'll be fine."

Flynn reached for the gearshift and set it to "D" the way Tucker had shown her. She hit the accelerator with her right foot and the truck lurched out into the road with a lot more acceleration than she'd been expecting. She screamed and hit the brake, sending Tucker shooting forward.

"Should have worn my seat belt," he said, a chuckle in his voice as he held on to the dashboard for support.

"Yeah, well, hindsight." Flynn took her foot off the brake and hit the accelerator, lighter this time, and toodled off onto the dirt road, clutching the steering wheel with white knuckles.

"Okay, now how long before we get to where we're going?"

"The cabin's about a mile or so down the road," Tucker said, glancing at the speedometer. "At this rate, it should be about an hour."

"Shut up," Flynn said, laughing as she punched it from five to ten miles an hour. "Hey. Dig me. I'm driving."

She felt his hand rub her shoulder affectionately. "Yeah. Dig you."

It was at that moment that there was a loud crashing sound, and glass sprayed over them from behind.

Flynn screamed and the truck careened as the wheel

flew from side to side under her hands. "Oh, shit! What'd I do wrong? What'd I do wrong?"

A pair of bright high-beam headlights came on behind them.

"I don't think it's you," Tucker said calmly.

"Who is that?"

There was a popping sound, and the driver's side-view mirror jerked violently and flew off the cab, banging into the truck before bouncing down the road behind them.

"Um, Tucker," Flynn said, trying to maintain as much calm as she could muster. "Is someone trying to kill us?"

"That's my guess," Tucker said. "Turn left and punch it."

The last fragment of calm left her.

"Are you kidding me?" she screamed, but before she had finished the sentence, Tucker had taken the wheel and stamped his foot down over hers.

"Ow, ow, ow, ow!"

"I'm sorry, I'm sorry, I'm sorry, I'm sorry!"

They lurched off the road and down a mild slope into what was thankfully a sparsely wooded area. Flynn pulled her foot out from under Tucker's and glanced behind them through the blown-out back window. The lights hadn't followed them. That was good. Flynn was sure that was good. That had to be—

Another popping sound came from behind them, and the truck jerked to the left.

"Oh, holy Christ!" Flynn yelled.

"It's okay," Tucker said, seeming oddly calm as he turned the wheel to the left, going with the momentum of the truck. They slid to the side, and Flynn screamed again.

"I need you to stop doing that," Tucker said.

"I need you to stop getting me killed!"

They skidded sideways for a bit, then the wheels gained traction. Tucker pulled the wheel to the right and they swerved between two trees, then bounced upward.

And then they were on the dirt road again, skidding to a stop in front of a cabin, with just enough room for the passenger side door to open. Tucker slammed the truck into park and grabbed Flynn.

"Time to go," he said, yanking her out with him. A moment later they were in the cabin and he was setting her down on what felt like a couch, but between the dark of the cabin and the blind panic, Flynn couldn't see anything. Her breathing came hard and shallow as Tucker's hands floated over her, touching her ankles, her legs, her arms, her face. It took her a moment to realize he was talking, too.

". . . okay? Does that hurt?"

She knew she should answer him. She wanted to answer him. She just couldn't.

"Flynn!" He grabbed her chin in his hand and forced her to meet his eyes. "Are you okay?"

She snapped back into the moment, and found her voice. "I'm fine. I'm fine. I mean, someone's trying to kill us, but other than that . . ."

Tucker's hands grasped her upper arms tightly, and she thought she heard him release a heavy breath. "You're okay? You're sure?"

Flynn concentrated. She couldn't really feel anything, but on the bright side, nothing hurt. "I think so."

Her eyes began to adjust and she could see the faint outlines of his eyes, his mouth, his hair. Everything came to her in bits and pieces, but it was Tucker, and he was okay.

They were alive.

Yay.

"Why would someone want to kill us?" she asked.

"I don't know."

"I'm a good person. I did jury duty. Twice. I give blood every six weeks. I don't kick puppies."

"Try not to take it personally," he said.

"And you seem like a fairly decent person yourself. Why would someone want to kill us?"

"Flynn, look, I need to go out there and see if they're still around. I need you to stay here and—"

"No!" She flailed, grabbing at his arm. "Let's just call 911 and—"

"My cell doesn't get service out here, and there's no phone in the cabin. I have to go—"

"You are *not* going out there. There is someone with a gun out there, and they don't like you."

"I'm gonna lock the door and take the key. If anyone knocks, don't answer."

People with guns knock? Who knew? Flynn shivered.

"If they're not gone already, I'm gonna draw them out. You need to stay here and be still and quiet, okay? You stay here."

She gripped his shirt with every bit of strength she had. "Don't you leave me!"

He gently pried her hands loose and held them in his. "Flynn, I have to. I'll be back. Two minutes, I'll be back. Count."

She gazed at him as her mind whirled. "What?"

"Count. You stay here, and you count to yourself,

quietly. Two minutes. One hundred and twenty seconds. Count. I will be back."

Flynn wanted to ask him if he was insane, but that would be a waste of time because obviously he was. His tone of authority calmed her though, and she did as he asked.

"One. Two. Three. Four . . ."

And he was gone. She heard him start up the truck and go back in the direction they'd come. She breathed slowly, deeply, her thoughts coming at her like sharpened spears.

Someone shot at us.

"Thirty-one. Thirty-two. Thirty-three."

We drove where there was no road. We could have crashed into a tree. I could be dead right now. Tucker could be dead.

It was right about then that she started to cry. Her hands shook violently, and she didn't even try to wipe at her face, taking odd comfort in the predictability of the *pat-pat-pat* as the tears fell into her lap. She counted.

"Fifty-nine. Sixty."

Where is Tucker?

She listened. There was nothing to break the silence but the sound of her own shaky breath. Tucker said he'd be back by one hundred and twenty. It wasn't that far away. She closed her eyes.

"Seventy-six. Seventy-seven. Seventy-eight."

Where was he? Was he dead? Had the maniac killed him? Was the maniac coming for her now? Why oh why oh *why* had she watched all those *Friday the 13th* movies? The chick in the cabin always got it.

Always.

"One hundred and three. One hundred and four."

She swallowed and stopped counting. She didn't want to get to one hundred and twenty, because if she got to one hundred and twenty and he wasn't back, that meant something bad had happened. So if she just never got to one hundred and twenty, that meant he was fine and would be back soon. She knew there was a hole in that logic somewhere, but she wasn't particularly anxious to find it.

The door opened and even though Flynn could see it was Tucker, she screamed anyway. She was finding it an oddly difficult habit to break.

"It's okay," Tucker said, sitting on the couch next to her. "They're gone. Whoever it was, they're gone. You're safe. It's okay."

She threw herself into his arms. "I'm gonna kill you for that later."

His hand cradled the back of her head and held her so close that his chuckle rumbled through her chest. "That's fine."

Her heart pounded, and she willed it to calm, but it didn't. "I think I'm freaking out. My heart is racing."

He pulled back and put one hand on her face. "It's okay. You're fine now. Just breathe."

"Okay." She gulped air frantically, tried to slow her breathing down, but couldn't. "Except I think I'm hyperventilating."

"What do you need for that? A paper bag, right?"

He started to get up, but she grabbed his shirt sleeve in a death grip and pulled him back down next to her.

"I think I'm hysterical. I always thought hysteria was bullshit, you know, because *hyster* is the Latin root for 'uterus.' Like women are the only people who ever freak out, but I don't care if it's sexist." She took another gulping breath and turned to him. "Tucker, I'm hysterical. And not in the fun way."

He put both his hands on the side of her face. "Don't take this the wrong way, but it might help if you stopped talking."

She shook her head. "I can't. I want to, trust me, but I can't seem to shut up." She turned to him, put one hand on his shoulder. "I think you're going to have to slap me, Tucker. That's what they do in the movies, right? They slap the woman who won't stop talking because she's hysterical. I think you need to slap me."

"I'm not going to slap you," he said.

"Then do something because I'm freaking out here!"

And he did. He pulled her to him and placed his lips on hers so forcefully that everything else went out of her head. Suddenly her whole world was him. He was everything she needed, more than air, more than light.

He was everything.

She took in breath through her nose and calmed as her heart fell into a reasonable rhythm. She dove into the kisses, tasting him with a desperate and overwhelming need that might have been frightening if she didn't have getting shot at to compare it to. Instead, she gave in to him, allowing the want and need to well up within her as she pulled his shirt up over his head.

For his part, Tucker kept pace, his hands flowing over her, finding her hips and her thighs and then starting again with her hair, moving down her body, his fingers running over her as though he was trying to commit the feel of her to sense memory. He pulled her shirt off and sent it flying across the room, and Flynn had the vague impression that it knocked something over, but they dove back into each other so fast that it was hard to comprehend anything except Tucker, the feel of him, the taste of him, the smell of him. He made it easy to block everything else out, to take comfort in him. It wasn't until she'd undone the top button on his jeans that he put his hand over hers, his breath sending her hair flying away from her face in ragged huffs.

"Flynn," he said, "maybe we need to slow it down."

Flynn shook her head. "It's life-affirming. Go with it."

He pulled her to him for another plummeting kiss, and she lowered his zipper. He groaned as she slid her hand along the hard length of him, and then he grasped her wrist.

"I'm not gonna try to stop you again," he said. "This is as gentlemanly as I'm gonna get."

"Good," she said, sliding his jeans and boxers off his hips. "Because it's getting on my nerves."

And once again, they rolled into it. She lowered herself down and took him in her mouth, letting her tongue curve around him, and he grabbed her shoulders and pulled her up.

"I thought you said you were gonna stop with that gentlemanly crap," she said.

"I am. But if you do that it'll be a short show. Trust me." He kissed her deeply, then, in as deft a motion as Flynn had ever witnessed, her jeans were off and he had her completely naked before him.

"Wow," she said.

"Thank you." On his knees before her, he rose up and kissed her gently, then lowered his mouth down to her breasts. She gasped at the sensation as it snapped through her like a live electrical wire, then tapped him on the shoulder.

"Look, that's a great idea for next time, but I'm really ready, like, you know, *now*," she said, not caring if the desperation showed in her voice.

"You sure?" he whispered gruffly.

In answer, she pushed him gently back by the shoulders until he landed on the knotted rag rug on the floor. She fell down on top of him, adjusted her position quickly, and sank him into her as forcefully as she could without hurting either of them. She released a groan as he filled her, moving herself up and over him, slamming against him repeatedly until all the fear and panic was gone, until there was nothing in her but him, until she screamed and fell on top of him, her body shuddering through the initial quake and all the aftershocks. She breathed heavily, her face against his chest, and for the first moment wondered what the hell she was doing. Vaguely, in the back of her head, she had the feeling that she'd done something wrong, but she pushed it away. She didn't want her presence of mind back, she just wanted to lie there forever, feeling his hands trailing over her back, playing with her hair, sweeping away the jagged edges that were trying to weasel their way back into her.

He cleared her hair away from her cheek and kissed it softly.

"Flynn," he murmured into her ear. "Sweetheart, I need to get up."

She held him tighter to her and closed her eyes. "No. Not yet. We're not done."

"You need a blanket," he said. "You're shivering."

"I'm not cold," she said, pushing herself up to look into his eyes. "And we're not done."

He smiled and reached up to tuck her hair behind her ear. "Yeah, we are."

She couldn't hide her surprise. "We are? But you didn't . . . Did you?"

He kissed the tip of her nose, then gently lifted her off of him.

Nope. He sure didn't.

"Wait." She sat up as he pulled on his jeans, adjusting himself as well as he could under the circumstances. "What are you doing?"

"I'm getting a blanket." In the dim moonlight streaming through the window, she watched as he walked across the room, opened a closet, and filled his arms with blankets. He walked back, flicked one out, and wrapped it around her shoulders. "Now, how about a fire?"

She shook her head. "How about you get those pants off? We're not done here."

"I'm fine," he said. "And you're still shaking. I think you're in shock."

He dumped the other blanket at her feet and went to the woodstove, in which wood had already been piled. One match later, it was beginning to blaze, and Tucker settled himself next to Flynn.

"We're not done," she said again over the lump in her throat as a tear tracked down her cheek. "We're not done."

"Not forever," he said, pulling her into his arms. "For now. What just happened was amazing, and wonderful, and something we both needed, and whether I came or not doesn't change that."

"But—"

"Shhhh," he said, hugging her tighter. "You're freaked out, and you're scared, and neither of us is thinking clearly. Let's just calm down for a minute, okay?"

Flynn leaned her head against his chest, but the raw edges were working their way back into her, and she felt more than restless. She felt wrong. She felt like she'd done something horribly wrong and she had to try and make it right, except she wasn't sure exactly how to do that. She raised up again to look him in the eye.

"I'm sorry. I didn't mean—" Her heart felt as though it was outside her body, raw and cold and beating despite itself. She shook convulsively in his arms, and it occurred to her that he might be right. She might be in shock. Emotions ran over her, bumping into her at every point, and she felt a tear fall down one cheek as she realized what she'd done wrong. "I wasn't using you, Tucker."

He guided her head back to lean on his chest. "Hey. You've got nothing to worry about, okay?" He ran his hands over her arms. "Just let me get you warm, okay?"

"But I wasn't . . ." Her teeth chattered. "I wasn't using you. You mean something to me. You—"

He wrapped the blanket tighter around her shoulders and leaned his face down in front of hers. "I know. Now for God's sake, shut up and let me get you warmed up, okay?"

It wasn't until that moment that she realized that she wasn't the only one who was on the edge here. In the firelight, she could see the desperation in his eyes, and she understood. All he wanted to do was take care of her. He needed it the way she'd needed him earlier.

She closed her eyes and leaned against him, allowing

herself to sink into his arms and let him carry her for a while. She listened to his heartbeat, still and strong and perpetual, telling her that as long as she could hear it, everything was okay. Her body relaxed, the shaking stopped, and after a short while, she fell asleep.

The first thing Flynn noticed when her consciousness returned was that it was dark; glancing at the clock on the wall, she guessed she'd been asleep for about an hour. Next, she took in the smell of the fire; deep, earthy, woodsy. Comforting. She took her time waking up, snuggling into the old couch, curling the blankets that had been placed over her into her fist that she tucked under her chin. When she finally opened her eyes, the first thing she saw was Tucker's back as he sat by the fire. His muscles moved softly under his shirt as he intermittently jabbed at the logs in the woodstove, and she could tell his mind wasn't on the fire. She stilled and watched him, content just to take in his movements and his existence in the same space with her.

Then, in a rush, the events of the evening came back to her.

The driving lesson, which had been sweet.

The being shot at, which hadn't.

And then of course there was the rampaging, desperate sex on the cabin floor.

Oh, God. Mortification stabbed through her, and she moved her hands under the blankets and confirmed her suspicion; yep, she was still naked. Trying to make as little noise as possible, she moved her hands around under the blankets, hoping to every force in heaven and earth that her underwear was caught up under the blankets with her somewhere.

Unfortunately, that didn't seem to be the case. She lifted her head slowly, trying to be deathly silent as she shifted one leg to the floor and fished for her clothes with her big toe.

"Everything's folded up on the other side of the couch," Tucker said, surprising her. "I'll keep my eyes on the fire until you're ready."

"Oh. Okay." Flynn held the blankets to her as she sat up and reached for her clothes. "Meaning, 'Okay, I'm putting my clothes on,' not that it's okay to turn around. I mean, not that it matters much now, I guess, considering . . . you know. The thing."

There was a slight pause, then he said, "What thing?"

She hooked her bra. "Stop it. You know what thing."

"Oh, *that* thing?" He jabbed at the fire, his head turned slightly toward her, but not so far that he could see her. "Don't worry about it. Never happened."

She zipped up her jeans. "Look, Tucker, I'll admit it's been a while for me, but usually I know when I've had sex." She put her shirt on and slid her hands under her hair, lifting it up from where it was caught under the shirt. She watched him for a moment longer, enjoying a few more moments when she could see him but he couldn't see her. Then, she said, "You can turn around now."

Tucker pushed himself up from the floor and brushed off the knees of his jeans, then tucked his hands in his pockets as he stood facing her.

"So," he said, one side of his mouth curling up into a sweet smile, "how about them Mets?"

Flynn crossed her arms, then uncrossed them, then

stuck one hand in her front jeans pocket, then pulled it out. Christ. She didn't even know how to stand. Her thigh muscles shook, calmed, and then shook again, which had always been a sign that her body was taking the hit for emotions her mind wasn't ready to process. She sat back down on the couch, pulling a cushion into her lap to hide her legs.

"The Mets suck," she said.

Tucker nodded, keeping his eyes on hers. "Yeah. Yeah, they really do."

Flynn concentrated on her fingers. Her manicure was pretty much ruined. Of course, that was the least of her problems right now.

"Flynn?"

She raised her eyes to Tucker. He smiled softly and moved to the couch, sitting down next to her but taking special care not to touch her, she noticed.

"It never happened," he said.

She tightened her grip on the couch cushion. "Tucker. It happened, okay? So stop trying to—"

"Hey." He put one finger under her chin and guided her to look at him, lowering his hand the second their eyes met. His expression was achingly in earnest, and she felt both intrigued and weirded out by this new, sincere Tucker. "It wouldn't have happened. If we hadn't gotten shot at, if you hadn't gotten hysterical, if I had slapped you instead of . . ." He gestured toward the knotted rug, then angled his body toward hers and leaned closer, speaking softly. "I don't think either of us would have chosen to have it happen that way if the circumstances hadn't been . . . extraordinary. So, you know, I think we deserve a clean slate. No embarrassment. No guilt. What do you say?"

"I say you're crazy," Flynn said, focusing her attention on pulling at a stray thread on the cushion as her leg muscles convulsed underneath it.

"I'm sorry." His voice was so soft, she wasn't sure she'd heard him right until she looked up and saw his face.

"Oh, please," she said. "What do you have to be sorry about? You didn't even . . ." She made a motion with her hands that wasn't accurately indicative of what she was talking about, but it didn't matter. She could tell by his light laugh that he got it.

"You have an unhealthy fixation on that," he said, taking her hands and lowering them back to the cushion in her lap. "And I have plenty to be sorry about. I should have stopped you if I didn't think you were thinking clearly. The problem was, I wasn't thinking clearly, either, and even if I had been . . ." He paused, shook his head. "I couldn't have stopped."

She tried to laugh, but her discomfort overcompensated with a decidedly unfeminine snort. "Well, any man and any woman in that situation would have been unable to stop—"

"You're not any woman, Flynn," he said, his eyes on the fire. "You had me since the second you got off that train. You know that."

"I do?" Flynn felt her breath catch on the words. "I mean, I did?"

Tucker turned back to look at her, surprise in his expression. He reached up and put one hand on the side of her neck, his fingers extending into her hair, as his eyes searched hers. "You didn't know that?"

"No," she said. "I thought you thought I was some spoiled little Daddy's girl sweeping into town to shut down the plant and send everyone home to cheating wives and starving babies."

"No." He watched her with that intent, sincere expression, and her legs shook again. "I never thought that."

She smiled, and he leaned forward and kissed her lightly, sweetly. It was the kind of kiss that said, *No rush. There's plenty more where this came from.* Flynn leaned into it, took comfort from it, and when they broke, her legs were calm.

How did he do that?

"So . . ." she said after a minute, "it never happened?"

He pulled her into his arms and she leaned her face against his chest, listening to the steady heartbeat within.

"Well," he said, "I figure we can do one of two things. We can talk the whole thing to death, feel embarrassed and guilty despite the fact that there's nothing we can do to change anything, let the awkwardness run its course and hope we come out okay on the other end, or we can say it never happened, wipe the slate clean, and have something to eat." He kissed the top of her head. "I think you know my vote."

Flynn snuggled deeper against his chest and stared at the fire. The fact was, right now, she didn't feel embarrassed or awkward at all. She felt calm, and comfortable, and happy. Somehow, Tucker had managed to fix everything before it had gotten too broken.

She had to find out how he did that.

She lifted her head and looked up at him with a smile. "Whatcha got in the basket?"

*   *   *

"So, you're going to break in *again* to return the laptop and the folder?"

"That's the plan," Jake said. Flynn's astounded face peered at him between the two candles that sat on the table. Her hair fell around her shoulders in wild waves, and the candlelight flickered warmly over her face. Despite the attempt on their lives and the totally botched lovemaking, he felt calmer and happier than he had in recent memory.

He was toast.

She leaned forward. "Explain to me again why you can't just give it to the police?"

Jake nudged the last plate of finger sandwiches her way. There wasn't much left—two hours of bringing Flynn up-to-date on the Chase situation had pretty much annihilated the picnic fodder. Still, there was something about watching Flynn nibble on finger sandwiches that never got old.

"Illegally gotten gains," he said. "Not admissible in a court of law. Gerard Levy—he's the sergeant at the Scheintown Police Department, my old boss—he's going to have to go in with a search warrant in order for anything to be worth anything legally. Let's just hope he doesn't ask me where I got the printouts."

Flynn nibbled her lip and shook her head. "Something's not right."

"Typically, when people are shooting at you, that's the case."

"Okay." She put her napkin down on the table, and pushed herself up out of her chair. "I'm going to say everything back to you the way that I understand it, because I'm pretty sure I'm missing something."

Jake sat back in his chair, crossing his arms over his chest. "Go."

She started to pace. "Okay. So. Chase is the head of the historical whatsis—"

"President of the Historical Preservation Society of Scheintown, yes."

"Okay. So, this society has healthy funding."

"About a million dollars a year, when you combine fund-raisers, private donations, and government grants."

"That's a lot of money."

He grinned. He liked watching her pace. "Your tax dollars at work."

"Okay, so Chase has been approving consultation fees for this historian guy to come up here and make sure everything's historically accurate."

"Professor Gavin P. Krunk, a specialist in post-Colonial architecture in upstate New York."

"Only he's been dead for . . . how long?"

"Fifteen years."

"Which is bad because unless Chase is able to transfer funds to the other side, the money for Krunk's consultation has been going somewhere else."

"You learn quick, Grasshoppah."

Flynn ignored him. He liked it when she did that, too. "And the laptop also had records for a subsidiary consulting company Chase owns?"

"Yes. With liquid assets equaling roughly the amount paid to Krunk over the last three years."

"In excess of fifty thousand dollars," Flynn said.

"Yep. Not so much that anyone would miss it, but enough to get Chase a good, relaxing stretch in the pokey."

Flynn sighed, walked back to the table, sat down, and grabbed her wineglass. "Except you don't think Chase did it."

Jake sat back in his chair and folded his hands over his stomach. "No. Fifty thousand over the course of three years? That's chump change to Chase. Also, why use the laptop that was stolen from evidence to keep the records? If he stole that laptop to keep the police from tracing that real estate scheme back to him, then he would have had it destroyed. Even wiped clean, the serial numbers would trace it back to him, which links him to stolen evidence. Chase is smarter than that."

Flynn put her wineglass down. "So, Rhonda's backup plan was that if the embezzlement didn't stick, he'd still be in trouble for stealing the laptop?"

"That's my theory. I just don't know why."

Flynn blinked. "She told you why."

Jake raised his eyes to Flynn's. "What? That bit about being in love with him? You believe that?"

"Hell, yeah. You say she's a mousy type, right? Guys like Chase don't even see girls like her, and she probably has no idea that she's way out of his league, anyway, because women are stupid that way. So, she cooks up a plan to get herself on his radar by being the faithful friend while he's in jail. It fits."

He stared at her for a moment, turning it over in his head. And the thing was, Flynn was right.

"Women are scary," he said.

"Well, we know she did it. She's got *Embezzling for Dummies* taped under her desk." Flynn motioned toward the manila folder that was sitting on the table, containing handwritten instructions outlining exactly how to embezzle the money from the historical society, written in what appeared to be a woman's hand. "And if she just wanted Chase to rot in jail, she would have gone to the police herself. This is the only thing that fits."

"Wouldn't it be easier to just get a pair of contacts and buy some new clothes if she wanted Chase's attention?"

"Sure, but we're dealing with a CWIL, here."

"A quill? We're dealing with a feather pen?"

"No. *CWIL.* Crazy Woman In Love. Freya coined the term. She tends to attract men that come with CWILs attached. It's a long story, but . . . yeah. Rhonda is a classic CWIL. She doesn't want to compete for his affection when she could lose. Her plan is to make it impossible for him not to love her." Flynn sat back, a self-satisfied expression on her face. "I'm totally right on this. Trust me." The satisfaction faded into worry. "But, the thing is, why try to kill us? Rhonda's the only one who knows that you've got the laptop, and you're playing right into her hands, so what's her beef?"

Jake shrugged. "If she knows I also have a folder full of information that basically implicates her in the crime, then I imagine that's her beef."

"Good point." Flynn shook her head. "Except, if she wanted us dead, we were sitting ducks. *Unarmed* sitting ducks. But she just shot and ran away."

"*If* it was Rhonda who shot at us. This is no time to jump to conclusions."

"Who else would it be?"

"A bad shot who tried to kill us and then got scared off," Jake said, "or a good shot who wanted to send a message."

"What message?"

Jake shrugged. "*I don't like you?*"

Flynn raised an eyebrow at him. "Do you think it's the same person who killed Elaine Placie?"

"Eileen Dietz," Jake corrected.

"Eileen. Elaine. Whatever. The only person connected to Eileen-Elaine is Chase."

Jake got up and started to clear the table. *Here comes the tough part.*

"Well, he's not the only one."

Flynn was quiet for a while. "What do you mean?"

"She screwed me over, babe. That speaks to motive."

She snorted, watching him to see if he was joking. A moment later, her face went serious. "Yeah, but you didn't kill her."

"I know that. You know that. But the police?" He shrugged. "They may not know that."

She pushed herself up from the table. "Of course they know that. They know you."

He stopped clearing the table and looked at her. "There's something I haven't told you, Flynn. That pan that they found with the body, the one that was dented and very likely the murder weapon?"

She nodded. "Yeah?"

He grabbed a plate and held it out to her. "You want the last petit four?"

She shook her head slowly, not taking her eyes off him.

"Suit yourself." He popped it in his mouth. "Anyway, the pan was from Mercy's kitchen. I wasn't working at the Arms at the time that Eileen-Elaine-Whatever was killed, but I ate lunch there almost every day. That speaks to means."

Even in just the light from the fire and the candles, Tucker could see her posture go tight and freeze.

"Exactly what are you saying, Tucker?"

He grabbed a napkin and wiped a wineglass. "Tracking the exact time of death is gonna be tricky after six months with the fishes, but they can estimate a fairly accurate window based on the last time anyone saw her. And, considering that I didn't start working at the Arms until sometime in April, that gives me the death row trifecta." He tucked the glass into the basket. "Means. Motive. Opportunity."

She advanced on him. "The police could viably bring you in for murder, and you're making jokes?"

Jake stuck the cork back in the wine bottle, then turned to face her. "Look, I didn't do it, which means the cops probably have evidence we don't know about that will point to whoever did. Chances are eighty-twenty I'll be questioned, fifty-fifty I'll be brought in, and maybe ten-ninety I'll be convicted of a murder I didn't commit. Going to the police with this information about Chase and Rhonda gives them more to go on, and I think it improves my odds. So, no, I'm not really worried about it and I don't think you should be either."

Flynn shook her head. "How can you be so casual about this?"

He walked around the table to her and reached out to touch her shoulder, but she jerked away from him.

"The best thing I can do for myself is keep a clear head, so that's what I'm doing. Gerard Levy is an old family friend. That's how I started out there in the first place, so that's something else I've got going for me. The chances are pretty good that I'll come out on the other side of this okay, so there's no need to panic."

Her stance softened a little, and he reached for her hand. This time, she didn't pull away, but she wouldn't look at him, either. He looked down at her hand in his and spoke.

"I want you to know that if you want to bail, go back to Boston, and let me deal with this by myself, I won't hold it against you."

Her eyes flashed with anger. "You think I would do that?"

He had to take a moment before answering her. "I think you'd be crazy if you didn't, Flynn."

She looked stunned, then hurt. "Well. Okay then. I'll just pack my bags and leave you here to deal with everything on your own."

"Don't misunderstand me," he said. She raised her eyes to his. "I don't want you to go. I'm handing this thing over to Gerard Levy and I'm out. I don't even care anymore what happens to him. But . . . you could have been seriously hurt tonight, Flynn."

"So could . . ." she started, but he held up his hand to stop her.

"I would have been asking for it. I've been so focused on getting back at Gordon Chase that if I'd been shot tonight, it would have been well earned. But you . . . you didn't sign up for that. And I'm just glad it didn't take you getting killed for me to finally get that some things just don't matter as much as I thought." He swallowed hard, surprised at how difficult it was to get the next part out. "And other things matter a lot more than I ever realized."

He reached for her, pulling her to him. Looking down

into her eyes, he felt sure that everything was going to turn out fine. He didn't know how; even if he didn't get wrongfully accused of murder, she was going to leave eventually. But he didn't want to worry about how it was all going to work out right now. It didn't matter. He leaned down to her and kissed her slowly, putting into that kiss everything he didn't know how to say, every question he didn't know how to ask.

Based on her response, he guessed her answer was *yes*. That had to be a good sign.

When they parted, there were tears in her eyes.

Bad sign.

"Hey," he said, wiping his thumb at a stray tear. "What's this?"

She rolled her eyes. "Allergies."

He didn't smile. "Flynn . . ."

She pushed away from him, turned, and grabbed the messenger bag.

"Dampen the fire and blow out the candles," she said as she headed out. "We've got some breaking and entering to do."

Chapter Twelve

♡ Flynn sat on her Nazi love seat in her flannel pajamas sipping a cappuccino she'd had Herman bring her
from the kitchen when she realized that, for the first time
since she'd been to Shiny, she'd slept a full night at the
cottage without Esther's interference.

Wow. 'Magine that.

She raised her eyes to the ceramic cows on the shelf,
lifted her cup to them in tribute, and returned her gaze to
the spot on the wall that she'd been staring at all morning, trying to sort out the big mass of ugly in her head.
First on the roster: the murder of Eileen-Elaine-Whatever,
and who might have really done it. Next was the attempt
on her own life, which seemed so surreal to her that part
of her still believed it had all been in her imagination.
Rounding out the bottom were Rhonda Bacon and Gordon Chase, twisted love gone trainwreck-ugly; the future
of the Goodhouse Arms; and her own future as a cog in
her father's real estate development machine.

And, hovering over all these things, Tucker.

She sipped her cappuccino and sighed. The night before had taken top honors as the best, worst, and strangest evening of her life. She and Tucker had hardly spoken at all when they broke into Chase's office to return the laptop and folder, and the conversation on the drive home had been stilted. He didn't ask to spend the night, she didn't even consider inviting him in, and the good night kiss at her doorstep had been cautious and awkward. It wasn't the Sex That Never Happened, Flynn felt pretty confident they'd nipped that in the bud. It was . . .

She dropped her head into her hand and groaned.

It was the crying.

As far as mood-killers go, crying when a man kisses you is right up there at the tippy top. She knew Tucker wanted to know what was wrong, but he wouldn't ask and she couldn't tell him. Even now, she wasn't entirely sure. All she knew was that when she'd kissed him, she'd thought about him going to jail and her going to Boston and had realized that this *whatever* they had between them was completely, totally, irrevocably doomed. Even if he didn't go to jail, she couldn't stay in a town like Shiny for a man she'd known for a millisecond. And there was no other reason to stay, which meant she'd have to leave, and maybe they'd try long distance for a while but the only thing in the world more doomed than a long distance relationship was a Hollywood marriage. Eventually Tucker would move on to live happily ever after with someone like Annabelle and Flynn would spend the rest of her life alone in one of Dad's antiseptic cookie-cutter condos.

She glanced down into her mug and momentarily regretted throwing out Esther's peppermint schnapps. This was definitely a drinking-in-your-pajamas–type day. Unfortunately, she was dry, the bar was closed, and there were no liquor stores within walking distance.

She'd checked on that the first day.

She lifted her cup to take another sip when there was a frantic knock at her door. She leaned back into the Nazi love seat and closed her eyes.

"It's Saturday," she yelled. "I'm off duty."

"Flynn Daly, I swear by all that is holy that if you don't open this door immediately I will kick it down!"

Flynn stared at the door, a small flame of happiness igniting within. She got up and walked over to the door, pulling it open and grinning when she saw the person on the other side.

"Well, I'll be damned," Flynn said.

Freya answered her with a glare, then stepped in and dumped the three large suitcases she was hauling inside the cottage.

"Oh. My. God. *What* have you been doing here?"

Flynn glanced around, not sure where to start. The ceramic cows? The lace? Getting shot at?

"So," Freya began, taking the cappuccino out of Flynn's hands, "I get home late last night from Tucson to find Dad waiting for me at the airport. The man has never picked up anyone at the airport in his life, so I assume it's the second coming or a tax audit or something equally catastrophic, but no." She sat on the love seat and looked up at Flynn. "It's you."

Flynn sat next to her. "Me? What'd I do?"

"Beats the hell out of me. All I know is he picks me up, talking about financial reports and missing money—"

"Missing money? What missing money?"

"—and how I have to get on the next train, leaving at *seven in the morning,* so I can come down here and help you sort out your little disaster." She took a sip of the cappuccino and motioned toward her luggage. "I didn't even get a chance to unpack. That second suitcase still has the robes from Tucson."

"You stole robes from your spa retreat?"

Freya sighed. "It's not stealing if they charge me, which they will when they do inventory. But the robes? Totally worth it. Anyway." She clapped a hand down on Flynn's knee. "So, what the hell is going on here, punkin?"

Flynn rubbed her eyes. "A lot, but nothing with the financials. I mean, I got him the reports yesterday even though my bookkeeper was out." Flynn tried to keep the mild bitterness out of her voice. "Wasn't he glad I got him the reports?"

"Glad? Are you kidding? He was totally pissed off. Apparently, there's some money missing or something and his preferred buyer is bugging him for third quarter financials despite the fact that there are enough records on this place to go back to roughly the beginning of time and—" Freya stopped, glanced at her watch, then looked back at Flynn. "Why aren't you dressed? It's one o'clock."

Flynn sighed. "I think I'm depressed."

Freya did not look amused. "You're kidding me with this, right?"

"No. Esther's been haunting me and I have no idea how to run this place and I killed myself to get those reports to Dad yesterday and he doesn't even appreciate it."

"Oh, honey. He appreciates it. He'll just never say so, because he's Dad. Do we need to go over this again?"

"No."

"Good. Now, how are things with your bartender?"

Flynn thought on that for a moment, and decided Freya wasn't ready for that whole story. "You know, maybe we should talk about that later."

"Fine. Get in the shower, get dressed, and we'll go to your office, sort this whole thing out." She bent her head to sip Flynn's cappuccino, but froze in mid-sip, her eyes caught on something on the wall. Flynn looked in the direction of her sister's gaze, then sighed.

"Oh, my God," Freya said, pointing at the cows. "What the hell are those?"

Jake put his feet up on Gerard Levy's desk, crossing them at the ankles as he sipped the standard-issue crap-ass police station coffee from a foam cup.

"So, that's pretty much everything," Jake said. "The whole mess is yours now. I wash my hands of it."

Gerard sat back in his cheap, avocado-leather, 1970s office chair. It squeaked like a hedgehog being sadistically violated.

See? Jake thought. *Nothing to miss about this place.*

"Okay. Try not to get killed in case I need you to testify at trial."

"I'll do my best." Jake pulled his feet down, set the crap coffee on the desk, and leaned forward. "Just one more thing before we officially go back on record."

Gerard raised an eyebrow. "More breaking and entering? I'm a cop, Jake, not a fucking priest."

Jake held up one hand. "Just entering. No breaking. She gave me a key, remember?"

Gerard stared Jake down for a long moment, then finally cracked a smile. "What is it?"

"The pan that killed Elaine?"

"Eileen."

"Whatever. Mercy's convinced it came from her kitchen, and I'm not one to argue with her."

Gerard laughed. "I've argued with the women in your family. I don't blame you."

Jake tapped his fingers on the desk. "Well, I think you might want to look in the direction of the Arms."

Gerard eyed Jake for a long moment. "Aren't you in that direction?"

"Generally, yeah. That's why I'm coming to you, Gerard. When you're called to testify at my trial, I want it on the record that I was completely forthcoming, just like any innocent man would be."

Gerard rose one eyebrow. "And this is all off the record, am I right?"

"Well, except for the part about being shot at. I think that should stay on the record."

Gerard eyed Jake for a while, then came to a decision and leaned forward.

"Preliminary forensic reports show that the blow was probably struck by someone who was right-handed. You're a lefty, right?"

Jake nodded, surprised by the rush of relief that ran through him. He didn't seriously think they would take him in for the killing of Eileen-Elaine-Whatever, but apparently some part of him had been anxious about it.

Gerard looked at him. "You're also over six feet, and based on the angle of the blow, we're thinking it was someone about six to eight inches shorter than you. You were never a suspect, but it was fun to watch you squirm there for a while."

Jake reached out and tapped Gerard's desk. "You're a good man, Levy. Don't let all that time you'll be spending in hell make you think any different."

Jake downed the last of the coffee and tossed the foam cup in the wastebasket next to Gerard's desk. Gerard stood up and walked around, holding out his hand.

"Thanks for the new information. I'll start working on that search warrant, and I'll let you know what happens."

Jake took his hand and shook. Gerard clamped his other hand over their joined ones and stared Jake in the eye.

"Officially, though," he said, "don't leave town."

Jake chuckled. "You love saying that, don't you?"

Gerard laughed and released Jake's hand. "It's the reason I took the job."

"The missing money is probably a glitch in the reservations system," Flynn said, leaning over Freya's shoulder as they both stared at the front desk computer screen. "Tucker told me he made a reservation once and they lost twelve thousand dollars. That's why Annabelle was the only one on the system, from what I understood. The second anyone else touched it, the bookkeeping got screwed up."

Freya leaned back in her seat. "Okay. Well, maybe we can start with the reservations system, then. Where is this Annabelle, anyway?"

Flynn took in a deep breath and stood up straight. "I don't know. She never showed up yesterday and hasn't answered her phone since."

Freya turned slowly in the chair and shot a hard look up at Flynn. "That's relevant information, don't you think?"

"I think it's just a glitch in the system, Fray. Annabelle's . . ." Flynn paused, trying to figure out how exactly to describe Annabelle. "She's really . . . perky."

"Perky people are the most dangerous kind. Never turn your back on a perky person. You know that." She let out a heavy sigh. "We'll look for a glitch first, but if we don't find a reasonable explanation by tomorrow, we're gonna have to call in the police to investigate perky little Anna-face."

Flynn smiled. "Thanks."

"Don't thank me. We're still up to our elbows in crap. Even if everything's on the up and up, it's no wonder the place isn't making a profit. Most of the rooms are empty, we've only got staff at the front desk from eight to five, Monday through Friday, which is laughable, and we're paying everyone way too much."

"You can't change that. These people do good work because they're valued, and if you take that away—"

"Flynn, what choice do we have?"

"I don't know." Flynn sat on the desk facing her sister. "Build a Web site. Get the reservations system online. Fill the rooms. Get some publicity. George Washington slept here, for Christ's sake. Eleanor Roosevelt planted the ash tree out in the courtyard. People love that stuff." She snapped her fingers. "And—oh! When I worked at the bakery, we did catering on the side. Our chef here is amazing, that could totally take off. And we could build in other side businesses. We could . . ." Flynn trailed off at her sister's expression. "What?"

Freya pushed herself up from the desk. "You know, it's going to take months to clear all this up, get things where they should be so we can get the full value out of the sale. And we're heading into winter, which is a slow season for tourism, so at best we won't see things really pick up until next summer. I'm going to need someone in here immediately to take care of things, get this place back on track."

Flynn felt disappointment rush through her. She was being replaced. Already.

She looked down at her feet. "Yeah. That makes sense."

Freya stared at her expectantly. "And?"

Flynn lacked the energy to be tested on her business acumen—or lack thereof—at the moment. "And . . . what? I don't know. I'm sure you and Dad will find the perfect person and everything will be fine."

Freya grabbed her purse and pulled out her cigarettes. "I want you on the next train back home, should be tomorrow morning sometime. I'll clean up here."

"Oh." Flynn swallowed hard. "Yeah. Right."

Freya nodded. "You can have Monday off if you want, but you should spend Tuesday in the office with Dad, get a feel for the place. I should be back by Wednesday, and we can get you really started then."

"Fine." Flynn nodded toward the computer. "But what about the thing? With the missing money?"

"I got it, babe. No reason for both of us to suffer out here in the middle of nature's freakin' wonderland, right? You go pack." Freya cocked her head to the side and gave Flynn an evaluating look. "Unless there's something you think you can do here."

Flynn stared down at the computer. The screen hosted two reports, side by side, one titled "Accounts Payable—Second Quarter" and the other "Accounts Payable—Third Quarter." It could have been written in Greek for all she could understand of it.

"No," Flynn said. "I don't think there's anything I can do."

"All right." Freya jerked her head toward the French doors. "I assume you have an outdoor smoking area?"

Flynn tried to hide her surprise. "Yeah. There's a gazebo with ashtrays out by the west wing."

"Good." Freya gave her a defiant look. "What? It brings down the value if people smoke indoors. I only do that in other people's properties." She turned toward the doors, her heels clipping against the ancient hardwood, sending the sound bouncing off the walls.

Flynn watched until her sister was out of sight, then sat down at the desk, tapping her nails restlessly against the wood. She didn't know why she felt so upset. Leaving was the only thing that made sense. Of course Freya wouldn't have her stay and run the place; she'd run it into the ground. Hell, she'd thought her father was talking about football when he'd mentioned quarters. Leaving was the only thing that made sense. There was only one reason to stay, but she'd only known Tucker for . . .

Her eyes filled quickly and she grabbed for the mouse, absently scrolling through the second quarter report, staring at the names that went by, barely paying attention to them as she remembered the way Tucker had looked at her in the truck the night before.

"Oh, my God, I'm pathetic," she whispered, reaching out to snatch a tissue from the box on the desk. She swiped at her face, knowing for sure that leaving was the absolute right thing to do. She hadn't known Tucker long enough to be this affected by him. It was needy, and stupid, and weird, and . . .

Wait a minute. She leaned closer and blinked the last

of her tears away, not believing what she was seeing. But there it was, right in front of her.

Gavin P. Krunk. She double-clicked on the record, and the computer whined, then spit up a report. Every quarter for the last three years, the Goodhouse Arms had been paying Gavin P. Krunk almost ten thousand dollars in consulting fees for restoration efforts.

Which didn't make any sense. There were no restoration projects going on at the Arms, and if there had been, they certainly wouldn't take three years to complete.

Plus, the consultant was dead. An additional wrinkle.

"Holy shit." Flynn grabbed the mouse and clicked into the third quarter report. She scrolled through for a while, then discovered that if she clicked on an arrow at the top of the "Payee" column, it organized them alphabetically. She scanned the names; Gavin P. Krunk wasn't listed.

"Holy *shit.*"

"Watch your fucking language," Freya said from behind her. "We have to set the example around here."

Flynn turned around, her face white. "How much money did you say we were missing?"

Freya crossed her arms over her stomach and shrugged. "Oh, I don't know, something in the neighborhood of ten thousand dollars."

Flynn glanced at the number next to Krunk's name on the payables report. "Was it maybe nine thousand three hundred and eighty-two dollars and seventy-three cents?"

Freya chuckled. "Sounds like the right neighborhood. You found it?"

Flynn hit the print button, and the printer in the corner

whirred in response. Freya walked over and stood behind her, looking at the screen.

"What's going on?"

"We need to call the police," she said. "I think you were right about perky people."

Freya put her hand on the back of the chair. "Of course I was right. I'm always right. How much did the bitch steal?"

"About forty thousand a year for three years," Flynn said, her mind racing as she made the connections. "And, possibly, another fifty grand from somewhere else."

"Wow." Freya shrugged. "Gotta hand it to her for ambition."

"Yeah." Flynn nibbled her lip, staring at the pages pumping out of the printer as she thought.

Annabelle. Sweet, innocent Annabelle was a thief. And, likely, the author of Rhonda Bacon's embezzling instructions. The big question now was why.

Freya's hand landed on Flynn's shoulder. "Hey."

Flynn jumped, her mind jerking back to the present moment. "Yeah?"

Freya nodded over her shoulder, in the general direction of the cottage. "Go pack your stuff. I'll call the police, but we'll probably have to go in and give statements tonight, so it's best if you're all set to go."

"Oh." Flynn felt the stab in her heart again as she got up from the desk and forced a big grin. "Okay. I'll see you back at the cottage later?"

"Hell, no," Freya said, her eyes on the computer as she reached for the phone. "I'm staying in one of these rooms. That place creeps me out."

Flynn forced a weak smile and headed out the French

doors. She hugged herself against the chill in the air as she crossed the courtyard toward her cottage, feeling oddly hollow, despite the fact that she knew that going back to Boston was the only reasonable thing to do.

She glanced over her shoulder at the Arms as she reached her porch, hearing her father's voice in her head.

Don't get attached, Flynn.

It had been good advice. Too bad she hadn't heeded it.

Chapter Thirteen

♡ Jake sat in the lobby of the police station, reading the latest issue of *People* and waiting for Gerard to come out and tell him why he'd been called in again less than two hours after he'd left. He hoped that whatever it was, was important. And didn't involve trading in his street clothes for a stylish orange jumpsuit.

He glanced at his watch. It was six-thirty. He pulled his cell phone out of his pocket and checked it; no messages.

Something was wrong.

Well, *maybe* something was wrong.

The night before with Flynn had been . . . incredible. Overwhelming. Awkward. Unfortunately, it had ended on one of the awkward notes, and that fact had been bugging him all day. He'd waited until the afternoon to call, and when he finally did Flynn hadn't answered her phone so he'd left a message. And now, she still hadn't called back. She had probably just been tired last night, and had probably just been busy all day.

On a Saturday.

He turned the phone over in his hands. He was *not* calling again. The ball was in her court. Leaving one unanswered message the day after their first time was appropriate and gentlemanly; leaving two was needy and weird.

He flipped the phone open.

Needy . . . and . . . weird.

He flipped the phone shut and had just tucked it back in his pocket when the door opened behind him. Jake glanced over to see Flynn walking in with a blond woman. He leaned forward to get up, then pushed back in the chair and struck a casual pose as her head turned his way.

"Hey," he said.

Flynn seemed startled at first, then smiled when their eyes met. She was happy to see him.

Everything was fine.

He knew it.

He hopped up off the chair, put his hand on her elbow and kissed her cheek. "How ya doin'?"

"Okay." She rubbed her arms, avoided his eyes. "How are you?"

Everything was *not* fine.

"Great." He smiled down at her. "You sure you're okay?"

Flynn opened her mouth to say something, but a thin hand inserted itself between them, extended toward Jake. His eyes trailed up the sleeve of a dark blue pin-striped business suit, past a delicate shoulder, and then finally up to a wide smile in the middle of a fine-featured face topped by golden curls.

"I'm Freya," the woman said. "Flynn's sister."

Flynn sighed. "Freya, this is Jake Tucker. He used to be our bartender. Tucker, this is Freya. Ignore everything she says."

Jake took Freya's hand and shook it. "It's nice to meet you, Freya."

"So you're the bartender?" Freya held on to his hand for a long moment, and Jake got the distinct feeling he was being sized up. Finally, she released his hand and tossed a small smile at Flynn. "Not bad."

"Okay," Jake said, then turned to Flynn. "So, what's going on? I got called in, but I don't know why. I'm assuming you being here isn't a coincidence."

Her casual smile didn't reach her eyes. "No coincidence. We found some missing money, and—"

"Flynn and Freya Daly?"

Jake looked up to see Gerard walking toward them, holding his hand out to Flynn.

"Gerard Levy." He shook Flynn's hand, then Freya's. "Come on into my office." He looked at Jake. "All three of you. We just got some new information, and we're going to need to take some statements."

Gerard led them into his office, where they all sat in a row across from him, like kids called into the principal's office for egging the driver's ed van. Before sitting down, Gerard dropped a mug shot printout on the desk in front of Flynn. Jake looked over her shoulder as she picked it up.

"Oh, my God," Flynn breathed.

Jake stared at it, then looked up at Gerard. "You've got to be kidding me."

He set the printout back onto the desk, where it was quickly snatched up by Freya.

"What? Who's . . ." Freya read off the sheet, "Candace Bellamy?"

Flynn shifted in her chair, obviously uncomfortable. "That's, um, Annabelle."

"Annabelle?" Freya said, her voice tight and her eyes blazing. "Annabelle-the-bookkeeper Annabelle? Annabelle-who-stole-a-hundred-grand-from-us Annabelle?"

Well . . . that was news. Maybe that's what was bothering Flynn. Jake touched her arm. "Annabelle stole from you?"

Flynn turned to him, still not meeting his eyes, and said, "Long story."

Nope. Annabelle stealing money from the Arms was a problem, but it wasn't *the* problem. He watched as Flynn's eyes went everywhere in the room but to him, and just as he was about to ask her again if she was okay, Gerard spoke.

"I did a check on Annabelle when you two called to report the possible embezzlement," Gerard said, nodding at Flynn and Freya. He reached his hand out, taking the printout back from Freya. "Candace Bellamy was arrested for fraud seven years ago, was sentenced to three years, served her time, got out early for good behavior. She legally changed her name and came here to work for Esther." He pulled another piece of paper out of the file, and set it before them. "This is a letter Esther wrote the parole board, explaining that Candace Bellamy was the granddaughter of an old friend, and that she wanted to offer her a chance to start a new life."

"Right here in River City," Flynn mumbled.

Jake chuckled.

She still didn't look at him.

Gerard cleared his throat. "I wanted to talk to you all together before getting your statements. There are a lot of crossed wires here I'd like to straighten out." He glanced down at the papers in front of him. "Okay. So. Flynn, you and Jake were involved in an independent private investigation of one Gordon Chase. Is that right?"

Freya held up one hand. "Um, what? Private investigation? Who's Gordon Chase?"

"Well, yes," Flynn said quickly, addressing Gerard. "I was assisting Tucker, who had gotten a tip from Rhonda Bacon that Chase was up to something. I went out on a date with Gordon Chase so he could break into Chase's office."

Jake leaned forward and tapped Gerard's desk with his index finger. "No breaking. Only entering. I had a legally obtained key."

"Yeah, I got it." Gerard turned his attention back to Flynn. "So, your involvement was limited to distracting Mr. Chase while Jake examined the evidence?" Gerard glanced at his notepad. "That is, until the shooting last night?"

Freya angled her body toward Flynn and slapped a hand down on Gerard's desk. "I'm so sorry, the *what*?"

Flynn patted Freya's knee. "Sorry, Fray. I meant to tell you about that. Somebody kinda shot at us last night."

"You *meant* to tell me? Getting shot at slipped your mind?"

"Well, I was surprised to see you, then there was the whole thing with the missing money from the Arms—"

Gerard cleared his throat. "It seems that Annabelle—Candace Bellamy—came up here to work for Esther after she finished her stint at the Tennessee Women's Correctional Facility about . . ." Gerard glanced at his paperwork. "Four years ago."

"Wait," Flynn said. "Tennessee. Isn't that where Eileen-Elaine-Whatever was?"

Gerard glanced at Jake, then shrugged. "Eileen Dietz was Candace Bellamy's roommate there for a brief while, yes."

"Oh, my God," Flynn said. "So, Eileen-Elaine-Whatever was here for Annabelle?"

"That doesn't make any sense," Jake said. "Annabelle going back to her roots, skimming money off the top at the Arms, fine. I get that. But why bring Eileen-Elaine-Whatever here? Why get involved with Chase?"

"She's a CWIL," Flynn muttered under her breath.

Jake looked at her. "What?"

Finally, she met his eyes. "Annabelle's a CWIL."

"Oh, dear God," Freya muttered. "That explains a lot."

Gerard tapped his desk. "Annabelle's a what?"

Jake tried to wrap his mind around what Flynn was saying. "So . . . what? Annabelle was in love with Chase, too?"

Flynn shook her head. "Not Chase. You. Chase hurt your family. So she went after him."

"That doesn't make any sense. If she wanted to help me . . . why use Elaine to steal the evidence that would get Chase off?"

"To put worse evidence on it, maybe," Flynn said. "Maybe she knew Rhonda Bacon was in love with Chase, and used her to set him up even deeper. Rhonda's a CWIL, too. Annabelle could probably spot her a mile off."

Gerard leaned forward. "I'm missing something."

"CWIL. Crazy Woman In Love," Freya said. "The only thing more dangerous and unpredictable is . . . well. Nothing." She turned to Flynn. "So, this is what you've been doing this week? Breaking into offices and dealing with prison people?"

Flynn turned to her sister. She seemed so tired and sad. What the hell was going on?

"I didn't know they were in prison," Flynn said, "and Eileen-Elaine-Whatever was murdered before I even got here."

Freya's eyes widened. "Murdered? Someone was *murdered*?"

Flynn shifted to address Gerard. "So, do you guys know who killed her?"

Freya tapped her hand on Gerard's desk. "I'm gonna need some liquor soon."

"It'll just be a few more minutes." Gerard looked at Flynn. "We don't know much, except that whoever killed her was about five-foot-six and right-handed."

"So, basically, half the town," Flynn said, then she brightened and turned to Jake, grabbing his arm. "Oh! But you're a lefty! Yay!"

Finally. Eye contact *and* a smile. Jake's heart lightened, and he grazed her fingers with his.

Freya sat forward. "Wait, you thought your *boyfriend* might have killed this woman?"

"No, *I* didn't think so." She pointed at Gerard. "*They* did. And he's not . . ." She withdrew her hand from his arm. "We're just friends."

Well. Whatever's wrong, it's definitely me. Jake sat back in his chair, and scanned his mind for what he had done to make her pull so far back. The night before had been weird and everything, but this . . . there was something more going on. As subtly as possible, he cupped his hand over his nose and mouth and checked his breath.

"Jake was never really a suspect," Gerard said. "Look, I called you all in here because we've got some things to cover. More specifically, some asses." He looked at Jake. "Yours in particular. I need you to go on record about all this. We've checked Annabelle's apartment, and it's been emptied. Rhonda Bacon has also turned up missing. I'm going to need detailed statements in order to get the search going full force. Chances are good your breaking and entering—"

"No breaking." Jake threw his hands up in the air. "What, do I need to get a T-shirt made?"

Gerard nodded. "Chances are good your *entering* in Chase's office is gonna raise some eyebrows, which means paperwork for me and possibly some charges against you, both of which are gonna delay my investigation. So it would help me a great deal if, in your official statement, you came straight to me with the information Rhonda Bacon gave you, and I'll obtain the search warrant based on your tip."

Jake raised an eyebrow. "Are you asking me to perjure myself?"

"Your father was a good man and a good friend. But the next time you fuck up, you go to jail."

"I guess now's a good time for me to shut the hell up, then." Jake stood up and shook Gerard's hand. Flynn and Freya stood as well. Gerard looked at his watch.

"It's getting late," he said. "If you want, you all can come in tomorrow morning and we can take your statements then."

"Oh, Flynn can't," Freya said. "She's going home to Boston tomorrow."

"What?" A jolt ran through Jake, and he looked to Flynn, but she kept her own gaze locked on Gerard's Swingline stapler.

"Okay," Gerard said. "Let me get the room set up and we'll take your statement, Flynn." He looked from Jake to Freya. "And I'll see you two in the morning."

"Fabulous," Freya said. Gerard left, and she touched Flynn on the arm. "I'm gonna go see if there's a liquor store within walking distance. The cabs in this town take forever."

"Um," Jake said, his eyes on Flynn, who still would not look at him. "There's a place about half a mile down Route 9."

Freya bent one knee, revealing a boot with a heel that looked like it had been made to spear prey. Jake nodded toward the lobby.

"I'll give you a ride in a minute," he said.

Freya glanced from Flynn to Jake, and then nodded. "Sure. Thanks."

She left, shutting the door quietly behind her. Flynn stood where she was, silent, apparently fascinated by the stapler. Jake sat back against Gerard's desk.

"So," he said. "Tomorrow morning, huh?"

Flynn raised her eyes, looking as though she hadn't heard him, then nodded suddenly. "Oh. Yeah. Freya's pulling me out. But, good news, there isn't going to be a sale. Not right away, anyway. We'll probably keep the place until at least next summer."

"Well, that's great," Jake said, taking a moment before adding, "So, why don't you stay and run it?"

She seemed surprised by the question. "Because."

Jake waited for her to follow that with a reason. When she didn't, he said, "Well, now I understand."

"Stop it, Tucker," she said, anger in her voice. "What am I supposed to do? I have no experience. I've been here five days and managed to get involved in both murder and embezzling. Dad and Freya, they know what they're doing. Me . . . I . . ."

He raised his eyes to hers. "And you can't think of any other reason to stay?"

She opened her mouth to speak, but nothing came out. Jake pushed himself up off the desk. "All right. I get it."

Her hand grabbed his and he stopped where he was, but for some reason, couldn't bring himself to look at her.

"I've only been here five days," she said. "I can't . . ."

Her voice cracked on the last word, and it damn near killed him. He turned to her and smiled. Just because he felt like he'd been hit in the gut was no reason to hit back.

"I know," he said quickly. "Of course you can't."

Surprise flashed over her face. "Oh. Okay. So . . . you understand?"

He scoffed, trying to sound as casual as he could. "Oh. Yeah. I mean, your life is in Boston. Mine is here. That was always the way it was."

"Yeah." She heaved a sigh, but didn't look much relieved. He widened his smile and pretended he was totally on board.

"We'll call. We'll e-mail."

"Sure we will." She offered a weak smile. "Of course we will."

He paused. "We're friends, right?"

"Yeah." She smiled back. "Good friends."

They held each other's gaze for a long moment, then Jake let his eyes wander over her wild hair. He was going to miss that hair. He reached out and tagged her lightly on the shoulder.

"Hey," he said softly, meeting her eyes again and trying not to let his disappointment show on his face. "I had fun."

Her smile disappeared. "Me, too."

The door opened and Gerard ducked his head in. "Flynn, we're ready for you. Jake, get the hell out of my office."

Jake nodded, then looked at Flynn. "I'll wait for you, take you and your sister back."

He kept his hand on the small of Flynn's back as he followed her out, then dropped it when they separated in the hallway. He watched her go into the interrogation room, the last bit of hope leaving him as the door closed behind her.

"Okay," a voice said next to him. He turned to see Freya looking up at him expectantly. "Where's that liquor store?"

Flynn hauled her suitcase out to sit by the front door. She'd already showered, changed into her comfy flannel pajamas, and laid out her outfit for the next day. All that was left was waking up at six the next morning—assuming she'd sleep at all tonight, which was one hell of an assumption—and head out to the train station. Tucker had promised to come get her in the morning, but when he'd dropped her and Freya back at the Arms, he'd made excuses about having things to do tonight.

Just as well, Flynn thought. *There's no point. Stick a fork in us, we're done.*

She crossed her arms over her chest and glanced around, checking for things she'd forgotten, but the only packable things in the room were Esther's cows and the brown liquor store bag Tucker had given her when he'd dropped her off. She'd known what was inside without looking, but hadn't wanted to take it out yet. Now, alone and facing a long train ride in the morning, it seemed the perfect time.

She tossed herself down in the Nazi love seat and grabbed the bag off the end table, then pulled out the bottle of Jameson's. She twisted the cap off, tossed it over her shoulder, and raised the bottle toward the cows.

"To you, Aunt Esther," she said, then took a swig. "It was fun."

She'd meant it sarcastically, but realized as she said the words that it *had* been fun. The old inn, the rose garden, the pumpkin risotto, even the painful date with Chase and the disastrous staff meeting . . . on some level, Flynn had enjoyed them all.

But mostly, she'd enjoyed Tucker. Tucker had been loads of fun.

She lifted the bottle again and took a long swig, wincing as the fiery liquid scorched its way down. A few breaths later, though, she was feeling warm and relaxed. The tension was leaving her shoulders and she sat staring at the bottle, allowing herself to replay the greatest moments of the last few days in her head.

Like the first time they'd met, when he smirked down at her at the train station and she'd wanted to hit him. That had been good.

Swig.

And the time that he'd busted down her door to save her from certain death at the hands of Tylenol PM and peppermint schnapps. Flynn chuckled to herself and lifted the bottle.

Swig.

She closed her eyes and went back to that night in the hotel room, remembered how her heart had raced at his touch, and how the butterflies inside had taken flight whenever he kissed her.

Swig.

Not that it mattered. Butterflies schmutterflies, she was not going to be one of those women who threw her whole life away for a man she'd known for a millisecond. Those women were stupid, and nine times out of ten they ended up pregnant, abandoned, and on welfare. Well, she wasn't absolutely sure about the statistics, but she was pretty sure the general picture was accurate.

She laid her head back on the Nazi love seat and felt instantly dizzy. She set the bottle by her side and released a long, deep exhale.

She was very likely going to regret this on the train ride tomorrow.

She pushed herself up from the love seat, not sure what she was going to do. She felt restless, and at the same time heavy with exhaustion. The room had a subtle, golden glow to it and . . .

Oh. Shit.

She glanced behind her. Her body was still on the love seat. She sighed, turned, and there was Esther, standing next to her.

"So, you're on your way, huh?" she said, nodding toward the luggage.

Flynn had never seen her aunt standing up before. The woman was short, less than five feet tall. Did ghosts shrink? she wondered.

"What's the matter? Cat got your tongue?" Esther glanced behind them at Flynn's physical body, sitting up and snoring lightly on the love seat, the bottle tucked between her arm and her hip. "Hooch got your tongue looks like."

"It's been a long day, Aunt Esther," Flynn said. "Is there something I can help you with?"

For the first time that Flynn had ever witnessed, Esther smiled a little. She turned and walked to the other side of the room. Flynn wasn't sure if Esther expected her to follow, but she found herself moving along with her aunt anyway.

Esther stopped in front of the shelf, running her fingers over, and sometimes through, the little cows, her expression full of mild affection.

"The first man I ever loved gave me these cows. His name was Harold Wilbur, have you ever heard of anything more unfortunate?" She chuckled. "We were at a county fair and he kept trying to win me those cheap little prizes at the booths, you know. He spent an hour trying to toss a ring over a beer bottle to get me a goldfish." She lowered her hand. "When I went to the ladies' room with my girlfriends, he ran into an arts and crafts booth and bought me these."

Wow, Flynn thought. *He must have been really desperate.*

"What happened to him?" she asked.

"Hmm?" Esther turned her head slightly toward Flynn, but kept her eyes on the cows.

"Harold Wilbur. What happened to him?"

"Oh, yes." Esther sighed. "He went off to war a few months later. He died in France."

Flynn was silent, feeling a sudden wash of sympathy and affection for Esther, but not sure exactly how to express it. It wasn't like she could put her hand on her shoulder or anything. Could she? To test, Flynn held out one finger and started to move it toward Esther's shoulder to see if it would go through. Before she got there, though, Esther turned and stared at her.

"What are you doing?"

Flynn pulled her hand away. "Nothing."

"Right." Esther sighed, then pointed to the cows. "I want you to have these."

"Hmmm?" Flynn glanced at the cows, then back at Esther. "You want me to, what, *have* have them? Like, take-them-with-me have them?"

Esther's face hardened. "I just told you these were given to me by the man I loved and you're acting like I'm asking you to take a blanket filled with smallpox."

"No, no. I'm sorry. I just . . . I mean, they're special to you."

"I assume your family intends to sell?"

Flynn nodded, feeling oddly guilty for not having thought earlier about how that would affect Esther. Of course, Esther was dead and/or a figment of her imagination, but still . . .

Esther's eyes drifted back to the cows. "When this place is sold, someone will come in here and they will box up my cows and deliver them to the Salvation Army where they'll be parceled off one by one, and no one will ever know that they ever meant anything." She shot a look at Flynn. "You're not a great alternative, but you're the only alternative I've got."

Flynn stared at the cows, surprised at how tight her throat felt. Maybe she'd developed some affection for the old lady. Maybe she was still a little drunk.

Maybe there was something in a story of a lost, hopeless love for which she had unusual sympathy.

She cleared her throat. "I'll take them."

Esther turned to her, eyebrows raised. "You will?"

Flynn smiled. "I will."

"Good." Esther shot a look back at Flynn's body on the couch. "Just sober up before you pack them. If you break them, I'll hunt you down in Boston and you'll never be rid of me."

Chapter Fourteen

♡ Jake had barely had a chance to knock on his mother's door Sunday night before it flew open, revealing a sad-faced Mercy.

"Hey, honey," she said, pulling him into a hug. As he reached to put his arms around her, his oldest sister Liv—also redheaded but easily four inches taller than Mercy—silently took the flowers from his hand and disappeared with them.

"I'm so sorry," Mercy said, pulling back and putting a hand on his face. "I heard."

Jake tugged at his tie. "About what?"

"About the big crash in the Dow last week." She hit him on the shoulder. "About Flynn, you dope."

He rubbed his shoulder. "Way to make me feel better." He smiled. "It's cool. I took her to the train station this morning. We're friends."

Mercy grimaced. "Oh, man. Friends? Yargh."

Jake shrugged. It had been twelve hours since he'd

dropped Flynn off at the train station, but he was still having trouble getting her absence out of his mind. He'd picked up the phone to call her a dozen times, but stopped himself every time. No point in prolonging the inevitable. They weren't friends. They never would be. The clean break was better for everyone.

No matter how much it sucked.

"Oh," he said, "and I'm letting go of the whole Gordon Chase thing."

Mercy's eyes widened. "No way. Really?"

"I handed everything I've got over to Gerard Levy. As irony would have it, it turns out Gordon's just another victim in this thing. If anything, I helped clear his name."

"Wow. That's great, Jake. I mean, I'd rather Chase spent the rest of his life rotting in jail, but for you, I think it's really best, you know?" She gave him a playful punch on the shoulder. "I'm proud of you."

Jake opened his mouth to respond, but was cut off by a shout to his left.

"Oh, my God!"

Jake looked up to see his mother clutching at her chest, her fist pulling at her *Where's my goddamn drink?* apron as she leaned against the wall and faked a heart attack.

"Don't die, Penny," he said, walking over to her and setting her right as he dropped a kiss on her cheek. "You'll miss your chance to make fun of my hair."

She grinned and reached for it, scissoring it between her fingers as she lifted it away from his head.

"Such a shame," she said. "We never could do a damn thing with that mop." She faked a frown and poked him in the chest. "And don't call me Penny. I may not be able to put you over my knee, but I can hire thugs to beat you up anytime I want."

"Is that roast beef I smell?" he said, leading Mercy and his mother into the kitchen. "And where's my goddamn drink?"

His other three sisters—Liv, the tall one; Sheryl, the sweet one; and PJ, the perpetually pregnant one—fluttered about the tiny kitchen while Mercy poured a glass of wine and stuffed it in Jake's hand.

Liv kissed him on the cheek. "Nice of you to join us, butthead."

"I'll drink to that," Jake said, lifting his glass.

"Oh, stop." Sheryl wiped her hands on her apron and shot Liv a disapproving look as she walked over to give Jake a hug. "We're happy to have you back. And we've all sworn not to bring up your job or your girlfriend."

"Or lack thereof," PJ shot out. She turned around as she stirred a pot and blew Jake a kiss. "I'd come over and hug you, sweetie, but I'm afraid my water will break if I move."

"Your water's been breaking every fifteen minutes for the past six years," Jake said. "I think I can handle it."

"Okay," Mom said. "Does everyone except PJ have something alcoholic?"

The room went quiet as everyone shuffled to retrieve their drinks and PJ grabbed a glass of ice water. Once they were all quiet with drinks lifted, Mom cleared her throat.

"To George," she said, "who can't be with us tonight because God is cruel and pianos are heavy."

Everyone laughed and drank, then Liv lifted her glass.

"To Dad," she said, "who always taught us to keep

our feet on the ground, but sadly never learned to look overhead."

"Hear, hear!"

"Cheers!"

Jake felt Mercy's free hand tighten around his, and he squeezed back.

"To Dad," Sheryl said, "who appreciated wit, wisdom, and Wurlitzers."

"Oh, groan," Mercy said, giggling as she lifted her glass.

Sheryl shrugged. "Ah, I meant well."

"To Dad," PJ said, "who I know would cut me slack on the toast tonight because my ankles are swollen up like freakin' basketballs."

The girls made sympathetic noises, then Mercy lifted her glass.

"To Dad," Mercy said, "because I know that he would be really proud of all of us, but mostly me."

Everyone drank. Jake caught his sisters exchanging a few surreptitious glances of worry, and he knew this moment was up to him. He lifted his glass, and the girls smiled and followed suit.

"To Dad," Jake said, "who proved that being buried in piano cases is not just for fat people anymore."

There was a short moment of silence, and the girls burst out laughing. Mom kissed him on the cheek and PJ cursed.

"Damnit, Jake," she said, hurrying past them. "You made me wet myself."

"Uh . . . sorry," Jake called after her.

Liv tucked her arm in Jake's and put her mouth by his ear.

"She's eleven months pregnant," Liv said. "Everything makes her wet herself."

"Well, okay," Mom said, clapping her hands. "Let's get this food on the table."

Mom, Sheryl, and Liv all grabbed a dish and headed into the dining room, but Mercy grabbed Jake's hand before he could do the same.

"I know this doesn't help at all," Mercy said, "but I really think everyone would have loved Flynn."

Jake smiled and nodded. "Yeah. I think they really would have."

Mercy leaned over and hugged him. "Maybe someday they'll get the chance. You know the fat lady hasn't sung yet."

She released him, then reached up and pinched his cheek. Jake smiled, grabbed the potatoes, and let Mercy lead the way, pretty damn sure that if the fat lady hadn't sung yet, she was certainly tuning up her pipes.

Flynn rolled over in her bed, unable to get comfortable. She'd never had a problem sleeping in before, but here it was, seven o'clock on Monday morning, and she couldn't keep her eyes closed. She had planned to spend the entire day in bed, the way she had yesterday, taking breaks only for the bathroom and Ben & Jerry's, but for some reason, this morning, her brain was in a whirl. She could blame it on the new apartment, which was white and clean and antiseptic even with her old, scuffed, mismatched, garage-sale furniture.

Still, she knew she could only blame so much on environment. If she could sleep in Esther's cottage, she could sleep anywhere. It wasn't the new apartment, and it wasn't being back in Boston.

It was her head. She just couldn't stop *thinking*.

She sat up in bed and punched her fists into the blankets. The cow creamers, all lined up in a row on her dresser, caught her eye.

They were judging her.

She blinked her eyes and stared at them a little longer. She was sure it was her imagination. They were cow creamers. They were kitsch. They were not capable of judgment.

Except they were.

Harold Wilbur's cows were *judging* her.

"Oh, shut up," she said, throwing her covers back. "What am I supposed to do, huh? I mean, really, what could I possibly . . . ?"

And she trailed off. She knew what she could possibly. She'd woken up with the idea at three in the morning, and that idea was exactly why she'd been tossing and turning ever since. All she had to do was haul her ass out of bed, open up that laptop Freya'd bought her, and get to work. Make it happen. Be a doer.

Still, she hesitated. First, it was a preposterous idea and her father would never go for it in a gazillion years. Second, she was all but guaranteed to fail. Third . . .

Well, third was more complicated. Third was the reason she'd spent the entire day crying in bed yesterday. Third was why she was scared to try, because if she tried and she failed and had to go through that good-bye all over again, it would hurt too much and she'd fall apart and become a woman who lives by herself talking to a bunch of cow creamers.

Third was Tucker.

The tears came instantly and she shook them away. See, that was the reason this idea was crazy. She was overly emotional about it already. No, the only reasonable, relatively risk-free choice was to suck it up and go to work tomorrow to learn how to buy and sell properties. Or learn how to do the filing for people who bought and sold properties. Whatever. It was the choice that made sense. It was the choice she'd already made.

But still.

She let her eyes travel back to the cows, which looked up at her with disapproval and disappointment and judgment and just general crankiness.

They kinda reminded her of Esther.

She took a deep breath and closed her eyes. There were two directions in front of her, and she didn't know which one to choose.

Unable to sit still any longer, she hopped out of bed and headed down her hallway to the bathroom. She'd take a shower, that's what she'd do. Showers were warm. Showers were comforting.

Showers had answers.

And even if she finished up nowhere closer to a decision than she was right now, at least she'd smell good.

That would be a definite improvement.

Richard Daly sat in his office, staring down at the neatly composed proposal his daughter Flynn had set before him. He had to admit, if it weren't for the fact that Freya was in the middle of New York State dealing with the Goodhouse Arms crisis, he would have thought Freya had helped Flynn. But he was pretty sure she'd done it on her own, because although it was well organized and nicely presented, it still seemed she hadn't quite grasped the concept of what a financial quarter was.

Flynn let out a big sigh and leaned forward. "So, what do you think?"

Richard leaned back in his chair and eyed his daughter. "I think it's almost five o'clock on a Monday afternoon. I have a dinner meeting in an hour. I'll have to let you know tomorrow."

He pushed himself up from his chair and held his hand out to show her the door, but she stayed seated.

"No."

Richard wasn't surprised very often, but this was one of the rare occasions.

"Excuse me?"

"No. I want an answer now. And I want the answer to be yes, because I have a train to catch in the morning."

Richard stood where he was for a long moment. If it had been anyone else but Flynn, even Freya, he would have shown them the door. But something about Flynn at that moment . . . she reminded him so much of her mother . . .

He cleared his throat and sat back down.

"You've got one minute," he said. "Convince me."

Flynn hopped up off her seat and began to pace in front of him.

"Okay. Here it is. I don't know anything about business. I have no idea what the difference is between cash and accrual accounting. I actually find *accrual* very hard to pronounce. I think I'd wet myself if I ever had to actually fire someone, and the very idea of chumming it up with someone over a game of golf makes me want to toss myself off the top of a building."

Richard glanced down at his watch. "Forty-five seconds."

Flynn stopped pacing. "I'll learn. I'll learn it all, and I'll learn it with a smile on my face. I don't know what kind of profit I need to make in order to make this a viable business venture for you, but if you give me a figure, come hell or high water, I will find a way to hit it."

Flynn paused, her eyes flickering up to his as if checking for reaction. He kept his expression blank.

"Go on," he said.

"Right. See, Dad, here's the thing. I love this place." She smiled as she said the words, and her face reddened. "I mean, I know I was only there for five days, but there was this rose garden . . . and the people there were . . ."

He watched as his daughter took a deep breath, steeled herself, and met his eye, all with an effort and resolve he'd never witnessed in her before. She had changed, was confident and in charge of herself where before she'd been like a little girl in her mother's shoes. Richard felt a shock of surprise as he realized that his little girl was a grown woman now.

When had that happened?

She stood before him, her posture straight as she met his eye. "I love this place, Dad. And I know that it seems rash to base huge decisions like where I'm going to live and work on five days of experience, but . . . well, hell. People have made crazier decisions based on less than what I feel for this place and sometimes it turns out okay. Sometimes, you can't rationalize why something is right. Sometimes, you just know it, you know it in your gut and your bones that this . . ." She held her hand out, gesturing toward the proposal on the desk. "*This* is it, Dad. I can't explain why, but I just know. And if you give me this chance and it turns out not to be what I think it is, then what have you lost, really? You're going to have to invest in it anyway to get the full market value. If it doesn't work, I'll clean up my mess and move on, but if I don't do this now I will never know for sure if I was right. And I really think I'm right about this."

Richard picked up the proposal and stared at the picture of the Goodhouse Arms on the cover, then dropped it back on the desk.

"Flynn," he said, "I appreciate your passion. I really do. But when you're talking to a business person about a business decision, it can't all be passion. There need to be numbers, and projections, and I'm sorry, but some of these ideas you have for side businesses don't make sense to me. You have to understand, when you're talking about business, you have to—"

Flynn leaned over and slammed both hands down on the edge of his desk. "I don't know how to do that. And I can't learn in the next fifteen seconds. All I can say is that I deserve this chance, and I can make it work."

Her eyes filled with tears, and Richard dropped his focus back to the proposal.

"I've already decided," she went on, "that if you say no, then I'll consider it Fate's answer. I'll accept that I'm just wrong about this, and I'll go work for you, and I will do the best job I know how. So, Dad, no pressure, but you're speaking for Fate. Please be very careful about your answer. Fate's a bitch when she's pissed off."

He nodded, his focus still on the proposal. He remembered a time when Flynn's mother had made a similarly passionate and irrational plea to open her own dance studio. Richard had given in then, because he'd never been able to say no to Veronica, and it had worked. There had been no guarantees, but it had worked, and Veronica had been happy.

And that had been worth a lot.

He took a long moment to think, then tapped his fingers down on the proposal, still keeping his eyes on the picture.

"I want you out here at least once a month to deliver a full report on what's going on. We'll review your progress with the property in six months and I make no promises about what decision I'll make at that time."

He pushed up from his chair, and before he was able to bring himself to look at his daughter, she had bounced into his arms.

"Daddy, thank you, thank you, thank you," she said. "I swear, it's gonna be great. I just know it."

Richard returned the hug as best he could, and then cleared his throat as he stepped back.

"I expect you to call if you have any questions, even if you think they're stupid. This is a lot of responsibility even for someone with commensurate experience, Flynn. It's not going to be easy."

Flynn smiled. "I'm up to it."

She turned and practically danced out of his office, and Richard stood staring at the door for a long time after she'd vacated.

She reminded him so much of her mother.

Someday, he'd have to tell her that.

Chapter Fifteen

♡ Flynn pushed her way into the lobby, barely able to stop herself from giggling as she did.

"Hello," a voice called from the front desk. "Welcome to the Goodhouse Arms."

Flynn blinked. A tall brunette in a neat blue suit extended her hand from behind the front desk and smiled warmly down at Flynn.

"My name is Cherise. How may I help you?"

Flynn took her hand.

"Flynn Daly," she said. "Is my sister . . . ?"

"Oh, yes." Cherise hit a button on the phone, and after a short pause, said, "Ms. Daly? Ms. Daly is here to see you."

Cherise grinned and nodded to Flynn. "You can go on in. But I just wanted to say how nice it is to meet you. I look forward to working with you."

"Um, me, too," Flynn said, then took the corner

around the front desk and opened the office door, carefully shutting it behind her.

"Where did you find her?" Flynn asked.

Freya kept her eyes on the laptop she was working on, but took the pencil out of her mouth so she could speak. "I headhunted her from The Boston Harbor Hotel. She's brilliant, knows everything there is to know about running a hospitality business. She's costing us an arm and a leg but she's worth every damn penny. Plus, bonus, not perky."

"Yeah, she's perfect." Flynn settled into the guest chair. "So, go ahead. Tell me. How cool am I?"

Freya looked up at Flynn, her eyes smiling. "Very cool. I still can't believe you got all that past him. You pulled out the pouty face, didn't you?"

"No. I presented a lot of really good ideas, and he's even going to let me do some of them. Like the catering business, and the wedding planning, and the private investigations business."

Freya's mouth dropped open. "Bullshit."

"I'm so serious. Tucker used to be a cop, and he was really good with all that stuff with Gordon Chase. So, I thought, you know, if we use these offices and Tucker agrees to stay on as a bartender and just do the P.I. stuff on contract, there's no additional overhead, and Dad said yes!"

"Did you just say 'no additional overhead'?" Freya asked, wiping away a fake tear, then grinning. "My baby's all growed up."

"Yeah, well, keep it to yourself. I haven't told Tucker yet. I haven't seen Tucker yet. I . . . um . . . have you seen him?"

Freya stared at her. "All this for a man, and you haven't even called him to tell him you're coming back?"

Flynn straightened up, pulling on her blazer. "I didn't do it for him. I really like it here." Flynn paused. "And we're just friends, anyway."

Freya chuckled. "Yeah. Right."

Flynn sighed in exasperation. "Well? Have you seen him?"

Freya shut the laptop cover. "No. Not since we dropped you off at the train station."

"Oh. Okay. Well." Flynn sat down in the office chair across from her sister. "So, everything okay here?"

"Now's not the time." Freya shut the laptop. "Your sweet little Annabelle screwed this place but good, but I think it'll recover. I e-mailed you all the reports. You can deal with it tomorrow."

"Good." Flynn wrung her hands in her lap. "So . . . do you think I should call him? I mean, you know, I have to offer him his job back and everything, so I should call him, right?"

Freya tucked the laptop in its case. "If you don't, I'll be forced to kill you."

Flynn grinned. "Okay."

Freya leaned forward as if to push up from the desk, but then she sighed and sat back again.

"I had a panic attack," she said.

Flynn went quiet, not sure what to say. Freya focused hard on the tissue box on the far corner of the desk.

"I thought it was a heart attack, but they said I was fine. Except, you know, in the head." She gave a weak laugh, but her smile faded quickly. "I didn't want to call Dad because I didn't want him to think I couldn't handle things, and I didn't want to call you because it was the middle of the night and the idea of you coming out from Southie just made it all worse." She paused, her eyes looking tired. "And there was no one else to call because I work twenty-four/seven like I'm trying to prove something only I don't know what I'm trying to prove, you know?"

"I'm so sorry," Flynn said. "I didn't know. I mean, you always seem—"

"I know," Freya said quickly. "That's my problem." She sighed heavily, then pushed up from her seat and slung the laptop bag over her shoulder. "I'm sorry I lied to you about Dad."

Flynn got up and pulled her sister into a hug. "It's okay. I don't care."

Freya hugged her back, then sniffed and released her. "Okay, enough of this crap. Go get your bartender, before you both make me crazy." She rolled her eyes. "Crazier."

Flynn laughed, and a horn honked outside.

"There's my cab." Freya stayed where she was, staring at Flynn for a long moment, then said, "Well, don't fuck it up."

Flynn smiled. "Love you, too."

Freya huffed, then leaned in and kissed Flynn on the cheek before making a hasty exit. Flynn watched her sister leave, then shut the door to the office.

Her office. But it would wait. First she wanted to get to the cottage and freshen up. And then . . .

Tucker.

Her heart leapt at the thought of seeing him again, and she grabbed her bag and hurried out the French doors and across the courtyard to her cottage. When she saw the figure standing on the porch, she thought at first it was

Tucker waiting for her, but when he turned around and hit her in the face with a *tink*ing smile, her disappointment came with a side of cranky.

"What are you doing here?" she said as she turned the knob on the door.

"Oddly enough, looking for you."

"How did you know I'd be here?"

"I called your father this morning. I would have picked you up at the train station, but I thought that would be presumptuous. Can I talk with you for a moment?"

Flynn pushed the door open and stepped inside, hurling her bag in and reaching to flick on the light.

"Say what you have to say fast and get out, Gordon," Flynn said. "I have things to do."

"Oh, what I have to say will be worth it," he said. "Trust me."

"What the hell is going on, Mercy?" Jake asked as his sister dragged him through the back hallway between the kitchen and the bar. "It's two in the morning. If it's fucking radishes, I swear, I'll kill you."

"It's not radishes," she said. "It's better than radishes."

"Wow. Better than radishes. That really narrows it—"

They pushed through the door into the bar and he stopped talking. The jukebox was playing, but the bar was empty, except for one table set up in the middle of the room with food and candles.

And Flynn.

Mercy giggled next to him.

"Now, don't you two worry about a thing," she said. "Just enjoy your meal and my staff will come in and clean it all out in the morning. Just relax. And have fun."

She scurried over to hug Flynn quickly, and then planted a kiss on his cheek on her way out.

"Don't screw it up," she whispered into his ear, then gave him a light slap on the shoulder to accentuate her point before leaving. Jake tucked his hands in his pockets and smiled.

"Hey, there," he said.

"Hi." She stepped out from behind the table and took a few steps toward him, the waves in her hair dancing in the candlelight. "I hope this is okay. I mean, I hope it isn't too much. I know it's late, but this was Mercy's idea, and once she gets going on something, it's kind of hard to stop her. I mean, I wanted to ask you to dinner, but she thought this would be . . ." She gave a nervous laugh. "I'm sorry. If you want to go home and go back to bed, I'll totally—"

He shook his head. "I don't want to go anywhere."

She went quiet and their eyes met and locked. He reached out and took her hand, examining her fingers, so light and delicate.

And right here with him.

"When did you get back?" he asked.

"This afternoon," she said. "I would have called, but—"

"I wish you had," he said, too worn-out from the last few days to not be honest. "I've been a fucking wreck."

Her face brightened. "Oh, you have? Me, too. I mean, I couldn't sleep, I—"

He pulled her to him and kissed her, his hands reaching up to touch her face, her hair, to know that she was really here, really back. The how and why of it could wait. He needed to feel her right now, and based on her response, she needed the same thing.

Thank God.

"I'm sorry," he said when he finally pulled back to catch his breath. "I interrupted you. You were saying?"

"I talk too much anyway," she said, pulling him in for another kiss. She smelled of vanilla and tasted like raspberries and in all his life, he'd never experienced anything this good. Now all he had to do was not screw it up.

How hard could that be?

"The music stopped," he said after a while. She pulled back, her eyes heavy-lidded.

"I only had two quarters," she said.

He smiled and touched her face. "Wait here a minute." He walked over to the jukebox, emptied his pockets, and made his choice, then walked back to her as the light piano tones of Sam Cooke's "Nothing Can Change This Love" filled the room.

"Oh," she said, clasping her hands to her chest. "I love this song."

"Can't go wrong with Sam," he said, taking her hand in his and bringing her fingers up to his lips for a quick kiss. "Can I have this dance?"

She nodded. He pulled her to him, wrapping his arms around her waist.

"I was thinking about coming up to Boston," he said as they swayed together to the music. "I had this grand vision that I would go up there and say something or do something to make you come back. But I couldn't think of anything good enough, so I sat home, drank beer, and listened to Willie Nelson."

"Ohhh," she said, smiling up at him. "That's so sad."

"You have no idea," he said. "I was this close to getting a dog, buying a pickup truck, and growing my hair out into a mullet. You saved me from a terrible fate."

She reached up and touched his hair. "You'd look good in a mullet."

"I appreciate that, but no one looks good in a mullet."

"You would," she said, then laughed. "Sorry. I'm just . . . I'm really glad to see you. I missed you, even though, you know, I know that's ridiculous because how can you miss someone you've only known for—"

He put his fingers under her chin and forced her to look him in the eye. "I missed you, too."

She smiled. "Good."

They danced in silence to the rest of the song, looking into each other's eyes and smiling like a couple of giddy teenagers. Jake didn't care. He'd be a stupid giddy teenager for this woman, and consider it a damn bargain. The song ended, and they stopped moving.

"Are you hungry?" she asked after a moment. "I know it's the middle of the night, but there's wine. And pumpkin risotto, of course. I think Mercy cooked up some quail. She went to a lot of trouble."

"Let's go." He took her hand and guided her to the table, pulling her chair out for her before picking up the wine and filling their glasses.

"So, I have to tell you what happened," she said, picking up her glass.

"I was hoping you would." He sat down, enjoying the sight of her happy face, practically glowing in the candlelight.

God, she was beautiful.

"I have plans for this place. And some things I'd like to ask you about. I did this whole big proposal for my dad and he thought they were good ideas. He's given me a budget for a new bookkeeping and reservations system—"

"Oh," Jake said sadly. "No more trained monkeys?"

Flynn grinned. "Anyway, we'll get a Web site, have an online reservations system, a full-time desk staff, all that jazz. But that's the boring stuff. I had these ideas, you know, for side businesses to fill out the bottom line."

Jake chuckled. " 'Fill out the bottom line.' I don't even know what that means."

"Me neither. But Mercy and I talked, and we're going to start a catering business on the side!"

Flynn giggled in excitement, and Jake loved every second of it.

"That's great, Flynn. Wow. Mercy's gonna love that."

"We've been scheming over it all night. She'll get an extra commission on top of her salary, and an opportunity to get out in the community and make her something of a local celebrity. We're talking local media opportunities and everything. It'll be great. I'm also thinking about doing wedding planning, because that gazebo in the rose garden? I mean, who wouldn't want to get married there, right?" Her eyes widened a bit. "I mean, when the time was right and the couple has been dating for more than fifteen minutes."

Jake reached over and patted her hand. "It's okay. I know it wasn't a hint."

She gave a sigh of relief and reached for the bread. "And then, the best idea of all . . ." She nibbled her lip, seeming about ready to burst with excitement. "A private detective agency."

Jake went still with surprise. "Wow. Really?"

"I know, it seems odd, right? But here's the thing. We use the offices we've already got, the cases are totally on contract, and you can bartend whenever you're not on a case. I mean, all you have to do is get a license, and then we're in business."

Jake played with the stem of his wineglass. "Was asking me about this a part of the plan?"

"Well . . . but . . . I mean . . ." she stammered. "You used to be a cop. And when we worked together on this Gordon Chase thing, it was really fun, so I thought, 'Hey, there's almost no overhead, why not?'" She looked at him, and he could tell by her expression that she was reading his pretty clearly. "So . . . why not?"

Jake straightened his fork on the napkin. "Well, for one, this time wasn't all fun. You got shot at."

"I'm sure that was a fluke," she said. "I mean, how often does your average person get shot at, right? Maybe once in a lifetime. So my once is already out of the way."

"And, two, I haven't said I wanted to come back as the bartender," he said. "You're kind of presuming a lot."

She put her bread down on her plate. "Well, yeah, but you'll need a regular job, right? Dad says it takes a while to build up any business, but something like this is really word-of-mouth based, and so it could be a year or two before—"

"Have you been hanging out with my sisters? I can get a job on my own, Flynn. I don't need you to fix my life."

Flynn stared at him for a long time. "That's not what I was trying to do. I was just trying to figure out how to dig the Arms out of the pit."

Of course she was. Jake reached for her hand. "I'm sorry. I'm being an ass about it. I know your intentions are good, and I'm not saying we can't talk about it, I just don't want to be committed to something until I've had time to think about it."

Flynn's hand went stiff under his, and he could tell by her face that there was something else she hadn't told him.

"Flynn?" he said. "What'd you do?"

She reached for her ice water and took a big gulp, then set the glass on the table. "I got our first client."

Jake sat back in his seat, trying to take that in. "But I don't have a license yet."

"Oh," she said. "Yeah. But that's just a little itty bitty fine, right?"

"Flynn, have you committed me to solving a case without consulting me first?"

"*Us*. I committed *us*. And it's not like I went out looking for business. It just landed in my lap, like kismet. Like it was meant to be. It's a lot of money and I need things to be profitable or my dad will yank me out of here in six months and . . ." She paused, then straightened her posture. "Yes. I made the commitment. And if you don't want to do it, that's okay. I can do it myself."

"You know," Jake said, "I think you just might be the type of person who gets shot at more than once in a lifetime. It's just a feeling."

Flynn put her hand on her forehead, as if warding off a headache. "I'm just going to spit this out because you're

already pissed off and I might as well get it over with."
She lowered her hand. "The client is Gordon Chase."

Jake stared at her, feeling like the floor had just fallen
out from under him.

"You want me to help Gordon Chase?"

"He was at the cottage when I got in this afternoon.
You must have just missed him. But anyway, it turns out
that Annabelle and Rhonda stole his money, too, except
they took all of it and now he's totally screwed."

Jake opened his mouth to speak, and Flynn raised her
hand. "Which is karmically proper and totally deserved.
But it's three million dollars, Tucker, and if we get it
back for him, he's going to give us ten percent. That's
three hundred thousand dollars. That's a lot of dollars."

Jake stared down at his fork, the tines seeming to
move in the flickering candlelight. "I can do the math."

"I'll be able to replace the money that Annabelle
stole, and get Mercy's catering launched, and the wedding planning." She sat back, staring at her hands as she
played with them limply on the table. "It will almost
guarantee my success, which means I won't get yanked
out of here after six months. This case is my security,
Tucker. Do you understand that?"

He raised his eyes to hers and nodded. "Yeah. I
understand."

She smiled lightly. "Thank you. We have a breakfast
meeting at nine o'clock tomorrow."

Jake laughed and shook his head, although he wasn't
at all amused. "No, we don't. I didn't say I'd do it. I said
I understood. Those are different things, Flynn."

"Fine. Then *I* have a breakfast meeting with him
tomorrow."

Jake tried to relax his jaw and speak calmly. "Cancel it, Flynn."

"You can't tell me what to do," she said.

"Oh, but you can run my whole life? You can make me help Gordon Chase, go to breakfast with him and act like he didn't get exactly what he deserved?"

She took a deep breath. He was angry; she looked totally pissed off. He'd never seen an evening take such a sharp turn so fast. It was amazing neither of them had whiplash.

"Look, I didn't just come back here for you. I need this to work, Tucker. I need it." She shook her head and took a deep breath. "All I'm asking is for breakfast. That's all. We don't have to make a decision now, just go and hear him out."

"What you're asking is for a lot more than breakfast," Jake said. "A hell of a lot more, and you know it. I don't mind letting the whole thing go, but I'm not gonna help the asshole get his money back. No. I'm not going."

"Fine. You don't have to go. But I'm going."

"Of course you are."

They stared at each other, the room dead silent. Her eyes filled with tears and she sniffled. Jake sighed.

"Flynn—"

"I'm not hungry," she said, pushing away from the table. "Tell Mercy I'm sorry I wasted her nice dinner."

"Flynn." Jake got up to follow her, but she only moved faster, and he stopped. She obviously didn't want him to come after her, so he wouldn't. He could respect her wishes. He could see things from her point of view. He could . . .

"Goddamnit," he muttered. He walked back to the

table and picked up his wineglass, staring into it for a while before looking back up at the door Flynn had gone through. He downed the wine, then slumped down into the seat and refilled his glass. He knew she wasn't coming back, but figured it wouldn't kill him to wait.

Just in case.

Chapter Sixteen

♡ Flynn sat in the Nazi love seat and stared at the cows. She hoped Esther appreciated her bringing the creepy things back. Flynn had no idea, she'd gotten all of five minutes' sleep the night before and Esther had shown up for none of it. Every slight noise had her rushing out to the front door, sure that Tucker would be there to either apologize or accept her apology. She didn't much care which. It wasn't until the sun rose that she finally gave up hope, and by then it was too late to sleep, so she'd just run a bubble bath and sulked until she ran out of time.

She glanced at the wall clock. Eight forty-five. If Tucker didn't show up within the next fifteen minutes to stop her, she was going to that breakfast with Gordon Chase. She could find a way to make it up to Tucker, but that three hundred thousand wasn't going to be knocking on her door again. The hard part was convincing herself that it wasn't the worst sort of betrayal for her to take money from a man Tucker despised with every fiber of his being.

Although it was. And she knew it.

There was a knock at the door, shaking her from the grip of her own thoughts. She glanced at the clock and her heart sailed; eight fifty-one. Guys like Chase were never early. It had to be Tucker. Suddenly her choice seemed so clear. After all, there were other ways to make money.

There was only one Tucker.

She hopped up off the love seat and ran to the door, wording her apology in her head as she pulled the door open.

Then she saw Chase's tinking smile and wanted to throw up.

"I'm a little early," Chase said. "Are you and Jake ready?"

"No," Flynn said. "Tucker isn't here, and I've come to a decision—"

Chase stepped inside and looked around. "He's not? Wow. I was really hoping I could take the two of you out. You're both so familiar with Annabelle and Rhonda . . ."

He trailed off, looking so sad and betrayed that Flynn almost felt bad for him, but then she realized that he was probably mourning the loss of his three million more than the loss of Rhonda Bacon.

"Look, Gordon," she said. "I'm sorry. I've thought it over and we just can't do it. You really should take this to the police."

"I can't take it to the police," he said quickly. Flynn crossed her arms over her chest and stared up at him. He broke within seconds.

"Okay, see, the thing is . . ." He sighed. "How do I say

this? I'd rather not bring these particular funds to the attention of the police, if you know what I mean."

Flynn's stomach turned. "Oh, God, Gordon. It's stolen money? Are you kidding me?"

He put one hand on her shoulder. "Not stolen. Just not necessarily obtained exactly legally. Look, I really need your help. I'll double your commission. Six hundred thousand dollars. You don't have to commit now, just let me take you out for breakfast and we'll talk. Just talk."

Six.

Hundred.

Thousand.

Dollars.

Flynn sighed. He looked so pathetic, she was so broke, and it was just breakfast. A breakfast that could be the difference between her being here for six months and being here forever.

With Tucker.

She closed her eyes, clenched her teeth, and said, "Okay."

"Wonderful!" Chase grabbed her by the shoulders and kissed her on the cheek. "Thank you, thank you."

She held up one finger. "It's just breakfast. I'm not committing to anything."

"Of course, of course," he said as he held the door open for her. He walked her to the street, where his town car was parked. She reached for the passenger side door, then noticed it was filled with bags.

"Are you going somewhere?"

Chase reached for the back door handle. "Yes, I have to catch a flight this afternoon."

She watched him, a niggle of suspicion sprouting in

her gut as he guided her into the backseat. "And what's the matter with your trunk?"

He grinned and shrugged. "It's . . . full."

He shut the door and she watched as he shuffled around to the driver's side. He put the key in the ignition and started it up. Flynn reached for the door handle and pulled.

Nothing.

"Um," she said as Chase pulled out into the street. "These back doors don't open from the inside?"

Chase shot her a guilty look over his shoulder. "Child safety feature."

"You don't have kids."

Chase shrugged and turned down Main Street. "Nope."

Should have listened to Tucker. Should have listened to Tucker. Should have listened to Tucker. She had a brainstorm, and reached into her purse, riffling through it but coming up empty.

"They're right here," Chase said, holding up her cell phone and her Mace key chain.

Stunned, Flynn looked back in her bag. "How did you do that?"

"I'm a thief and a liar," he said. "I have skills."

Skills, she thought as she watched the lovely country pass by her window. *Uh-huh.*

"You gonna tell me where we're going at least?" she asked finally.

He met her eyes in the rearview. For what it was worth, she could tell he was at least mildly conflicted.

"There are some men in this world who can be poor,

Flynn," he said as they pulled onto the highway. "I don't happen to be one of them."

"Damnit," Jake said and snapped his cell phone shut. Flynn wasn't answering at home, and her cell was going to voice mail. He'd left a few messages, but didn't tell her exactly what he was doing. He figured, after what he'd put her through the night before, it was the sort of thing better said in person. He leaned forward in the backseat of the Suburban and tapped Gerard Levy on the shoulder.

"About how much longer before we get there?" he asked.

Gerard glanced at his watch. "Forty minutes, maybe."

"And you're sure they're both there, right?"

"We can't be sure of anything. We activated the Lo-Jack on a car we think they might have stolen. I've got a good feeling about it, but who the hell knows?" Gerard eyed Jake suspiciously. "Look, Jake, I called you out of courtesy. My ass could very easily get burned for bringing you along."

"If it's any comfort," Jake said, "I'm a private detective now. It's for an official case."

Gerard huffed. "Who's the client?"

Jake shook his head. "You wouldn't believe me if I told you."

Gerard chuckled. "Okay, I know I've said this before, but I'm saying it again. SWAT goes first in case they're armed, then once they've secured the place, I go in. When I give you the okay, you get fifteen minutes with them to get your information, and you're gone like you were never there, you get me?"

Jake nodded, flipped his phone open again, and started to dial.

"I got you."

He put the phone to his ear and sat back again.

Hi. You've reached Flynn Daly. I'm sorry I'm not here to take your call—

"Damnit," Jake said, and snapped the cell phone shut.

Flynn blinked as her eyes adjusted to the dim light in the small house. Chase's shoulder was digging into her gut and she wished she'd eaten before she left just so she could boot all over his backside.

"Bastard asshole," she grunted, struggling against him again, but unfortunately, Chase was stronger than he looked. She had made his extracting her from the car a royal pain in the ass—she highly doubted he'd be having sex again in the near future—but in the end, he'd clocked her in the head and knocked her out, and by the time she woke up, she was over his shoulder, being hauled up a dirt path with nothing but trees and a downward view of Chase's bastard ass to focus on.

She tried to look for some defining characteristics in the landscape, but didn't catch any. She knew they were somewhere in the Catskill Mountains, but they'd traveled on little side roads for so far that she'd completely lost her bearings. Even if she got away from Chase and got her cell phone—if she could get service way out here, which was unlikely—she wouldn't know what to tell the police.

Or Tucker.

She closed her eyes and banished all thoughts of Tucker. If she thought of him, she'd get all emotional, and she needed to maintain her pissed-off-ness if she was going to stand a chance against Chase.

They moved up a porch and Flynn heard the sound of a door opening.

"Ooompth!" she said as Chase tossed her down on the old wood floor. She started for the door, but Chase grabbed both of her arms and held her in place. She managed to get a good grunt out of him when she jabbed at him with the heel of her boot, but it wasn't nearly as gratifying as the kick to the balls she'd delivered earlier.

Ah. Good times.

"Annabelle!" he called. "We're here!"

"Oh, you're kidding me!" Flynn yelled. "You're delivering me to Annabelle McCrazy?"

"And then she gives me my McMoney, yes," he said. "Sorry, Flynn. I like you and everything, but I don't do poor."

"Where's Jake?"

Chase whirled around, taking Flynn with him, and they both came face-to-face with Annabelle holding a gun on them.

"Crap on a cracker," Flynn muttered.

"Hey, Flynn!" she said, smiling brightly. "I'm so sorry about all this, but there just wasn't any other way. I promise it'll all be over soon, though, okay?"

Chase shoved Flynn down on the couch that sat between him and Annabelle, and pointed a finger at her.

"She's crazy, but she's a good shot. Don't move." He turned to Annabelle. "Where's Rhonda?"

"She's in a car out back, waiting for you," Annabelle said. "Where's Jake?"

"He didn't make it," Chase said. "Now give me my money."

"Oh, man," Annabelle said. "I need Jake."

"Call him. Tell him you've got a gun on Flynn. He'll be here in a shot."

Annabelle thought on that for a moment, then shrugged. "Yeah. I guess that'll work, too."

"My money?" Chase said.

"Rhonda has all the information." Annabelle tossed him a set of keys. "You don't take her, you don't get your money. You know the drill."

Chase gave her a look of pure loathing. "You both are insane."

Annabelle smiled at him, but the smile didn't quite reach her eyes. "Tick tock, Gordon. You're losing interest as we speak."

Chase muttered something under his breath, then turned and rushed out the door. Annabelle grinned and bounced over to sit on the other end of the couch from Flynn, the gun trained on her.

"Poor Rhonda," Annabelle said. "It's so sad, you know? And she could have done so much better. A nice haircut, a little lipstick, she really could have been something, you know?"

Something niggled at the back of Flynn's brain. "Could have been?"

No sooner were the words out of her mouth than a tremendous boom came from outside, followed by a second, smaller explosion. Annabelle used one hand to pull back the curtains, then giggled.

"Oh, yay!" she said. "It worked!" She let the curtains fall back. "I got the plans off the Internet, and you just never know how those things are going to go. Good thing there's nobody around for five miles or there'd be cops all over this place, and that'd be no good." She nodded toward the window. "Wanna see?"

Flynn tucked one finger behind the curtain, her heart pounding in her chest. Outside she could see the dark outline of a car engulfed in flames at the far edge of the driveway.

"Holy shit," she said, and pulled her shaking hand back from the curtain.

"Cost of doing business," Annabelle said, a sad look on her face. Then, suddenly, her expression brightened and she tapped Flynn on the knee with her free hand. "Hey, wanna make a phone call?"

They'd just pulled off the highway when Jake's phone rang. He yanked it out of his pocket, not bothering to check the caller ID.

"Flynn?" he asked. "Where have you been?"

"I think where I am is probably more important." Her voice was blank and flat. Was she still pissed off at him? Probably. And she had a right. He could only hope she'd get over it when he told her what he was doing.

"How did the breakfast go?" he asked.

"Not well."

Jake felt the first strings of alarm ripple through him. "Flynn? Are you okay?"

"Ow! Quit it!" she said, her voice remote, and then louder, "Tucker? You still there?"

Jake gripped the phone tight in his hand. "Flynn? What's going on? Where are you?"

Flynn rattled off an address and Jake's heart sank. He tapped Gerard on the shoulder.

"Punch it," he said.

"What?"

"They've got Flynn!" he yelled. Gerard tapped the driver and gave a small nod, and the sirens went on.

"Flynn?" he said into the phone.

"She says no cops," Flynn said. "Just you."

"All right," Jake said, making eye contact with Gerard. "Fine. No cops."

Gerard motioned for the driver to shut the sirens off.

"Flynn, what happened?"

She sighed. "Well. It turns out I was right about Annabelle being in love with you. And you were really right about Chase." He heard her voice crack. "But we don't have to worry about him anymore, because he's dead."

"He's what?"

"He's dead. So is Rhonda."

He shook his head, trying to put the pieces together in his head. "You mean Annabelle's got you?"

"She's a CWIL with a gun. The worst kind."

A gun? Jake rubbed at the back of his neck. "Flynn, I'm coming, okay? I'm already on my way. You just hang in there. I'm coming."

"I'm so sorry, Tucker, I—"

The phone cut off.

"Flynn? Flynn!"

Silence. Jake slammed his phone shut and put his face in his hands, trying to stay calm. Annabelle wanted Jake, so she wouldn't hurt Flynn until Jake got there. And once Jake was there, he could protect Flynn. So it was going to be fine. It was going to be fine.

". . . phone number? Jake!"

He raised his head to find Gerard yelling something at him.

"What?"

"Did you get the phone number?"

Jake opened his phone and scrolled through the ID list, then nodded.

"Good," Gerard said. "We're gonna need that when we get there."

He opened his own cell and made a call. Jake caught random words like "negotiator" and "hostage situation" but mostly all he heard was Flynn's voice.

I'm sorry, Tucker.

He'd bet his life he was sorrier.

"Breathe into this," Annabelle said, holding out a small paper bag to Flynn. Flynn reached out a shaky hand and took it, breathing into it slowly as Annabelle sat down next to her. She had been able to hold on to her pissed-offness until she'd heard the panic in Tucker's voice when he'd told her he was coming for her. If Tucker was worried, she knew she was good and screwed.

"He loves me, you know," Annabelle said, rubbing Flynn's back with one hand while holding the gun on her with the other. "I've been there for him all along. Eileen wasn't supposed to get him fired. She was just supposed to get the laptop. She did it on purpose, you know. Went after him like that. She was always jealous of me."

Flynn pulled the bag away from her face. "You know, if you want me to calm down, maybe you could cool it with the crazy, okay?"

Annabelle pushed up from the couch. "I'm sorry,

Flynn. I know you have feelings for him, too. And I never wanted you to get hurt in this. Chase got what he deserved for hurting Jake the way he did and Rhonda . . . well, poor Rhonda was just never going to get it, you know? But you . . . you're an innocent. And I know that, but you have to understand that he loves *me*, okay?"

Flynn tried to resist opening her mouth, but the shock of knowing that two dead people were charbroiling in the driveway had put her in a very surreal, very stupid place.

"So, what's your plan? You put a gun to my head and make him tell you he loves you? Of course he's going to do it. It won't make it true."

She put the bag back over her mouth, concentrating on the crinkling sound it made when she breathed to keep herself from passing out.

"Oh, honey." Annabelle stared down at her. "You are nobody. You're a blip on the radar. Before you came, everything was fine. He would have asked me out ages ago, but Esther told him not to."

Flynn gasped into the bag, and lowered it again. "Holy shit. You killed Esther, didn't you?"

Annabelle's eyebrows knit for a second, but then she smiled in understanding. "Oh, not for that. She'd been snooping in my books, which meant that sooner or later she would have figured out what I was doing, and let me tell you, I did not want to go back to jail. Do you know what kind of girls are in jail? Girls like Eileen Dietz." She sat down next to Flynn again and patted her knee. "I was so freaked out when I thought you'd had the schnapps, by the way. You, they would have autopsied, and it would have been hell to explain an overdose of heart medication with you."

Flynn felt her chest explode with rage. "You crazy bitch."

Annabelle stood up and put her hand to her chest, tears springing to her eyes.

"There's no need to get personal," she said. "I just did what I had to do, Flynn. Do you think I like this? Do you think I feel good about this? I don't. I'm just doing what I need to do. This has been really difficult for me, you know."

Flynn raised the bag to her face and concentrated on breathing in and out.

In and out.

In and out.

Annabelle paced back and forth, whispering something to herself that Flynn couldn't hear over the crinkling of the bag. Which was just as well.

Because the bitch was crazy.

Jake had darted out of the car before the Suburban came to a complete stop, and was oddly surprised when he felt Gerard yank him backward.

"The negotiator isn't here yet." Gerard put both hands on Jake's shoulders, clamping down tight. "You wait."

"Fuck the negotiator." He stared up the dirt road. According to the map, the house was less than half a mile away. Through the autumn-thinned woods, he could see the outline of a white house, and a column of thick black smoke.

"Jesus Christ," he muttered.

"I know this is hard, but this is not your operation, Jake," Gerard said. "There are people coming who know how to handle this type of situation. Unless you want to get Flynn killed, you need to let them."

Jake broke free of Gerard's grip, but didn't run up the dirt path. Instead he focused his rage and kicked a sizable dent into the side of the Suburban.

"I'll pay for that," he said.

"Don't worry about it." Gerard stepped closer and put one hand on Jake's shoulder. "We'll convene here, make the call, and send you up once we have proof of life. That's the plan."

Proof of life. The words sliced through him, but he nodded.

"Yeah," he said. "Yeah. Okay."

Jake's cell phone rang. He exchanged a glance with Gerard, then checked the caller ID. He held it up for Gerard to see and answered off his nod.

"Flynn? You okay?"

Annabelle's voice bounced through the line at him.

"Jake! It's so good to hear your voice."

"Is Flynn okay?"

"Oh, she's fine, but . . . sweetie, I said no cops. Didn't she tell you no cops? We can't really talk this out if there are police around. I won't be able to concentrate, and I have some really important things to say."

He shook his head at Gerard, and Gerard closed his eyes and swore. "I'm sorry, Annabelle. They were with me when you called."

Annabelle sighed. "It's okay. It's not your fault. But they know I've got Flynn, right? And a gun? And they know I'll kill her, right?"

"Annabelle," he said, "don't."

"I don't want to," she said. "But I will if I have to. Can

you tell them to go away and then come on up alone?
We're kinda running out of time."

"Let her go, Annabelle. I'll be on my way as soon as I
know she's safe."

"Jake, if she's safe, those policemen are gonna come
and get me and then we won't have any time to talk. I'm
so sorry, I just can't. You understand, right?"

He leaned one hand on the Suburban and dropped his
head, clutching the phone to his ear. "I need to talk to her
first. I need—"

"Oh, what? Proof of life?" Annabelle giggled. "Right.
I saw that movie. Here."

There was some shuffling, followed by a strange crack-
ling sound, and then, finally, he heard Flynn's voice.

"Tucker?"

Every muscle in Jake's body tightened. "I'm on my
way. Nothing is going to happen to you, okay?"

"Chase is dead. Did I tell you that? I told you that,
didn't I? So is Rhonda. And Annabelle? Is crazy."

Jake's heart cracked listening to her. She sounded so
scared. He tried to inject calm into his voice. "Yeah, babe.
I know. It's gonna be okay."

"Chase said she was a good shot. I'm inclined to believe him."

Jake flashed back to the night in the cabin.

So, who shot at us?

*A bad shot who tried to kill us and then got scared off,
or a good shot who wanted to send a message.*

"I think maybe I should have stayed in Boston," she
said.

"I'm going to get you out of this," he said. "Nothing is
going to happen to you."

"Hi! Me again!" Annabelle's voice came back on the line. "Jakey, you really have to send the police away. I'm so sorry. Look, I'll give you one minute, okay? Starting . . . *now!*"

Jake flipped the phone shut. "Go. Now."

"Jake—"

"Game's over, Gerard. If you stay here, Flynn dies. And the only way you're going to stop me from going up there is to shoot me yourself. It's your operation. Your call."

Jake was halfway to the house when he heard the Suburban pull away behind him.

Flynn folded up the paper bag neatly and set it by her side. Her breathing had returned to normal. She found that she could forget the smell of the burning car outside by concentrating on the shapes of the water stains in the ceiling.

One of them looked kinda like Vladimir Putin.

Annabelle put down the binoculars and shoved the heavy drapes shut over the window, settling the room into a dark gloom that seemed appropriate.

"Oh, yay! They're gone," Annabelle said. "Thank God. That could have been so messy, you know?"

Flynn nodded. Finally, the urge to talk back had left her. She knew that Jake would be walking through that door in a moment, and he would save her and then some lucky therapist's kid was going to be lousy with ponies off of Flynn's monthly bill.

See? she thought. *Everyone wins.*

There was a knock at the door. Annabelle smoothed her

hand over her long blond curls and grinned like a teenager on prom night.

"Come in!" she called, and stood next to Flynn.

The first thing Jake saw was Flynn sitting on the couch, her hands tucked primly between her knees. He started for her, but froze when he saw the gun, which Annabelle raised and pointed directly at Flynn's head.

"I'm sorry, Jake," Annabelle said, "but we're kinda running out of time, so I need you to tell her."

Jake stared at Annabelle. "Tell her what?"

Annabelle laughed, but her smile soon faded. "That you don't love her. That you love me. Then I'll have to kill her, which is a shame, but we can get away, and I have scads of money. I've got two tickets on a flight to Buenos Aires that leaves in . . ." She checked her watch and made a face. "Oooh. Three hours. That's kinda tight. So . . . go ahead."

"Wait," Jake said, holding his hand out. "Annabelle, I'm not going to let you kill her."

"I know. It sounds horrible, I know. But these people, they kind of deserve it. Esther was going to send me to jail, which is not nice. Eileen made you lose your job. Gordon Chase was a complete waste of humanity. Rhonda betrayed the man she loved just to get him to love her back, which, yeah, that was my advice, but she took it, you know? And Flynn . . ." She looked at Flynn and sighed. "I liked Flynn, but she tried to take you away from me, so this is really her own doing."

Keeping her eyes on Jake, Annabelle cocked the gun. He held his hands up.

"Don't, Annabelle," he said. "I'll go with you. Fine. Just don't shoot."

Annabelle leaned her head a little to one side, looking like a dog who was unsure what she had to do to get the treat. "But you don't love her, right? I mean, it's always been me, right? The only reason why you and I aren't together is because Esther told you not to ask me out, right?"

"What are you talking about?" Jake said. "Esther and I never talked about you."

"But you did. She told me. She said that you liked me, but Esther told you not to ask me out because she didn't want employees dating."

Jake shook his head. "Annabelle, she never told me not to ask you out."

Annabelle's face contorted in confusion. "What? Well, then . . . why . . . ?"

Flynn sighed. "She was being *nice*. She probably knew Jake would never ask you out and she felt sorry for you, you freakin' whackjob."

"Flynn," Jake said, warning tight in his voice. "Why don't you let me do the talking?"

Flynn threw her arms down at her sides. "I'm gonna die. I need to bite my tongue, too?"

Annabelle's eyes filled with tears, and the gun shook slightly in her hand. "It's not true, Jake. It's not true. You love me. You just . . . Esther . . ."

"Christ, Annabelle," he said, trying to keep his voice even. "You don't have to kill her. I've only known her for a week. I've known you a lot longer than that and I do care about you. But we need to talk this out, and I can't talk if a gun is pointed at someone. Put it down."

"See?" Annabelle said, her hand steadying as she held the gun on Flynn. "I told you he didn't love you."

Jake glanced at Flynn, and she met his eyes and gave him a slight, knowing smile.

Give them what they most want, or show them what they most fear.

"No," he said, but Flynn had already stood up.

"If you're gonna shoot me, Annabelle, then quit the sniveling and shoot me," she said. "But if you think for a minute that Jake is ever going to love you, you're batshit crazy."

"Ignore her, Annabelle. Look at me," Jake said, sidling closer. Annabelle's focus was totally on Flynn. If he could just get between Flynn and the gun . . .

"You're so obsessed with whether he loves me or not. Who cares? What does it matter? I'm not your problem, Annabelle. Your problem is you. He's never going to love you, whether I'm in the picture or not. That's all there is to it. It's just never going to happen."

Jake watched as Annabelle tucked a shaking finger inside the trigger.

"Get down!"

Flynn took the cue and darted to the floor just as Jake bent down and launched himself at Annabelle's midsection. The gun went off and chunks of ceiling fell over them.

"Flynn! Get out!" he yelled as he grabbed for Annabelle's hand, grasping it by the wrist as the gun went off again. He heard a crash and a scream behind him.

"Flynn?!?" He tried to look for Flynn, but Annabelle almost got free from under him.

"He loves me!" she screamed, her eyes wild. She

cracked him in the head with the gun, and he grabbed her wrist and banged it against the floor as hard as he could. He heard the crack of bones, and Annabelle screamed. The gun slid from her grip and without letting her go, he shifted one leg out to kick it out of her reach.

He put one hand on the floor to push himself up off of her, but hands grabbed him and pulled him away before he could get to his feet. The hands released him and he realized that they belonged to two SWAT guys. He had no idea when the cops had come in, but the room was suddenly filled with uniforms. He turned around and frantically searched the room.

"Flynn!"

He felt a hand on his shoulder, and whipped around to see Flynn behind him. He pulled her to him, one hand cradling the back of her head as he held her tight, drinking in the feel of her alive in his arms.

"Thank God you're okay." He pulled back, holding her by her upper arms and glancing over her body. "Are you okay?"

She smiled, then slowly shook her head. "Don't think so."

She bucked in his grip, and that's when he felt the slipperiness under his left hand. He put his right arm around her waist to catch her.

"I need a medic!" he yelled as he guided her to the couch.

"On the way!" a voice yelled back.

"I'm shot," Flynn said, her voice high and calm. "I'm pretty sure I've been shot."

Jake leaned over her right arm, trying to get a good

look in the dim light. All he could see was a growing dark patch on the sleeve of her sweater.

"Flynn . . ." He glanced over his shoulder and shouted, "A medic! Now!"

He rolled up the sleeve of her sweater and used it to put pressure on her arm, blocking out her gasp of pain as he did what needed to be done. The blood seeped out from under his hand, dripping into a small pool on the couch. It was a lot of blood, and it was coming fast; Annabelle had hit an artery.

"You don't look good, Tucker," she said.

"I'm fine." He raised his eyes to hers and forced a smile. "You're gonna be fine, too. I've seen worse paper cuts."

"Oh, I'll bet." Her voice was frail. "Hey, Tucker. You wanna hear something funny?"

"Always." He kept the pressure on her arm, and tried to look casual. "What is it?"

"I love you."

He looked up, not sure how to respond, not even sure if he heard her right.

She chuckled. "Don't worry. I'm not gonna shoot anyone over it or anything."

"Flynn . . ."

A light smile fluttered on her face. "I know it's only been a week, but there are people getting crispy in a car outside and I was held at gunpoint and it occurs to me that life is just too freakin' short, you know? I love you, and I just want you to know that."

Tucker bit the inside of his cheek and concentrated on maintaining the pressure on her wound. "Anything you need to tell me, there will be plenty of time to tell me later."

She raised her good arm and put her hand on his wrist.

"I want you to know now. Just in case—"

"Knock it off, Flynn." He looked her in the eyes. "You're gonna be fine."

"Oh. Of course."

He reached up with his free hand and touched her cheek. "When you wake up on the other side of this, after I give you a healthy ration for scaring the shit out of me, I'll tell you that I love you, too."

"You don't have to say that," she said. "It's okay."

"Flynn . . ." His voice shook on her name and he took a moment to steady it. "Flynn, if I was the kind of guy who'd say that when he didn't mean it, I would have said it to Annabelle."

She thought on that for a second, then offered a weak smile. "Good point."

Even in the dim light, he could see how pale her face was, and it scared the shit out of him. He smoothed some hair away from her face, and stared into her eyes, anchoring himself in them. "I'm not just saying it, Flynn. I love you."

"Well, yeah," she said, smiling. "I mean, who wouldn't?"

Then her eyes closed and Jake turned his head toward the door and screamed, *"Where is my fucking medic?"*

Chapter Seventeen

♡ Flynn glanced behind her at her body, lying still in the hospital bed. Then her eyes went to Tucker, sleeping by her bedside, one hand resting on her lower arm to alert him if she moved. It was dark out, way past visiting hours, but he was there. She smiled. All that stuff they say about unconscious people knowing their loved ones are with them? It was true.

Huh. Dig that.

Flynn sensed someone at the foot of her bed, and turned her attention away from Tucker to see Esther standing next to her bed.

Wow. That woman was really short.

But something was different about her. She looked younger. Happier. And unlike all their other visits, the light that accompanied her was white.

Flynn smiled. "You're here."

"Of course I'm here." She motioned toward the sleeping Flynn. "Did you think I'd miss this?"

"Guess not." She watched Esther's smiling face for a moment, overwhelmed by affection and sadness.

This day had been just full of surprises.

"So," she said, feeling an odd lump in her throat despite the fact that she was disembodied at the moment, "I assume by the fact that you're here and not in the cottage that you're free now?"

Esther nodded. "I am."

"Because I solved your murder, right? I freed you, didn't I? How much are you digging me right now?"

"Less and less as time goes on," Esther said, but then smiled and nodded toward Tucker. "You should wake up. Put the poor man out of his misery."

"I've tried," Flynn said. "I can't. I think it's the drugs."

"Okay. Well. Since we've got a minute . . ." Esther paused, daintily smoothing out the sleeves of her ghostly dress. "I'd like to say that despite how rude you were to me, I have risen above it, and I left something for you."

Flynn bopped up on the bed. "Oh! Is it a ghost pony? I've always wanted one of those."

"No," Esther said, pursing her lips.

"Well? Where is it? I want my gift."

"You'll get it soon, and when you do, you'll know it's from me."

Before she could remember that they were both disembodied, Flynn reached out for Esther's hand, and was surprised to feel it solidly there. It was warm, and the white glow spread to encompass Flynn's fingers as Esther squeezed back.

"Wow," she said, sniffling. "Those are some powerful drugs. I'm kinda sad to see you go."

"If you work on that mouth of yours," Esther said, her

eyes misting a bit themselves, "you might just turn out okay."

Flynn laughed, gave Esther's hands one last squeeze, and released them. "Tell Harold Wilbur I said hi."

Esther nodded, then turned and walked away.

Crazy old goat, Flynn thought as she wiggled her fingers in the direction of the wall Esther had just walked through. *I'll miss you.*

I heard that, Esther's disembodied voice called faintly.

Flynn's vision went black, and her body felt suddenly heavy. She took in a deep breath and opened her eyes.

She was in the hospital room. Awake. Alive.

Tucker stirred in the seat next to her, as if sensing her consciousness. He lifted his head and smiled when his eyes met hers.

"Hey," he said, his voice soft.

"Hey yourself," Flynn croaked, then coughed against the scratchiness in her throat. Tucker grabbed a pitcher from the bedside tray, poured her a cup of water, and sat on the bed, holding it out for her to drink. When she was done, he put it on the tray and looked down at her.

"How are you doing?" he asked.

"I don't know. How am I doing?"

"You're gonna be fine." He gave a weak smile. "The, uh, the bullet hit an artery, and you lost some blood. A lot of blood, actually. They medevacked you out here to Albany and put you in surgery and they, uh, they fixed you. Your arm's gonna be sore. It'll be a while before you can play golf again."

"I hate golf."

"Hey, well, then it's a win."

Flynn took a deep breath. "How are you? Are you okay?"

Tucker raised his eyes to hers and she could see the answer to that question.

"Tucker . . ."

"Well," he said, lowering his eyes again, "I tell ya, I don't know what I'm gonna do to top this. First I get you shot at, and then I get you actually shot. I'm really struggling to figure out what our next date should be. How do you feel about naked skydiving without a parachute?"

"I like the naked part." She reached out and put her hand on his. "You know this isn't your fault, right?"

He huffed. "Then whose fault is it?"

"Annabelle's," Flynn said. "Speaking of which, they took her down, right?"

"Yep. She's rotting in a cell as we speak."

Flynn smiled, but Tucker's face didn't reveal the slightest trace of amusement.

"Hey," she said. "Stop it with the miserable, okay?"

"All you asked was for breakfast. If I had gone—"

"Hey," she said forcefully. He raised his eyes to hers, and once she knew she had his attention, she smiled. "Never happened."

"What?" he said, his voice an incredulous whisper.

She spoke slowly, so he'd know she meant what she was saying. "It. Never. Happened."

"Flynn, that doesn't work here. You could have—"

"Look," she said, "we can sit here and torture ourselves about it. I can feel bad that I very easily could have gotten you killed, and you can feel bad that I got a glorified paper cut, wc can talk it to death and hope we come out okay on the other end . . ."

Tucker allowed a small smile at this, and Flynn wound her fingers in his.

". . . or we can agree that it never happened, you can kiss me, and we can move on."

Tucker stared at her for a long moment, his eyes glimmering in the dim moonlight.

"Flynn . . ."

"I think you know my vote."

Finally, Tucker smiled, leaned forward, and kissed her lightly on the lips, but pulled back way too soon.

"Good. We're agreed," she said.

"Yeah." He rubbed his hand over his eyes, obviously tired. "Um, Freya and your dad were here, but I sent them back to the hotel to get some rest."

"My dad was here?"

Tucker nodded. "Yeah. He flew in the second we got a hold of him."

"Wow," Flynn said. "Good."

"Yeah," Tucker said, smiling, "I told the nurses I was your brother so they'd let me stay."

Flynn laughed. "Well, how's that gonna look when they walk in on us making out?"

Tucker chuckled. Flynn reached up with her good arm and grabbed a fistful of his shirt, pulling him down toward her for a long, comforting kiss. A moment later he pulled back and smiled down at her, and finally the darkness was out of his eyes and the perma-smile settled on his lips and he started to look like her Tucker.

My Tucker, she thought, and she shivered under the force of the emotion that rushed through her.

"Are you cold?" He hopped up off the bed and grabbed a bag from under the bed.

"I'm fine. Come back."

He lifted the bag up, set it at the foot of her bed, and riffled through it. "No, when your dad and Freya were here with you, I got a little restless, so I drove back to the Arms and got some of your stuff. You know, the comfort of the familiar aiding with the healing process and all that stuff. Ah, here we go."

He pulled out the purple afghan. *Esther's* purple afghan. Flynn had seen it so many times, and it had never once occurred to her that it would be real.

But of course it was.

She laughed and took it from him, amazed at how soft it was under her fingers. "Oh, my God. Where'd you get that?"

He glanced at it, confused, then looked back at her. "It was in the bottom drawer of the armoire. It's yours, right?"

Flynn stared at it for a long moment, then reached out and took Tucker's hand in hers.

"Yeah," she said, swiping at a happy tear. "It's mine."

About the Author

LANI DIANE RICH lives in upstate New York with her husband, Fish, and two daughters, Sweetness and Light. (Names changed to protect the innocent. Although the husband knew what he was getting into.) She grew up in a small town in the mid-Hudson Valley very much like Shiny, but that's where her life and the setting and events of *Crazy in Love* diverge. For instance, Lani has never been shot at, she's never had chats with dead relatives, and she's never inherited a multimillion-dollar hospitality business. If she had, this book would have taken a lot longer to write. So, it worked out for everyone.

Lani can be found on the Internet at her Web site (www. lanidianerich.com) and at Literary Chicks, the group blog she shares with Michelle Cunnah, Eileen Rendahl, Beth Kendrick, Whitney Gaskell, and Alesia Holliday (www. literarychicks.com). You can contact Lani at lani@lani dianerich.com. She thanks you for buying this book, and thinks you are very, very pretty.

THE DISH

Where authors give you the inside scoop!

♥ ♥ ♥ ♥ ♥ ♥ ♥ ♥ ♥ ♥ ♥ ♥ ♥ ♥ ♥

Book Group with
Lani Diane Rich, Diana Holquist,
Eve Silver, and Mrs. McGrunt

Mrs. McGrunt: Welcome to the Liverpool Public Library. We're here to discuss *War and Peace* by Leo Tolstoy . . .

Diana Holquist: Oh, about that. See, I kind of got to reading Lani Diane Rich's new release *Crazy In Love* (available now) and I couldn't put it down.

Eve Silver: No way! Me too! The one about Flynn Daly who inherits a historic inn *and* her dead aunt's ghost. Awesome.

Diana Holquist: And that cute bartender, Jake. That scene where he picks her up at the train station and pretends he's not there for her—the sparks really fly!

Lani Diane Rich: You know, that actually happened to me.

Eve: The cute guy, the sparks, or the train station?

Lani: Okay, none of it. But I wish it did.

Diana: Especially the cute guy . . .

Mrs. McGrunt: *War and Peace*, ladies! Now, on page 797 . . .

Lani: Did anyone read Eve Silver's *Demon's Kiss* (available now)?

Diana: Is that the one with long, confusing Russian names?

Eve: God no. My sexy new release is about Ciarran D'Arbois, a lethal, seductive sorcerer determined to save the world from demons while saving himself from the darkness invading his soul.

Diana: Oh, I loved *Demon's Kiss*! The demons try to use Clea Masters to break down the wall between the human and demon realms.

Lani: And Clea unwittingly threatens everything Ciarran is. She steals his magic—and his heart.

(Deep sigh from all three authors.)

Mrs. McGrunt: Ladies? *War and Peace*?

Lani: Ya know, in Diana's new book *Sexiest Man Alive* (available now), Jasmine has a major war with herself when she finds out that the one man on earth destined to be her "one true love" is the world's hottest movie star. She thinks there's no way she can live that sort of life.

Eve: She sure does find peace in his bed for a while.

Lani: And satisfaction. And bliss.

Diana: And a Ken doll. Er, guess you gotta read the book to understand that part.

Eve: But when the paparazzi catch them and everything falls apart—it was so touching.

Mrs. McGrunt: Touching *and* sexy! Those gypsies sure know how to ride the wild fantastic! That young man on the cover in his teeny towel sizzles. Hoo-ah! You don't even have to open *Sexiest Man Alive* to enjoy it. *Hey, big boy, I'll hold that towel for you* . . .

Lani, Diana, Eve: Mrs. McGrunt!

Mrs. McGrunt: Okay, okay, so I didn't read *War and Peace* either. I was going to, but then I saw Lani's *Crazy in Love*. How hot was that love scene in the cabin, huh? And Eve's *Demon's Kiss* just had me from the start. I'm such a sucker for a dark, tortured hero. And then, I had to re-read that scene in Diana's *Sexiest Man Alive* where they're backstage and . . . well, wowza!

Lani: Let's blow this stuffy library, get a latte, and discuss some hot, sexy, fun romance novels.

Eve: I'm there! And all you readers should join the group by reading these three awesome new releases.

Diana: They're all on the shelves this month. So don't miss a single one.

Mrs. McGrunt: Okay, ladies, let's make a break for it! We can hide behind this enormous *War and Peace* tome. Cover my back. Go! Go! Go!

Happy reading (and discussing)!

Love,

Lani, Eve, and Diana

Lani Diane Rich

Eve Silver

Diana Holquist

www.lanidianerich.com
www.evesilver.net
www.dianaholquist.com

More Forever romances . . .
From authors who'll make you laugh
And fall in love . . .

Lori Wilde

"A unique voice that will soar to publishing heights."
—*Rendezvous*

THERE GOES THE BRIDE
0-446-61845-4

YOU ONLY LOVE TWICE
0-446-61516-1

MISSION: IRRESISTIBLE
0-446-61515-3

LICENSE TO THRILL
0-446-61366-5

CHARMED AND DANGEROUS
0-446-61367-3

Kelley St. John

"Fast-paced, sexy, and witty."
—*Booklist* on *GOOD GIRLS DON'T*

TO CATCH A CHEAT
0-446-40122-6

REAL WOMEN DON'T WEAR SIZE 2
0-446-61721-0

GOOD GIRLS DON'T
0-446-61720-2

AVAILABLE WHEREVER BOOKS ARE SOLD.

*Want to know more about romances at
Grand Central Publishing and Forever?
Get the scoop online!*

GRAND CENTRAL PUBLISHING'S
ROMANCE HOMEPAGE

Visit us at www.hachettebookgroupusa.com/romance
for all the latest news, reviews, and chapter excerpts!

NEW AND UPCOMING TITLES

Each month we feature our new titles
and reader favorites.

CONTESTS AND GIVEAWAYS

We give away galleys, autographed copies,
and all kinds of fun stuff.

AUTHOR INFO

You'll find bios, articles, and links to personal
websites for all your favorite authors—and
so much more!

THE BUZZ

Sign up for our monthly romance newsletter,
and be the first to read all about it!

**If you or someone you know
wants to improve their reading skills,
call the Literacy Help Line.**

WORDS ARE YOUR WHEELS
1-800-228-8813